Jenna looked down at her sleeping son

She was uncomfortably aware that there were some things she couldn't give Jay. Things only a father could understand and face with a son. She kissed Jay lightly on the forehead. "I'll do the best I can for you," she whispered as tears filled her eyes.

Returning to her room, Jenna sat on the side of her bed. She needed someone to talk to. Someone to tell her everything would be all right. She thought of Ty, then dismissed the idea. She'd already woken him up once. She was determined not to bother him again.

She sighed. Something inside her wanted to depend on Ty—perhaps because he'd been so close to Jimmy—but she knew that wouldn't be fair to anyone. No matter how important he'd become to her and Jay, the fact remained that he was a Texas Ranger.

She'd lost one husband to his oath to protect and serve. She would not lose another.

Dear Reader,

After writing seven Temptation books, I've put my heart into something new—*A Ranger's Wife,* my first Superromance novel.

I've written about men in law enforcement before, but I find the Texas Ranger to be a unique example of the true-life hero. I enjoyed putting an honorable man in conflict with his heart's desire—the woman he wants. Ty promised to take care of his best friend's widow. And he's pretty sure taking care of her doesn't include falling in love...but some things can't be helped.

A Ranger's Wife is also the emotional story of Jenna Taylor whose husband, a sheriff's deputy, was killed in the line of duty. Now, two years later, she must find a way to put her life—and her young son's—back together again.

Her husband's best friend, Ty Richardson, has tried to help her do just that. He's the man she turns to when the nights are too silent and tomorrow too uncertain. But Ty is a Texas Ranger and Jenna knows she cannot invite him into her life. She's lost one man to a bullet. How can she take a chance on losing her heart to another lawman?

I hope you enjoy *A Ranger's Wife.* I like to hear from readers. Write to me at: P.O. Box 441, Bowie, MD, 20718.

Sincerely,

Lyn Ellis

A RANGER'S WIFE

Lyn Ellis

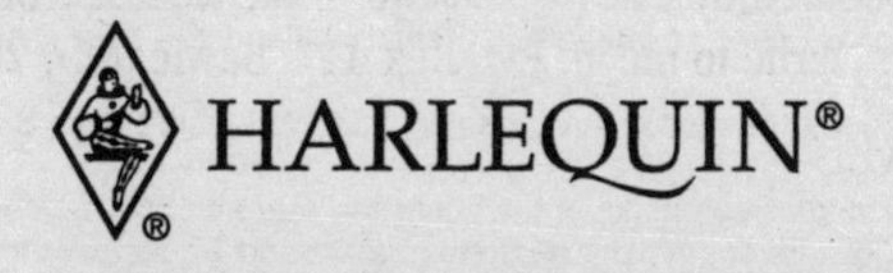

TORONTO • NEW YORK • LONDON
AMSTERDAM • PARIS • SYDNEY • HAMBURG
STOCKHOLM • ATHENS • TOKYO • MILAN • MADRID
PRAGUE • WARSAW • BUDAPEST • AUCKLAND

ISBN 0-373-70867-X

A RANGER'S WIFE

This edition published by arrangement with Harlequin Books S.A.

Visit us at www.romance.net

Printed in U.S.A.

To Laura Shin—together again.

CHAPTER ONE

RANGER TY RICHARDSON'S memory of that disastrous day two years ago was as clear as a blue, Texas spring morning, and each time the images came back to him, he could hardly breathe. The shooting, Jimmy's blood on his hands, the hospital, seeing Jenna's heart break with every word he spoke: those were the memories he would carry forever.

There was no comfort after someone you loved died. Ty knew that. But he'd done his best. He'd said the words, he'd helped bury Officer James A. Taylor and he'd held Jenna in his arms because he'd promised her husband he'd look out for her.

Not long after he'd lost his best friend and fellow officer to bad luck and bad guys, fate had given Ty a welcome reprieve. Jenna had gone back east to her family. That should have been the end of it.

Then the first of her letters had arrived. Neatly addressed envelopes containing her loneliness, heartbreak over the past and fears for the future. Worries and doubts she'd confessed she hadn't been able to confide to anyone else, and questions he couldn't answer with any natural talent for consolation. But he'd been unable to ignore her letters. And he could sympathize with not being able to say the words out loud. So he'd answered them.

But now Jenna Taylor, his best friend's widow, was back in town. And he couldn't ignore *her*. He'd never been able to in the past. Something in her spunk, her smile, her love for Jimmy had always affected him.

Ty opened his desk drawer and randomly chose one of several envelopes stacked inside behind his current case files. Even as he opened it and pulled out the crisply folded sheets, he knew he was stalling.

Sometimes I can barely move, I miss him so. I thought if I left Texas, if I left all the familiar faces, the familiar places Jimmy and I had been together, that I could go on alone and be happier.

But running hasn't helped. I've brought everything with me, the memories, the love and the heartache. As surely as if I'd packed it all in a bag and loaded it in the car along with my son.

Ty ran a hand down his face and sighed. His own chest felt tight in response to what Jenna had written. He understood about trying to outrun pain. He missed Jimmy, too.

He'd thought if he read some of her letters again

he would know what to say to her when they spoke in person.

He wasn't good with face-to-face. Not unless it had to do with apprehending criminals or interviewing murderers. His ex-wife had testified to that particular failing of his in no uncertain terms and in front of a judge. Then she'd gotten her divorce decree and moved to California.

Might as well get it over with, Ty decided as he refolded the letter and slipped it back in the drawer. Standing, he settled his Stetson a little lower over his eyes and headed for the parking lot. If he'd had an appointment to meet his maker he couldn't have been more jumpy…or reluctant.

He had to go. His honor was at stake. He'd made a promise as a friend and as a Ranger. But that didn't mean he had to like it.

Forced to stop at a red light a few minutes later, Ty sighed and rubbed his tired eyes. He'd been out late the night before on a homicide case, but he couldn't claim fatigue as an excuse. He needed to get a grip. He could do this. He'd delivered the worst possible news to Jenna—that her husband was dead. Anything after that should be a cakewalk.

The light changed, and Ty pressed the accelerator. He should have been the one who died that day. If he could have stepped in front of Jimmy and taken the bullet in his place, he would have felt like he'd done his duty to his friend and to the State of Texas. Hell, he had no one depending on him. Okay, almost no one—only old Kirby, his ex-wife's granddaddy. But being left behind to comfort didn't seem very useful. Besides, it was damned hard.

Ty turned into the sleepy residential neighborhood by habit. He'd been to Jimmy's house a hundred times, along with other Department of Safety officers, for Sunday barbecues and Saturday football games. He'd driven past the house at least fifty more times since Jimmy had died, just to keep an eye on it.

But now Jenna was home.

Back then he knew *he* had no words to "comfort." After the funeral he'd stopped by, but each visit felt strained and formal, as if neither of them knew what to say. Jenna seemed like a sleepwalker, and Ty was reluctant to be the one to wake her to the grim realities of widowhood. He'd watched his mother struggle for years after his father died suddenly of a heart attack. Better to be stunned than aware of all the birthdays and holidays to come that would be faced alone.

And then there was Jimmy's son, James Jr. As difficult as it had been to console the boy's mother, Ty had formed an easy relationship with James Jr. Ty knew how it felt to lose a father and be forced to grow up overnight. He remembered the multitude of questions that had remained unanswered when his own father died, all the pain he'd had to hold inside so he wouldn't cause his mother to cry.

Ty had intended to be there to help the boy, just as he intended to look after Kirby. Instead, he'd helped send Jenna and James Jr. off to her family.

Before they left, he had made sure both understood that if they needed him, they only had to call.

But he hadn't expected the letters.

> James Jr. told me he dreamed about his father last night. Then he asked when we could go home to see him. I told him that he would only see his dad in dreams from now on, and we both cried ourselves to sleep.

Dammit to hell.

Half a block from Jimmy's—no, from Jenna's house, Ty slowed the car and studied the differences. The place had come to life again. Instead of looking closed up and empty, the windows were open. There were a few toys and a bright red, kid-size pedal car left abandoned in the shaded driveway next to a burgundy minivan. Somebody had cut the grass.

An onslaught of guilt and anger ran through him. Why was he alternately anticipating and dreading seeing Jenna Taylor again?

Because of the letters.

That thought spooked him enough to make him drive past the house without stopping.

That's the real problem, isn't it? he thought in disgust as he cruised down the street. His trained eyes studied the familiar neighborhood, but the truth poked through all his carefully constructed defenses until it hit the mark. *You* want *to see her,* his conscience gleefully attacked. *You* always *wanted what Jimmy had...a family...*Jenna. *And you remember some of those letters by heart....*

I feel so empty and alone tonight. I've been lying here in this quiet house, in the middle of my empty bed, remembering Jimmy's touch, his loving. My body is proving that I'm still alive, even though my heart wants to argue.

I never thought of it before, but you must have missed your wife like this after the divorce. So I thought you'd understand....

Ty understood, all right. He'd spent several sleepless nights understanding exactly what she'd meant. But he hadn't been thinking about his ex-wife—he didn't miss Mary Jo—he'd been thinking about Jenna. She'd gotten to him by pouring out her heart in those letters. Now he didn't know how to face her.

He rolled to a halt at the stop sign and signaled the car opposite him to go first. He wasn't in a hurry to circle the block. That would lead him back to Jimmy's house and Jimmy's wife. The woman he wouldn't have even considered before because of her vows, and the widow he couldn't have now because of his promise to Jimmy.

Well, hell, he decided as he turned the corner on his way back to where he didn't want to be. He knew how to do his duty. He'd taken Kirby on for whatever years the old man had left. And that's what Jenna was, a duty. As long as no one ever knew she made him tongue-tied and tangle-footed he could keep his promise to Jimmy and leave his honor intact.

JENNA WAS BENDING over a big, open, half-empty box when the phone rang. As she straightened, she heard her son's footsteps racing down the hall.

"I'll get it, Mommy!"

Jenna chuckled. If the person on the line was another salesman, he was going to get an earful of Jay's six-year-old enthusiasm.

At least he *had* some enthusiasm.

She was still searching for hers. She shook her head. Maybe she'd find it packed in one of these boxes. If she just kept looking… She'd come back to Texas with the intention of starting a new life. Walking back into her former home had been a shock, but she'd recover. Jay's laughter echoed from the kitchen, and Jenna couldn't help but smile. Thank God she still had her son, even though he'd decided on his own that he didn't want to be called James Jr. anymore.

At first his stubborn insistence about the change had hurt, but Jenna had decided to go along. It had to be difficult having everyone solemnly calling him by his father's name. James Jr. and two of his friends, John and Jake, had proclaimed themselves the Three *J*s, like the Three Amigos. James Jr. had called himself Jay ever since.

They were both making a new start.

"Mom! It's my *kinda* aunt Sharon."

Jenna did laugh then and headed for the kitchen. "Your kinda aunt, huh?" she asked as she ruffled her son's fine dark hair.

"How long will it take for you to really be my aunt?" Jay asked the woman on the phone. He listened in total concentration. "That long?" Then he brightened and offered the phone to his mother. "She said maybe by Christmas."

"Hey, Sharon," Jenna said into the phone.

"I'm going outside," Jay called as he took off toward the front door.

"Remember, stay in our yard away from the street," Jenna cautioned.

His "I will" came back punctuated by the slamming of the front storm door. Jenna returned her attention to the phone and the woman who'd become her best friend.

"How are you coming along with settling in?" Sharon asked.

"Oh, fine. Unpacking keeps me busy." She considered confessing to her lack of enthusiasm but decided to keep it upbeat and talk about the future—not the past. "Have you heard anything?"

Sharon laughed, and Jenna could almost see her friend's mischievous features. According to Sharon, the two of them were in cahoots, but Jenna felt as though Sharon had saved her life. Her future anyway. Sharon, a woman who'd been married to the same man for twenty-five years, had gotten a divorce close to the time Jimmy had been killed. Her divorce, in her words, had been a "declaration of independence.'' The two women had met through a neighbor after Jimmy's death. As soon as Sharon learned Jenna was coming back to Texas, she'd decided to take her on as a project. They both could learn to stand on their own, together.

''We can go look it over on Friday,'' Sharon said triumphantly. ''The agent finally tracked down the owner. I'm so excited I could spit.''

''Uh-oh. You'll have to remember, no spitting in the restaurant, please. First of all, we don't own it yet and, secondly the Health Department would close us down before we got started,'' Jenna teased. Then, hearing a car pull up outside, she stretched the phone cord and stepped into the hallway to look through the glass front door. When she glanced outside, she froze… Her heart seemed to rise in her chest before plummeting to her stomach. Elation to…embarrassment. ''Hey, listen, I've got to go,'' she said, hearing her own voice go breathless.

''What's wrong? You sound funny.''

Jenna did her best to keep her voice normal. ''Oh, nothing,'' she lied. ''I've got a Texas Ranger in my front yard.'' She watched as the tall Ranger, Ty Richardson, got out and squatted to speak to her son. She blinked her stinging eyes, determined not to lose control.

She hadn't seen Ty for nearly two years. Since she'd run away from Texas. But she'd heard from him during that time.

After she'd mailed the first envelope, she'd been sure writing to Ty was a mistake. But he hadn't forgotten her—he'd answered her grief-filled letters. She was different now, stronger than the broken-hearted woman who'd written him. And looking back on all the things she'd told him because he was Jimmy's friend, because she didn't have to talk in person, she struggled with embarrassment. How could she look him in the eyes after baring her soul?

"I'll call you later for details on the meeting," she promised Sharon so she could get off the phone.

"Okay, I guess. Do you want me to come over there?"

"No," Jenna said, watching her son show Ty his new plastic baseball bat. A ripple of pain resurfaced. It hadn't been Jimmy's captain who'd come to tell her the news; it had been her husband's best friend. She remembered Ty's haggard features under the harsh fluorescent light of the hospital corridor. He'd looked half-dead himself, but it was Jimmy… *He's already told me my husband is dead. What news could be worse than that?* "I'm fine, really," she assured Sharon. "I just need to go see what he wants."

"All right," Sharon said slowly. "Call me later and we'll talk about Friday."

"You got it."

After Jenna hung up, she pressed a hand to her chest, closed her eyes and took a deep breath. She was determined to retain her composure. In the past year she'd learned to deal with the pain of Jimmy's death. She'd come back to Texas to begin again.

As she felt her pulse pound in her temple, she recognized that a part of the feeling threatening to overwhelm her was…excitement. Her enthusiasm seemed to be returning in a rush. Coming home had been a difficult decision. Her family had been against it. But she couldn't spend her life in the limbo of grief. She had Jay to think about.

Something in Ty's letters had given her the courage to follow her heart. And the moment she'd walked back into her own house, she'd known she'd made the right choice. She could now face her future.

> You know, Jenna, the future is a funny thing. I used to plan and do my best to outsmart tomorrow or the next day. Now that I've lived through a good bit of my tomorrows, I realize that a high percentage of the things I worried about didn't happen. Other things happened that I didn't like worth a darn. But mostly, my worrying was for nothing.

A piece of the complicated puzzle of her past was now standing in front of her son. She realized she *wanted* to see Ty Richardson if for no other reason than to let him know she'd gotten through the hardest part, and to thank him for helping her.

Calmer now, she took slow, steady steps down the hall. A framed mirror on the wall caught her attention and she glanced at her reflection. Out of reflex one hand came up to sift through her short hair, and she experienced a pang of regret. Jimmy had always loved her long honey-colored hair. She'd cut it right after leaving Texas, in an inept attempt to rid herself of the memories and pain. It hadn't worked. She'd taken the pain with her and come to realize she needed to keep the memories alive. Jimmy's son needed to remember his father and to grow up in Texas as his father had.

So she'd returned to San Angelo. The city streets and buildings had stayed the same, but her appearance still surprised her. She looked like a different person. She'd changed inside, as well. What would Ty Richardson think?

She pushed open the door and Ty looked up. The Stetson shaded his hazel eyes, but she could clearly see the wariness in his expression. Jenna almost felt sorry for him. *He must hate this.* She knew men weren't very good at emotional support and grief. She'd experienced a lot of well-meaning but clumsy male efforts to comfort her. But at least Jimmy's law-enforcement buddies had tried. The wives she'd spent most of her time with when Jimmy was alive suddenly seemed afraid of her, as if her grief could penetrate their lives and take their men away, as well.

She'd felt some of Ty's reluctance in his letters. Instead of discussing the emotional roller coaster she was strapped in to, he'd kept her sane by writing about normal things, about the minutiae of living in the real world.

I picked up an old mutt on the road yesterday. Darned thing was just about on its last lap of chasing cars. He looked relieved when I offered him a ride into town. He sat up in the seat like an out-of-state tourist and in some ways was a better companion than a few of the partners I've had. At least he wasn't trying to start a conversation or tell me how to drive. I took him out to Kirby's place and Kirby named him Buster. The two of them should be a proper pair.

Ty had never discussed her grief. He'd listened...or more accurately, he'd read her words, then he'd brought her back to everyday pleasures and problems. Watching her son talk man to man with him was another small gift.

Ty finished what he'd been saying to Jay, then slowly stood as Jenna walked down the front steps. She'd forgotten how tall he was.

In the few seconds before they spoke, Jenna had the crystalline memory of Ty and Jimmy arguing and laughing over a UT football game one Saturday afternoon. They'd bet a six-pack of beer and two extra large pizzas on the outcome, but the game had ended in a tie. She hadn't seen Ty smile since. He'd been her husband's best friend and he'd stood next to her, expressionless as a guard at Buckingham Palace, at the very public, very official city funeral for Officer James A. Taylor. A renewed sense of loss for all concerned caused Jenna's voice to falter.

"He—hello, Ty."

He touched his hat and nodded. "Jenna." His gaze ran over her face as if he was looking for the woman he remembered, or the woman in her letters, then he added, "Welcome home."

"Mom? Can Mr. Ty show me how to hit some balls? He said he used to play baseball with my dad."

"Thank you," Jenna acknowledged to Ty, before coaching her son. "Of course he can, sweetie, but let's let him get all the way into the house first." She figured Ty must have a reason for stopping by. Shifting her attention back to him, she asked, "Would you like to come in?"

"Sure," he said. But he didn't look the least bit sure. Jenna thought again about how difficult this must be for him. For all intents and purposes, the only thing they really had in common was Jimmy. And Jimmy was gone.

"So, how are you doing?" Ty asked as he followed Jenna into the house.

Jay moved to stand next to her, and out of habit Jenna combed her fingers through his hair before answering. "We're doing well," she replied automatically before turning to look at Ty. He'd removed his hat and stood in the door like a soldier at parade rest. It made her uncomfortable to see him acting like a stranger. Two years before, she'd considered him part of her family. And after his letters, he'd become a part of *her*. "Please—" she gestured toward the living room "—have a seat."

Then she remembered half the room was still strewn with empty and ready-to-be-emptied boxes. Jay had used them to build a fort or a tree house—sans the tree. She shrugged helplessly and moved ahead of Ty to push boxes out of the way. ''There's a rug and a coffee table under here somewhere,'' she joked. ''At least they were here when I left.''

''Don't bother,'' Ty said as he tossed his hat on the couch and reached to take the empty boxes out of her hands. ''You don't have to straighten up for me, I'm not really—'' Ty's hand brushed hers and everything stopped. They ended up both holding the boxes and staring at each other. ''Company,'' Ty finished.

He looked as nervous and uncomfortable as a prom date. After a moment of silent inertia, Jenna felt a bubble of laughter rising inside. The image of her and Ty having a tug of war over a handful of cardboard shifted the moment from the sublime to the ridiculous. ''That's right.'' She smiled. ''I forgot.''

''Hey, Jay? How about taking some of these empties out to the curb for me?'' Jenna pushed a box toward her son with her foot and again tried to take the others from Ty's hands. She couldn't budge them.

Ty looked at Jay. ''How 'bout I give you a hand there, buddy?''

Defeated, Jenna let go and opened the front door for the two of them. ''Stay out of the street, Jay,'' she added for good measure. She'd made safety a habit. After what had happened to Jimmy, she'd be damned if she'd lose her son by inattention to details.

Jay's answer was swallowed by the thumping of the box he was kicking in front of him and his excited questioning of a real live Texas Ranger.

THE TEXAS RANGER WAS GLAD to be out of the house for a moment. Ty had gotten through the initial clumsy hello, then nearly lost it. All the words and emotions he'd read between the lines of her letters came rushing back at him. Her letters may have been about Jimmy, but they were written to *him.* That fact was a source of pain, and of pride. He wasn't sure which one would win out. When his hand had slid over Jenna's, his first impulse had been to pull it back as if he'd touched a hot stove.

A stove would be safer.

He'd forgotten the exact color of her eyes, but with her hair cut short, feathering around her face, the clear blue of her gaze had surprised him. Ty didn't like surprises. There was enough awkwardness between them. Thank goodness Jenna hadn't noticed or taken offense. He'd felt like some kind of sleazy lecher even though the contact had been unintentional.

Thank goodness for the boy, Ty decided as he helped James Jr. put the cardboard boxes inside each other in a neat stack. "Why does your mom call you Jay?" Ty asked to make conversation.

"Because my dad is dead," Jay said without

looking at him. "I'm not James Jr. now. I'm just Jay."

Ty stopped. "I see. And what do you think about that?"

"It's okay. My grandmom cries when she calls me James Jr. I like Jay better."

Ty stooped to be at the boy's level. He suddenly found himself staring into eyes so much like Jimmy's he was startled. *Jimmy's son.* "It's a man's prerogative to choose his own name." He put out his hand and waited for the boy to shake it. "I'll call you Jay and you call me Ty, okay?"

The grown-up action of shaking hands with a Texas Ranger seemed to please him. He nodded enthusiastically. Ty pulled his wallet out of his back pocket and removed one of his business cards. He showed it to Jay.

"Here's my card. You see my number at the bottom?"

Jay nodded.

"Well, you call me if you need me. Or if you just want to talk. Okay?"

"Okay," he answered, and Ty stuck the card in Jay's shirt pocket.

"Do you have any kids?"

Ty shook his head.

"Don't you want some?" Jay persisted.

"I'm not married anymore," Ty said in answer to the boy's question, hoping he wouldn't have to explain the complexities of d-i-v-o-r-c-e to a six-year-old. He pushed to his feet, but Jay wasn't finished.

"Did your wife die?"

Ty ran a hand over his face to ease the tightness in his jaw and to give him time to think of a suitable answer. He wasn't used to the unleashed curiosity of children.

"No, Jay. She didn't die. She moved away."

Jay seemed to think about that for a moment, then he brightened. "Maybe she'll move back, like we did."

The last thing Ty wanted was for Mary Jo to move back, but he couldn't tell Jay that. Ready for the conversation to end, Ty started toward the house. "Maybe so," he said noncommittally. "Maybe so."

CHAPTER TWO

BY THE TIME they'd walked back to the house, Jenna was in the kitchen filling glasses with ice.

"What can I get you to drink?" she asked. She stepped into the hall and added, "We have water, soda, orange juice and milk."

"Can I have root beer?" Jay asked.

"*May* I, and yes, you may. And what would you like?" she asked Ty.

"Root beer sounds fine to me," he answered.

She moved past the counter and indicated packs of plastic forks and paper plates. "I won't get the dishes completely unpacked until tomorrow at the earliest. I was planning to grill some hamburgers and hot dogs in a little while. Would you like to stay and eat with us?"

Thankful for something that would keep him from staring at this new version of his best friend's wife, Ty said, "Only if you let me do the grillin'."

"That can definitely be arranged." Jenna smiled. "The charcoal is right there beside the door."

Watching Ty and Jay prepare the grill in the backyard gave Jenna a pang of regret. It should have been Jimmy out there with his son. But when

Ty instructed Jay to stand back while he lit the coals, the way any father would, Jenna regained her peace of mind. She was grateful to have Ty give some male attention to her son.

She gathered the plate of hamburgers and hot dogs, and the cooking utensils before pushing through the screen door. Flames were shooting out of the grill as she crossed the yard, and Jenna made a show of standing back. "Should I dial 911?" she asked.

Ty looked serious for a moment, then answered, "No, the firemen would eat all the hot dogs." Then he nudged Jay. "You said you like hot dogs. You think you might want to be a fireman when you grow up?"

Instead of answering, Jay said, "My daddy was a policeman. I'll show you." Then he took off at a run for the back door.

Jenna knew what Jay had been in such a hurry to retrieve, but she didn't mention it to Ty as he took the plate of hamburgers from her. The initial flames had died down, and he began preparations to cook.

"He seems to be getting along okay," Ty said as he rearranged the coals.

Jenna didn't answer immediately, and Ty turned toward her. "He is doing okay, isn't he?"

Pushing back her hair, Jenna sighed. "I think so. It's hard to tell. I know he misses his dad."

Ty looked away. "Yeah, I expect he does."

''He comes up with any excuse to talk about him,'' Jenna confided.

Just then the screen door banged and Jay sprinted toward them clutching a framed picture. ''This is my dad,'' he said, shoving the picture toward Ty.

Jenna watched as Ty wiped his hands on a towel before squatting and taking the picture from Jay. It was a photo of Jimmy looking young and earnest and indestructible on the day he'd graduated from the police academy.

Jenna had given Jay that picture to keep in his room for two reasons: one, to remember his father and be proud of him, and, two, because Jenna hadn't been able to hang the picture and be reminded every day what had taken Jimmy from them. She wanted to remember him as her husband, as Jay's father, not as a conscientious police officer.

Ty stared at the picture of his best friend and felt his chest tighten. Jimmy was dead, and here was his son clinging to all he had left.

Ty felt Jenna's eyes on him but he couldn't look up; he had to give Jimmy's picture his complete concentration. Jay was watching him expectantly.

''Did anyone ever tell you you look like your dad?'' Ty asked the little boy.

''My grandmom,'' Jay said, but he didn't sound as if he believed her.

''Well, you do. Your eyes are just like his, see?'' Ty held up the picture for Jay to study, and from the corner of his eye he saw Jenna turn quickly and walk away. He wondered if he'd done something wrong already. He'd barely been here an hour.

"Are you okay?" he called to her.

Without turning, she nodded and waved a hand in their direction. "I'll get everything else ready. Bring the burgers in when they're done."

Thirty minutes later Ty followed Jay into the kitchen and plunked down the plate of grilled food. Jenna looked a little subdued but she gave them both a smile. Soon the three of them were eating and making polite conversation. When Ty mentioned that the food was as good or better than any restaurant, Jay brought up his "kinda" aunt.

"Mom and Aunt Sharon are buying a rest-urant," he said proudly.

"Really?" Ty asked and looked at Jenna, thinking the boy must be mistaken. *A restaurant?* She'd never mentioned buying a restaurant in her letters.

Instead of denying it, Jenna gave her son a fake frown and made a qualification. "Well, we haven't bought it yet. We're going to look it over on Friday and speak to the owners."

"Why would you buy a restaurant?" Ty asked out loud, still fumbling with the concept.

Jenna glanced down and ran a finger along the condensation frosting her glass of root beer before answering. "Sharon and I want to go into business together since both of us are on our own."

The sound of "on our own" stuck in Ty's mind. He wanted to tell her she wasn't alone, but other words came out before he could help himself. The farfetched idea of going into business sounded wonderful; it also sounded crazy. "Do you know anything about running a restaurant?"

In the silence that followed, Ty could tell by the stubborn look on Jenna's face that he'd wandered into forbidden territory.

"Sharon and her former husband used to have a diner years ago. She waitressed and he cooked, and she's always wanted to try it again." Her words sounded as cool as the hands-off look in her blue eyes.

Ty knew he should quit while he was ahead but he'd promised Jimmy. He also knew better than anyone that Jenna was in a vulnerable state of mind and could probably be talked into anything. So, even though it was the last subject he wanted to discuss, he brought it up. "You never mentioned this in your letters. Have you ever worked in the restaurant business?"

It wasn't fair to remind her of how much she'd revealed to him. No matter how reluctantly he'd been drawn into her life and her concerns, he'd jumped in—over his head. Now he found he didn't like the feeling of being left out.

Her cool look became downright frosty. "I waitressed in college. I can cook."

"They're gonna cook breakfast and lunch," Jay added. "And I get to work there, too."

"But—" Ty began.

"We have the capital, and this is a good location. There was a successful business there up until one of the owners got sick and had to shut it down. We can make it successful again.''

''Where?''

''It's the old diner right off the exit at Route 82,'' Jenna said, defrosting a bit. ''Just down the road from the Everhardt plant.''

Ty thought for a minute, trying to picture the location. Then he remembered. ''You mean the diner with the giant doughnut out front?''

''That's the place.''

''And I get to help make the doughnuts,'' Jay said before taking a triumphant slurp of root beer.

Ty decided to back off until he had more information. The only way he knew of to find information was to ask questions. Not necessarily the most obvious questions, since they had a six-year-old audience.

''Is this some kind of female conspiracy?'' he asked, narrowing his eyes suspiciously.

Jenna smiled then, and Ty felt her warm reaction down to the toes of his Justins.

''In a way it is,'' she answered, before grinning at her son. ''Except for Jay, that is.''

''Do you like doughnuts, Ty?'' Jay asked.

''Of course I do. All police officers like doughnuts. The academy considers them one of the major food groups.''

''My daddy loved doughnuts,'' Jay said.

A sharp spear of guilt skewered Ty. Here he was sitting at Jimmy's kitchen table smiling at Jimmy's son and Jimmy's wife—no, widow. His best buddy was dead.

He'd finished his meal. He wiped his hands on his napkin, took one last swallow of root beer and pushed to his feet, trying not to look too obvious. He picked up his used paper plate and searched for the trash can. He had to get out of here. He had to go someplace and remind himself that he wasn't supposed to gather up the scattered plans for the future and move into Jimmy's family. He was only supposed to be there *if* they needed him.

"I'll take care of that," Jenna said. She took the plate from his hand and stacked it on top of her own. "Is everything okay?"

"I have to get going," he said. He knew his sudden departure was strange but he couldn't explain it. He briefly touched Jay's shoulder. "We'll have to hit some balls another time, buddy. See you later," he said, then forced himself to look at Jenna. "Call if you need anything, okay? I've gotten used to hearing from you."

After one searching gaze, she nodded.

He couldn't tell if she was sorry to see him leave or glad to be rid of him. And for once in his face-it-head-on life, he decided he didn't want to know.

A PLUME OF DUST TURNED golden by the setting sun trailed Ty down the dirt road to old Kirby's place. He wasn't sure how it had come about, but he'd made a habit of driving out once or twice a week to make sure the old man hadn't, as Kirby put it, "gone toes up." Buster the dog, Kirby's new best friend, met Ty as he rolled to a stop and opened the car door.

Ty grasped the bucket of chicken he'd picked up at a KFC on the way out and tucked it under one arm before he bent to give the lanky hound dog a pat on the head. "Hey there, Buster. Looks like stayin' in one place agrees with you. First time I saw you, you were all bones and ears." He thumped the dog's barely visible ribs. "You're fillin' out."

Buster's tongue lolled in what looked like canine agreement. Then the dog stretched upward to sniff the bucket of chicken with interest. Before he could do any more, the screen door opened and Kirby stepped out onto the porch. Buster made a beeline for him. It didn't take a genius to see the bond between the stray dog and the old man.

"Appears you two are gettin' along," Ty said as he moved up the steps.

"Yep. We've come to an agreement," Kirby answered. "I buy food. He eats it. Never seen a dog that stayed hungry all the time."

Ty struggled not to smile. "I'll be glad to help out with the cost, if that's a problem."

Kirby harrumphed and glanced down at the dog sitting at his feet. "I can afford him. But I don't tell him that, so he won't get too comfortable. If I go toes up, who's gonna feed him?"

"I suspect that would be me," Ty volunteered, thinking that Kirby just might outlive them all.

He'd already buried his wife and two sons. The only family he had left was Mary Jo, and she'd run off to California. Of the many things Ty's ex-wife had left behind in Texas, the one that surprised him the most was her granddaddy. As far as Ty knew, M.J. never even wrote or called the old man.

"Have you heard from Mary Jo?" Kirby asked. It had become part of their routine. Kirby acted like M.J. was making plans to come back to Texas, like living in California could never be all it was cracked up to be. Problem was, Kirby had it wrong. M.J. would never come back to Texas as far as Ty could tell. And that was fine with him. He'd quit trying to explain that to Kirby a long time ago.

"No, sir. Not yet."

"Well, you mark my words," Kirby said with confidence, "any day now she'll be heading back."

"If you say so."

Kirby stared at him for several seconds, then continued. "I've got the baseball game on. Come on in and sit awhile."

Glad to get off the uncomfortable subject of his ex-wife, Ty nodded and removed his hat. He handed the bucket to Kirby. "I brought us some supper. What's the score?" he asked as he followed Kirby inside.

Ty had a difficult time keeping his mind on the game even though the Rangers were winning. Jenna kept interrupting his thoughts. She'd gotten thinner while she'd been away, and with her hair cut short she looked ten years younger than he remembered.

Unless you looked into her unsettling blue eyes. That's where you'd find the pain she'd put into her letters. But when she'd smiled, Ty had had a hard time remembering his own name. And the boy—

"You want another piece of this chicken?" Kirby asked, shaking the bucket to gauge how many pieces were left. "You haven't eaten much. You're not sick, are you? You'll start to look like that scrawny dog if you don't perk up."

Buster, the dog in question, raised his head off his paws and watched the bucket of chicken as if he had high hopes of being included in the offer.

"No, thanks. I'm fine. I had a big lunch," Ty lied. He'd actually had an early dinner, with Jenna and Jay. "You keep it for later."

The third baseman hit a home run, and Ty found it difficult to get excited by a three-run lead. He watched as the entire team gathered at home plate to high-five the hitter, then sighed and took a swallow from his can of soda. He should have gone back to his place instead of coming out here. He didn't give a damn about the ball game, and old Kirby had Buster to keep him company. But somehow, after he left Jenna's, the last place he wanted to be was home alone.

A crazy and dangerous thought.

He'd gotten used to living on his own. It had been four years since he and Mary Jo had split. He knew how to cook and do his laundry. He knew how to fill his hours with the kind of work that made the world a little better place—or at least a world with some measure of justice. His job took top priority in his life. What difference did it make that Jenna Taylor was back in San Angelo?

It just meant there would be no more letters....

There seems to be a conspiracy of silence here. My family wants to see me, to ask me how I'm doing. But none of them wants to talk about Jimmy. They don't want to upset me, see me cry. I wish they'd understand that I need to talk about Jimmy. I need to find a way to let him go gradually—instead of having him disappear like he never existed.

But I can talk to you.

Remember the time Jimmy tried to ride that bull? How much did you guys bet? If you hadn't already taken him to the emergency room and had his wrist set before you brought him home, I would have killed you both.

Damn.

CHAPTER THREE

"MOM? MAY I GO with Rusty and his dad to the store?" Jay yelled from the front door. "He said we could get ice cream."

Jenna dried her hands on a towel as she walked from the kitchen to the hall. When she glanced out the front door, beyond her son, she could see his new friend Rusty and a man who had to be Rusty's dad standing in the yard. An unfamiliar sedan was parked in the driveway.

"Why don't you introduce me to Rusty's dad," Jenna said as she dropped the towel on the hall table and ushered her son out the door. She was glad Jay had found a playmate in the neighborhood, but she wasn't about to allow him to run off somewhere with strangers.

"Hi," Jenna said as she approached the two visitors.

"This is my mom," Jay announced.

"Hi, I'm Rich Martin, Rusty's dad," the man said as he offered his hand. He indicated a house up the street. "We live in the third house on the right. The blue one with white shutters."

''It's nice to meet you. I'm Jenna Taylor. Now, what are you guys up to?''

Rich chuckled. ''Well, my wife, Nancy, is expecting and she asked me to pick up some ice cream from the Dari-mart. I thought these two might like to ride along and get a dipped cone. You're welcome to come along, too, if you like.''

''Ah, no. Ice cream I can resist,'' Jenna answered. ''Of course when I was expecting Jay, there were a lot of things I couldn't pass up.'' The memory of Jimmy driving the well-known path to the Burger King caught her off guard. He'd been so tolerant of her cravings. She gave Rusty's father one star for not complaining. ''When is your baby due?''

''Not until October,'' he said with a sheepish smile.

''There'll be a lot of trips to the Dari-mart between now and then,'' Jenna said. ''Unless, of course, her tastes change.''

Rusty tugged on his dad's pants to get his attention. ''Dad? Can we go now?''

Rich put his hand on his son's shoulder, then looked at Jenna. ''Can Jay ride along?''

Jay's face was a comical mix of hope and disinterest. Jenna couldn't see any reason why he shouldn't be included. ''Sure,'' she said.

Jay and Rusty simultaneously yelled, ''All right!'' and ran for the car.

''Make sure you mind Rusty's dad,'' Jenna

called to her son. "Oh, let me go in and get you some money."

"Don't bother. I'll buy. We should be back in about forty-five minutes," Rich said. As Jenna followed him to the car, he instructed the boys. "Both of you in the back seat and put your seat belts on." Then, as if he'd read her mind, he stopped before getting in behind the wheel. "I'll look out for him."

Jenna chalked up another star for a dad who knew how a mom felt when her child went with someone she didn't know well. "Thank you."

Watching them drive away only gave her a slight twinge. Rich seemed like a down-to-earth guy who loved his family. When he'd mentioned his wife and her condition, Jenna could see the love in his eyes.

She'd had that once—a loving husband and father for her son. A whole family. She'd been struggling so with the loss of Jimmy she'd never considered the possibility she could find that love, that wholeness again.

Now that she'd been reminded, she realized she wanted a traditional family, for herself and for Jay.

Rich's wife was pregnant with a second child. Jenna touched her own flat stomach and for a moment allowed herself to dream of having another child, a baby sister for Jay. She couldn't do that unless she remarried.

Jenna glanced down the residential street. All these houses, filled with families of every different sort. She and Jay were still a family, but if they wanted a man in their lives and a new little sister, she'd have to seriously think about dating. She wouldn't meet the right man in her front yard.

That would have to wait awhile, Jenna conceded as she headed back to the house. She hadn't even gotten everything unpacked yet.

TWO DAYS LATER Jenna smoothed down the fabric of her skirt before she turned to help Jay out of the minivan. The real-estate agent stood waiting for them under the awning of the defunct Donut Wrangler Diner.

"Cross your fingers," Sharon instructed Jay. Then she looked at Jenna. "Are you ready for this?"

"Ready as I'm going to be," Jenna answered nervously. They'd driven over together to bolster each other's confidence. So far, everyone she'd confided their plans to had grave doubts about their success. Jimmy's mother had come right out and said she thought the idea was foolish. How could Jenna raise a son and run a restaurant? her mother-in-law wanted to know. How could Jenna put what little money she had into a high-risk business venture, rather than plan for James Jr.'s future?

Jenna didn't want to think about *not* getting the diner. The future belonged to her, as well as to her son. She'd always provide for him no matter what she had to do. But the idea of being her own boss, of investing in something that would be hers, was too powerful.

For moral support, she glanced at Sharon as they started up the steps. Sharon winked, as if to say everything would be all right. *We can do this.* With that thought in mind, Jenna introduced herself to the agent and shook his hand.

TY KNEW HE WAS BUTTING IN. After spending several hours with a victim's family in their lawyer's office discussing the merits of an old fraud case, he'd been left with an open afternoon. A Ranger could take on any case he deemed solvable, but in his opinion there wasn't enough new evidence to reopen the case they'd discussed. He'd told the family to call him if any other information came up. Then he'd tried his best to stay busy in his office, to schedule a meeting, round up a suspect—anything to keep him away from the diner. But he'd failed. He knew Jenna would be there, looking the restaurant over with her friend. He felt honor bound to ensure she wasn't making a mistake.

As he pulled into the cracked, nearly empty parking lot of the Donut Wrangler Diner, the first thing he noticed was that the doughnut out front needed a fresh coat of paint. The next thing he realized, was that the diner had no neighbors. It had been built on a solid two-lane road with a fair amount of traffic, but it stood on its own pretty much in the middle of nowhere. You could see the doughnut for miles. He parked between it and Jenna's minivan.

The door was unlocked, so he let himself in. The interior seemed dark and deserted. It had been built in the fifties, and the serving area consisted of lime-green vinyl-covered booths with only six tables. A counter with matching vinyl stools ran the length of the place, and the original artwork—several framed prints of running horses—still hung on the wall. A dusty jukebox stood like a forgotten sentinel at the end of the room.

He heard voices coming from what must be the kitchen and headed that way.

"This equipment was updated around ten years ago. The wiring is up to code and—" The agent stopped talking when he saw Ty in the doorway.

"Mom, it's the Texas Ranger!" Jay exclaimed, and ran forward.

"Hey, Jay," Ty said as he bent toward him. "I thought we agreed that you'd call me Ty."

"Yes, sir—Ty. Did you come to help us make doughnuts?"

"We won't be making any doughnuts today," Jenna said, claiming Ty's attention. She was staring at him, looking more surprised than angry.

After a long silent moment, Ty felt the need to explain his presence. "I was in the area, so I thought I'd drop by," he said lamely. "It's been a while since I stopped in this old place for coffee."

The woman next to Jenna cleared her throat, spurring Jenna to action.

"Oh, Ty, this is my good friend, Sharon Kellerman, and the real-estate agent, Mr. Farley. This is Ty Richardson. He's—he was a friend of Jimmy's."

"I thought we were about to be carted off to jail," Sharon said, and smiled. After one thorough head-to-toe glance she shook his hand. "I'm Jenna's not-so-silent partner."

"Good to meet you," Ty replied, then shook hands with the agent. "You, too, Mr. Farley." Silence fell over the group again.

"Don't mind me," Ty said finally to the agent. "I'm not here on official business, just as a friend of the family. Go on with what you were saying."

Mr. Farley continued his tour of the grills and the fryers, but Jenna had a hard time keeping her mind on business. She'd almost had a heart attack when she'd looked up and seen Ty in the doorway.

He just surprised you, that's all, her mind tittered. *Get over it.*

When Jay got restless, Ty suggested that the two of them should check out the jukebox so Jenna and Sharon could see the rest of the place. Jenna was grateful for the suggestion. With both of her distractions occupying each other, she could think a little straighter.

They toured the walk-in cooler and the small office hidden in the back. They discussed plumbing and public-bathroom access. By the time they'd gone full circle and joined Ty and Jay again, Jenna couldn't think of any more questions to ask.

But Ty had one. "Why has this place been closed up and vacant all these years?" he asked.

"Well, now, that's a story," Mr. Farley replied. "The diner has been empty because the owners weren't interested in selling until recently. Evan and Ruth Sanders ran the place for years before Ruth started having some health problems. At first they only intended to close it for a few months. They owned the building, so being shut down wouldn't be a hardship. They even had some renovations done during that time."

Mr. Farley shook his head. "But that was almost ten years ago, and Ruth's condition has only gotten worse. They think she had a stroke or something—has trouble with her memory." The agent looked at Jenna and Sharon. "I think Evan's finally decided that keeping the diner won't help her. I've known them for years and I told them I'd try to find a buyer."

"That's so sad," Jenna said.

"It is that," Mr. Farley agreed. "If you want to meet with Evan and ask more questions, I'm sure he'd be happy to help you."

"Thank you," Jenna said.

"We'd like some time to talk this over," Sharon added. "How about if we call you in the morning?"

"That'll be fine. You folks look around and take your time." He pulled the key to the front door out of his shirt pocket and handed it to Jenna. "Lock up when you leave. You can return the key next time we meet." Then he smiled. "That is, unless you decide to buy the place."

After saying his goodbyes, Mr. Farley drove off.

Before the dust settled behind him, Sharon gave a Texas-style whoop, picked up Jay and spun him around until he was laughing. "What do you think of our new restaurant?" she asked him between giggles.

"Don't hold back, Sharon. Tell us how you really feel," Jenna joked.

"It's not *new*—it's old!" Jay declared.

"It's new to us," she answered, and set him back on his feet.

Ty was conspicuously quiet but he stared steadily at Jenna.

"What do you think?" she asked, unable to exclude him.

One broad shoulder came up in what looked like a shrug. "I think I'd want to talk to the owner before I decided. How much are they askin' for it?"

"A hundred and twenty thousand with terms," she answered.

Jay bounded over and clamped his arms around her thighs. "Can we buy it?" he asked, as if the diner were a toy at the grocery store.

"We'll see, honey," Jenna answered automatically.

"I think we can swing it," Sharon said with more confidence than Jenna was feeling at the moment. "Depends on what kind of terms we can negotiate." She held Ty with a serious gaze. "Most of the equipment in here is in great shape. It doesn't matter that it's been sitting a few years. And if the owners are ready to get rid of it, they'll deal."

"Then I would say it depends on the deal," Ty answered carefully.

"NOW, WHO IS this Texas Ranger again?" Sharon asked a little later.

Jenna glanced toward Jay in the back seat before answering. He was ignoring them, busy with the toy they'd gotten at McDonald's on the way out. "I told you, he was a friend of Jimmy's." Jenna had met Sharon after Jimmy's death. She wasn't sure why they'd never discussed Ty before. Jenna guessed it was because she'd been trying to keep before and after the funeral separate. To let go of the past and move into the future. Except for Ty.

"Is he married?" Sharon persisted.

Jenna thought about that for a moment. She knew what Sharon was getting at, but she was wrong. Instinctively she was sure Ty wasn't the type to fool around with his friend's wife. But still, she searched her memory for any incident between her and Ty while Jimmy had been alive that might have seemed too friendly.

Nope. Nothing. Ty had become her friend *after* Jimmy was gone.

"No, he's divorced. He's been a friend to me—to Jay and me—since Jimmy was killed."

"What I wouldn't give to have a friend like that." Sharon sighed dramatically. "A single flesh-and-blood Texas Ranger. He could leave his boots on my welcome mat anytime. Or take me prisoner—"

"It's not like that," Jenna protested even though her conscience had to admit she'd noticed him, not just as a friend, but as a man. That made her nervous. She wasn't ready to think about Ty—about any man—that way. "He's only being nice...."

"Don't get upset," Sharon soothed, then patted Jenna's knee. "I was just teasin' you. Well, sort of teasin' you. The part about being his prisoner was the truth." She laughed. "That man needs to have his tail feathers ruffled. He's way too serious—and too good-lookin'. You suppose he'd be interested in an older woman?"

Jenna had to laugh. Out of the several things she'd noticed about Ty, none had anything to do with his age. She'd never stopped to think about it before. If she had to guess, she'd say he was older than Jimmy. He seemed older anyway.

"I have no idea what kind of woman he'd be interested in. But if I were you, I'd think twice about ruffling anything on a man who wears a gun."

She almost added that she ought to know—she was married to one. But she wasn't married anymore, and with God as her witness, she silently swore she'd never marry another man who wore a gun for a living. She had Jay to think about. She couldn't live with the uncertainty, with the possibility that she and Jay could lose someone else to violence.

"Mom? Can I have a gun like Mr. Ty's?"

Along with Jay's question, another unsettling

thought presented itself in full Technicolor, and she nearly slammed on the brakes in reaction. It was the image of Jay growing up to be like his father, of him applying to the police academy instead of college. She glanced in the rearview mirror and watched her son hit one of his Beanie Babies over the head with a rubber wrench from his tool kit. Picturing him as a grown man wearing a badge and a gun sent a rush of terror through her.

She worked to keep her voice even. ''You just got a new baseball bat. One thing at a time, kiddo.''

The real answer was—no. *Never.* Starting right now, she'd begin steering Jay away from his father's career. Her son was not going to end up a dead hero like Jimmy. Not as long as she had breath in her body. No matter how noble Ty made it sound in his letters.

My uncle was the county sheriff years back. He always told me I'd either grow up to be a criminal or a lawman. He threatened to whup the former out of me and pushed me toward the latter. I guess he got his wish. He used to take me to the police firing range with him when I got tall enough to see the targets. The day I became a Texas Ranger was the happiest day of his life. I wish my father had been there to see it, too.

Never.

CHAPTER FOUR

"FIRST WE'LL HAVE TO CLEAN and repaint the place," Sharon said as she wrote on the legal pad balanced on her lap. "We can do some of that ourselves, but the exterior will have to be contracted." Oblivious to Jenna's fearful thoughts, Sharon brought her back from worrying about the future to the reality of planning it. "Then we have to hire a cook, work out a menu and set up accounts with suppliers."

Without taking a pause, she changed directions. "Have you decided what to do about Jay? Still planning on keeping him with you?"

Jenna swallowed. Maybe Sharon could read her mind after all. She'd already defended her decision to Jimmy's mother; she hoped Sharon wouldn't force her to do the same. "I know it's crazy. He'll be seven soon and starts school in August, but until then, I want him with me."

Sharon watched her for a moment before nodding. "I understand. Well, if he can handle being stuck in the restaurant most of the day, then I can handle having him there." She smiled. "It's been a long time since my boys were that little. After all, how much can an 'almost' seven-year-old eat?"

"That depends on whether doughnuts are involved...." Jenna answered.

"Ugh. I forgot about that. I'm not sure making doughnuts from scratch is going to be cost effective. Maybe we should have them delivered."

Ready to admit she hadn't had any experience making doughnuts, Jenna fell back on what seemed like a good idea. "What do you think about what Mr. Farley suggested?"

Sharon looked up from the list she was composing. "Which part?"

"About meeting with the owners, getting their advice."

"I think that's a fine idea. Ten years is a long time to be out of a business, but so is twenty. That's the last time I— Well, the last time Dean and I were in the restaurant business." She frowned before returning to her list. "I'll call them when we get back to your place—see if they're agreeable to meeting with us."

AS IT TURNED OUT, Evan Sanders was very agreeable. Not only did he have the answers to several questions Jenna and Sharon asked, but he also offered them a lease-purchase agreement they couldn't refuse. The only thing he couldn't provide was a good doughnut recipe. The man who'd been their original cook had passed away five years before. By the following Friday, however, Jenna Taylor and Sharon Kellerman were the proud owners of the Donut Wrangler Diner.

"We need to have a victory party," Sharon said, throwing an arm around Jenna as they walked up Jenna's driveway after signing the final papers.

Jenna started to agree, then realized how long it had been since she'd thrown any kind of party. Long enough that she wasn't sure how to go about it. Her life had changed so drastically she hardly recognized the woman she used to be. And at this point the only people she would want to invite to a victory celebration were Sharon, Jay and...Ty. Not a very impressive number for a party.

"Maybe we should forego celebrating until we get this thing off the ground," she replied.

"Still worried?"

"Of course." Jenna laughed as she hooked her arm around Sharon. The apprehensive part of her mind pondered the possibility that it was too soon to celebrate because she and Sharon had just made a huge mistake. But under the obvious fear, Jenna could feel the unmistakable current of excitement. Maybe she'd found her enthusiasm after all. Too soon to tell which would win out. "We have so much to do, I can hardly grasp it."

Sharon contemplated that for a moment. "All right, then. We'll save the party for opening day. But today's achievement calls for dinner out—on me." She winked. "We have to start checking out the competition."

Later, after dinner and getting Jay into bed, Jenna

slipped between her own covers and pulled them up to her chest. On the one hand she felt exhausted. It had been an exhilarating day, and she'd had a hard time getting Jay settled down. It was the happiest she'd seen him since they'd returned to Texas. His happiness naturally elevated her own.

On the other hand, now alone in her bed, she felt restless. As if she'd forgotten to do something. She played back the evening through her mind. Dinner had been fun—she and Sharon planning their own menu with a little help from Jay. The only thing missing had been Ty. Rushed along by Sharon's desire to celebrate, she'd forgotten to tell him the good news.

Without thinking, she reached for the phone.

"Ty Richardson." Even at ten o'clock at night, with that familiar, professional tone to his voice, he still seemed to be on duty.

"Ty? It's Jenna."

A moment of silence followed a slow indrawn breath. Then she heard him move, the distinct slither of sheets rustling over skin. Guilt spread through her.

"Did I wake you?"

"No." His deep voice said otherwise, but he was clearly wide-awake now. "Is something wrong?"

"No, nothing. I—" She felt like a rat. A rude rat, who would call and wake a friend just because she wanted to share some good news that could have waited until morning. "We got the restaurant," she finished weakly.

"What?"

"The Donut Wrangler. It's ours."

"Congratulations."

"I'm sorry for calling so late. I'll let you go back to sleep—"

"Wait a minute." She heard what sounded like him dragging pillows into a pile behind his back. "I'm awake now, don't run off. What kind of deal did you get?"

His question forced Jenna to smile. Leave it to a man to worry about the deal. Ty was determined to look out for her. Some other time that might concern her. But at this moment, late in the evening, alone for the first time all day, his interest felt good. After explaining the terms and answering a few straightforward questions, Jenna found herself confessing more than she'd intended.

"You know Jimmy's mother is against this."

"Now, that doesn't surprise me," he said slowly. "I'm sure she means well."

"Do you think Sharon and I are crazy? It's hard for me to decide anymore." She dreaded the answer because she knew he'd tell her the truth.

"Yeah. I suppose I do." She heard a gruff laugh that softened the words she hadn't wanted to hear. "But I guess it's something you need to try. And you know what they say about tryin'...."

"What's that?"

"Tryin' is a waste of time. Just do it, whatever *it* is, and get it over with."

"Gee, thanks, I think," Jenna said. "But you're

right, this is something I have to do. For Jay's future, for mine…" She caught herself explaining the obvious. They both knew the emptiness her future held…without Jimmy.

Several moments of silence passed. Enough time to make Jenna feel completely exposed.

"You'll do fine," he said. The confidence in his voice almost made her believe it. "And you have friends. I don't know how to cook, but I make a heck of a good customer. You fix the doughnuts, and I'll send all the lawmen I know."

"Thank you, Ty, for being a friend. Jimmy was right about you. He always said you were one of the good guys."

"Well, I suppose I have my moments. You stop worrying and get some sleep."

"Okay, I will. Good night."

"Night."

Ty hung up the phone and rubbed his forehead to ease the frown there. Jenna's call bringing him out of a restless sleep had almost had him reaching for his pants and his gun. Sleeping naked had its disadvantages in an emergency.

But it hadn't been an emergency. She'd simply wanted to talk, to tell him her news. That was worth waking up for. Now, however, he was wide-awake and after hanging up the phone he didn't know what to do. No use rolling over and trying to go back to sleep. The thought of Jenna, lying in bed alone… thinking about *him* drained every ounce of fatigue from his body.

Don't even go there.

He flipped back the sheets and reached for a pair of sweats. He'd go watch the news, maybe make a sandwich. As he headed down the hall into the kitchen, he wondered if he ought to get a dog to look after. That would keep him occupied when he couldn't sleep.

"Sorry, Jimmy," he said under his breath as he switched on the kitchen light and did his best not to think about Jimmy's wife....

JENNA HAD ROLLED OVER and switched off the light before she realized what she'd done. She'd called Ty, late at night without thinking about how she might be interfering in his life. What if he'd been with a woman? He was a bachelor after all. She could feel warmth rising in her cheeks at the thought. How embarrassing. She'd never even asked him if he had someone special in his life.

It was time she grew up and stopped treating him like a brother. He wasn't her brother. He was her husband's best friend. He had his own life. He always had; she'd simply forgotten that point when they'd been writing. Well, not completely forgotten. She'd asked him once, what he did when he was off duty.

> Sometimes I go have a beer at the Caballero over toward the military base. The beer is cold, and they have pretty waitresses. There's usu-

ally a few guys from the sheriff's department looking for a game of pool in the back.

Jenna wondered if he'd gotten to know any of those pretty waitresses personally. Something about the image of Ty dating made her uncomfortable. Probably because it was none of her business. She didn't need to know, or want to know unless he felt compelled to tell her. And that was the end of that.

She squirmed around until she found a comfortable position, then drew in a long breath and closed her eyes. "I miss you, Jimmy," she whispered into her pillow. But no tears came this time. The last thing she heard as she drifted off to sleep was the echo of Ty's voice, *You'll do fine.*

THE STEADY BANGING COMING from the restaurant kitchen might have given Jenna a headache if she'd had time for one. She glanced out the window she was cleaning and watched the shimmer of summer heat rise from the pavement as a telephone-company van pulled into the lot. A trickle of sweat ran down her back as the van parked between the plumber's three-quarter ton and the electrician's pickup.

"Hey! We should have a phone soon," she called to Sharon. "Telephone man is here."

Sharon stuck her head around the doorway from the kitchen. "Great, I need to get started on our list of suppliers." A trio of loud bangs punctuated her words, and she winced. "That is, when it's quiet enough in here to use a phone and cool enough to think. We should have electricity in another hour or so.''

Banned from helping with the work going on in the kitchen, Jay left the crayons and paper he'd spread on the table of one booth and dashed to the open front door. He watched with interest as the man got out of the van and put on his tool belt. ''Look at all his tools. Mom, can I be a telephone man when I grow up?''

''Yes,'' Jenna answered unequivocally. She'd buy him the tool belt herself. She'd had a heck of a time keeping him out of the way of the workmen. So far he'd wanted to be a plumber, maybe a ''lectrician'' and definitely a grown-up. ''You can be lots of things,'' she added, determined not to pass up any opportunity to ease him in a safe direction. *Anything but a policeman.*

Jenna gave the window a final wipe, then gathered her cleaning supplies to move to the next one. They couldn't start painting until the workmen had finished, so she'd decided to get the majority of the dust out of the place. It was hot, sweaty work and they'd have to clean again after painting, but Jenna felt the need to do something constructive. She blotted the moisture gathering around the sweat band on her forehead. One more window and she'd start on the jukebox.

She stopped long enough to greet the phone man and to introduce herself and Jay. Barely two minutes later, another car pulled into the parking lot. A man Jenna didn't recognize got out and stared at the front of the restaurant as if he couldn't believe his eyes.

It was far too early to hope for potential customers, so when Sharon came into the dining room carrying a box of trash, Jenna stopped her. "Do you suppose that's one of the cooks who answered the ad?"

Sharon glanced with interest in the direction Jenna indicated, then frowned. She was looking at the man as if he were some kind of varmint. "Ignore him," she said finally. "He used to be my husband."

"Your *what?*" But Sharon kept walking. After depositing the box in the Dumpster outside, she crossed the parking lot to speak to the man. Jenna looked a little closer. She guessed he was somewhere in his early fifties, a solidly built five foot nine or so. A good match for Sharon's buxom five foot seven.

Sharon had never talked much about her divorce or her ex. She seemed determined to begin a whole new life and let the past go. The past didn't seem to be cooperating, Jenna thought as she watched the two face off. Actually Sharon did most of the talking with her ex alternately staring at her in disbelief or shaking his head as if she'd lost her mind completely. Jenna hoped there wouldn't be cause to dial 911. They didn't have a working phone yet.

"WHAT ARE YOU DOING HERE?" Sharon asked, her exasperation buzzing around her like a cloud of bees. She had the urge to sting somebody herself. Even though they'd been divorced nearly two years, Dean kept tabs on her just the way he had when they'd been married. She hadn't liked it then, and the divorce meant she didn't have to put up with it now. "Who told you about this place? I'm gonna put their hide on the menu."

Squaring his shoulders, Dean almost grinned. "I have my sources, and I'm here because I couldn't believe my ears when I heard you were going back into the restaurant business."

He looked tired, but Sharon couldn't let that sway her. In the last few years of their marriage, he'd always been tired. Tired, and as he continually reminded her, getting older.

"Well, now you know. And I don't want to hear any argument. I've already signed the papers."

Dean scratched the back of his neck and sighed. "Yeah, I know about the signin' of papers." He squinted at her. "And I suppose you sank all the money from the settlement into this place. Well, that's my money, too, and I can't let you go into something like this without some advice. You're not twenty years old anymore and—"

"Stop right there," Sharon said as she held up a hand to halt his words. Dean hadn't changed a whit. It made her want to grab him and shake him. "That's *exactly* the kind of advice I *don't* need. Contrary to popular belief, I'm aware of my age. But I also know I'm not *dead* yet, which is what you seem intent on convincing me of."

Unable to face more of the same old argument, Sharon spun away. But after two steps she stopped and turned back. "If you have any real advice, rather than the kind designed to undermine what I'm trying to do, then you're welcome to give it. Otherwise, don't come around here. Go home and count your gray hairs."

Sharon strode back to the diner determined not to turn around again. She saw Jenna watching from the window and inwardly sighed. It was time to tell her partner a little of her history. Not that she thought Dean would cause trouble. He wasn't like that. But since she and Jenna were in this together, Jenna needed to know more of the story, more of the reason why she was determined to make the Donut Wrangler succeed. She had to prove a point, to herself and to Dean.

Jenna's eyes were full of questions when she met her at the door. "Is everything okay?"

"Yeah." Sharon dusted her hands on her jeans and glanced toward the parking lot. Dean was still standing in the hot sun with his hands stuffed in his pockets gazing at the restaurant as if he wasn't sure what to do. Right then, his expression looked more like one of her son's than her husband's. Er, her *ex*-husband's. He'd been such a fireball when they'd first gotten married....

"He just came by to give me a hard time," she said, then felt a stab of contrition. "Actually I think he came by to see the place, and me."

"Why doesn't he come in?"

"I told him he couldn't until he had something good to say, instead of telling me all the things he thinks will go wrong."

Jenna nodded in understanding.

The whine of a high-speed drill droned from the kitchen, cutting off any further normal conversation. Sharon raised her voice in order to be heard. "We'll talk about it later." She patted Jenna on the shoulder and headed back to her work in the kitchen.

THE SUN WAS LOW in the sky before the partners had time to sit and talk. The workmen were gone and the air conditioner was doing its best to counteract the waves of near-hundred-degree heat left over from the middle of the day. They even had the lights on, though the doughnut outside remained a dark circle in the sunset.

Jay had finally worn himself out an hour before and was currently sound asleep on one of the bench seats. Jenna dug around in the cooler they'd brought and presented Sharon with a cold soda. She chose a bottle of water for herself.

"Here's to hard work and success," Jenna said, figuring that description just about covered their day. Much of the accumulated dirt had been cleared away, and the place smelled like lemon oil and Windex. The dining room almost looked ready for human habitation, and the kitchen had been wired with two new 220-volt electrical boxes. There was still some cleaning left to be done in the bathrooms, but that would have to wait.

Jenna felt like a dustbin herself. She hadn't done so much manual labor since her move back to Texas, and she knew she'd feel it in the morning.

"I'll drink to that," Sharon said, and popped the top of the soda can. After taking a long drink, she added, "Don't tell anyone, but right now I feel as old as I am."

"I know what you mean. Once we start painting, we're both going to wish we'd opened a dress shop."

"Nah," Sharon said with a laugh. "We've put our eggs in the right basket. Just because we can't currently lift that basket doesn't mean anything. Tomorrow is a new day."

Jenna watched the smile fade from Sharon's face as she gazed out the window. "That's what I kept trying to tell Dean."

"What's that?" Jenna asked.

Sharon set down her soda and ran a tired hand through her hair. "Sometime about five years ago, Dean suddenly got the idea that he was old. And not just him. He thought both of us were, 'too old to do this,' 'too old to do that.' I thought it had to do with something at work, maybe he'd been passed over for promotion or a raise." She looked Jenna directly in the eyes. "I thought it was a mood that would pass. I used to try to tease him out of it. But his pessimistic outlook didn't go away after he retired. He was convinced that any week now he would drop dead or get some dreadful disease.

"He even started lecturing our sons on what they should do while they were still 'young.'"

"Was he having health problems?" Jenna asked. She remembered her own father having to be convinced he couldn't do all the things he used to do because of a weakening heart.

"No, that's what made me so mad. He's healthy. Strong as an ox and just as thickheaded. So, I divorced him."

Jenna almost spit out her water. She managed to swallow before asking, "You divorced him because he said he was old?"

"Sounds loony, doesn't it?" Sharon smiled again, briefly. "My mother still doesn't understand it. I'm not sure if I can explain. You see, I'm a person who believes in hope." She shook her head. "Not just believes. I thrive on hope. When my kids were young, I had so many dreams and good wishes for them. Sure, I worried, but it was the hope that kept me going.

"Once our boys were grown, I had *hoped* Dean and I would start up a life for the two of us. There was so much we couldn't do when the kids were home. We had the money and the time. But Dean…"

Jenna thought of her own preoccupation with a dark future and shivered inside. A loss of hope. Suddenly that sounded like an excellent reason for a divorce. She'd come back to Texas to rekindle her own faltering hope. In order to do that, she'd have to ignore her painful past and go on.

"Anyway," Sharon continued, "I have more life left in me, and several things I still want to do." She smiled at Jenna again. "Thanks to you, I have high hopes for our partnership and—" she glanced around the room "—in the Donut Wrangler, such as it is. Dean and I put our hearts into the restaurant we owned—he cooked and I waited on customers and we made it a success. You and I can do that, too."

Headlights flashed through the front windows as a car turned into the lot. Too tired to move, Jenna looked at Sharon and sighed.

"I sure hope we have this many people in and out of here when we actually open the doors and serve food." She squinted to see the driver, but the car was too close to the building. "Can you see anything? I'm too tired to move."

Sharon got off her stool and sauntered over to the window. "Well, it looks like that tall, handsome Texas Ranger, along with someone else."

"Ty?" Jenna squeaked. She lowered her gaze to inspect her clothes, wondering if she was as grimy as she felt. Then she remembered the dirt-smudged sweatband around her forehead and groaned. She stood and had covered two steps toward the bathroom before Ty walked in the front door.

"Hello, Ranger," Sharon said.

Ty stopped and touched the brim of his Stetson. "Miz Kellerman." Then his gaze locked on Jenna.

"Please pardon our mess," Sharon went on graciously as if she were the lady of a manor. "Come on in."

Jenna was a little more conscious of how she must look after a day of pushing dust. She brought one hand up to slide the sweatband out of her hair. "Hey, Ty. I'll be right back." Then before he could answer, she left.

Jenna turned on the light and stared at her reflection in the bathroom mirror. It was worse than she'd thought. Her face was smudged with dirt, a crease mark from the sweatband spanned her forehead and her hair… Oh, God, her hair looked like she'd been swimming in the ocean all day—alternately plastered down and sticking up.

She groaned again before turning on the water to wash her face.

"WHAT'S THE MATTER with Jenna?" Ty asked Sharon.

"Oh, we weren't expecting visitors, that's all. We're both a little on the shabby side after working in here all day. Who's your friend?"

Ty turned to Kirby. "This is Kirby Watson. Kirby, this is Jenna's partner in crime, Sharon Kellerman."

"How do?" Kirby said.

"Hello, Kirby. I'm flattered you remembered my name, Ranger," Sharon challenged.

"I'm good with names," Ty countered. "It goes

along with my job.'' He was beginning to see that Ms. Kellerman was a handful.

''You two have a seat. We have some soda, juice and water in the cooler. Would you like something?'' she asked.

''Not me,'' Ty answered. ''How about you, Kirby?''

''No, thanks.'' Kirby glanced at Sharon. ''Ty told me you ladies were opening up a diner. You mind if I look around?''

''Go right ahead, just watch out for the junk.''

As Sharon showed Kirby some of the high points, Ty sat on a stool. It worried him that Jenna had run out of the room when he came in the door. But he figured after she'd called him and interrupted his sleep, he had a right to stop by and see how things were going. It had been a last-minute decision to bring Kirby. They'd been on their way to dinner when Ty decided he wanted to show the old man the diner.

Returning from the kitchen, Sharon and Kirby were walking near the booths when Kirby said, ''And who's this?''

''That's my son.'' Ty turned toward Jenna's voice. She closed the distance and put a hand out to Kirby. ''I'm Jenna Taylor, and this sleeping whirlwind is Jay. I think we finally wore him out after working in the heat all day.''

Kirby graced Jenna with a smile. ''Kirby Watson, and I know just how he feels. After a long day I tend to fall out for a nap on any flat space.''

Then Jenna's gaze was on Ty and for some reason his insides took a dive.

"Hey, Ty."

"Jenna," he said. He searched her features for any trace of displeasure that he'd intruded. He found none. As he watched, though, she raised one hand and ran it through her wet hair. She looked as if she'd been rolled in the dust then left out in the rain. Unfortunately for Ty, it only made her more attractive. He liked a woman who wasn't afraid to get her hands dirty.

"I'm sorry everything is such a mess. We weren't expecting—"

"I know. Don't worry about it. We just stopped by for a minute on our way to dinner."

Jenna relaxed slightly. Her hand swept the room. "So, what do you think? We have lights, air-conditioning and running water."

Ty considered that for a moment. He couldn't help but tease her. "Well, I think all three of those things are a darned good idea."

Jenna rolled her eyes, and Sharon laughed. "We thought so, too."

"Are you girls gonna have pancakes on the menu?" Kirby asked. "I'm a pecan-pancake fiend."

"I think that could be arranged," Sharon answered with an enticing smile that could probably melt butter from across the room. "Are you plannin' on being a regular customer?"

"Sign me up," Kirby said with a wink.

Ty almost choked. He'd never seen Kirby flirt with a woman before. There seemed to be life in the old man yet. Ty thought it best to change the subject before things got too out of hand.

"We came by to ask you out to dinner. You must be starving after working here all day."

"Oh, no," Jenna said quickly. "I mean, we can't. We're filthy and I have to get Jay home, cleaned up and in a real bed."

"Are you sure? I don't mind a little dust."

Jenna seemed to fade before his eyes. "Honestly, Ty. I'm exhausted. We were just getting ready to pack up and go home."

Ty stood up and nodded. "Okay. We can at least help you with that."

"We sure can," Kirby agreed.

"If either of you men is available tomorrow, we're having a Saturday-afternoon painting party," Sharon said as she moved around the counter. "The more, the merrier."

After a couple of trips to the car with the cooler and Jay's box of toys, Ty left Kirby and Sharon in the parking lot and went back inside. Jenna was bending over Jay, getting ready to pick him up.

"Here, let me take him," Ty said. He nudged Jenna aside and scooped up the sleeping boy. "Hey, Jay," he said so the child wouldn't be startled. Jay shifted in his arms and murmured in his sleep.

"Daddy..."

Ty froze and met Jenna's eyes. They widened

slightly. For a moment Ty thought she looked winded, as if she'd taken a blow. But she quickly shrugged it off and offered him a tired smile.

Daddy…

CHAPTER FIVE

> Sometimes I look at Jay and see Jimmy in his eyes. It's almost eerie. But then, part of Jimmy is in Jay and that's comforting. We didn't lose him completely.

TY'S HANDS tightened on the wheel as he drove home. When Jay had mistakenly called for his daddy, Ty felt as if a slab of granite had been lowered onto his chest. He'd sworn to be there for Jay and for Jenna. He would do anything he could, get them whatever they needed. But the boy needed the strong arms of his daddy to carry him, and Jenna needed…her husband.

Jimmy was the one thing Ty couldn't give them.

He wondered what Jimmy would do if Ty had been the one who'd died, and Jimmy were standing in his shoes. The closest thing he could remember had been years back. They'd been called to a suicide. A farmer on the losing end of a series of bad crops had taken things into his own hands and ended the struggle for money with a shotgun. He'd had the crazy idea that he could make it look like an accident so his family would collect the insurance money.

Most of the other law-enforcement personnel had come in, done their job efficiently, then left. Ty remembered Jimmy taking some extra time, sitting down with the widow and two grieving children and explaining to them how their father's death wasn't their fault. That the man had chosen the only way he could see out of a situation, that he hadn't known how much it would hurt them or how little it would help them.

Ty shook his head. If people could read his thoughts, they'd probably say, "Damn, he's making Jimmy into a saint." He could almost hear his friend laugh.

Another memory surfaced—Jimmy, Lucas Angelo and Ty were trying to steal a pig one night for a practical joke. When they'd first planned to get the pig, put it in a burlap sack and deliver it to one of the local pig-in-a-poke politicians, Jimmy had laughed and said, as usual, "piece of cake." By the time they'd chased that pig for an hour in the dark, the mud and the pig patties, Jimmy had threatened to shoot it for barbecue and send a picture of a pig instead.

No, Officer Jimmy Taylor was no saint.

And neither was Ty.

How much more could he do for Jenna and Jay? When he'd seen Jenna smudged and exhausted, he'd wanted to put his arms around her, take her home, make sure she ate, rub her back....

Whoa.

He was pretty sure that when he promised to look out for Jenna, back rubbing had not been included. That would be his hormones talking. And he had to disconnect the conversation somehow…

Maybe he'd been without a woman too long, but at the moment he wasn't in the mood for visiting the Caballero. And going home would give him too much empty time to brood about Jenna. He needed to keep his mind on business—his own business. He acted on the idea by turning left at the next crossroad. He'd ride down a few of the back roads known to be prime locations for a *pachanga.*

Originally a south-Texas tradition, the *pachanga* had migrated north along with the killer bees and several law-enforcement officers. The object was to find an out-of-the-way place in the mesquite to set up a barbecue grill and a few coolers. A place where any and all off-duty lawmen were welcome to sit on the tailgates of pickup trucks, drink beer, eat fajitas and shoot the breeze. It harked back to pioneer days of gathering around the campfire to hear news.

It looked as if he'd hit the jackpot tonight. With a nearly full moon rising on the cloudless eastern horizon, it was easy to spot several trucks and cars parked out in a field near the old north-south crossroad of Highway 32. He was sure he'd know most of the men, and the ones he didn't he'd meet tonight. Ty slowed his car, then eased it off the road and over the hard-packed soil.

He glanced at his watch. It read eight-thirty. Most of the eating would be done by now, but the talking ought to just be getting started.

As he closed the car door behind him, he settled his Stetson a little lower on his head. He'd left his gun stowed securely in the trunk and wasn't wearing his badge.

Two men standing near the bed of a black pickup stopped talking as he approached. One of the men raised his long-necked beer in acknowledgment. "Evenin', Ranger," he said.

Ty nodded. "Evenin'." He didn't know the man's name but he'd seen him before, probably in the sheriff's office. He continued on toward the center of the gathering. A spurt of laughter reached him on a warm draft of smoke-and-dust-tainted air. Will Temple, the Green County sheriff, greeted him.

"We've got the wild bunch out here tonight," the sheriff said. "If we're not careful, somebody might call the law." Chuckling at his own humor, he stood, offering Ty his hand. "Good to see you, Ranger."

Ty shook hands and nodded. "What are you boys up to?" He pivoted slightly to survey the other men.

"Any of you men don't know him, this is Ty Richardson. He's the Ranger for this county." The sheriff turned back to him. "We've got beer in the box, hard stuff on the back of that truck and probably a few fajitas left in the pan. What can we do you for?"

Since he'd already eaten dinner with Kirby, he passed on the fajitas. "I believe I could sip on a little tequila if you have it." He could use a stiff belt after struggling with his damned "feelings." Why did women say they wanted men to search their souls? It was damned uncomfortable. One of the men close to the bar set up on the tailgate of the other truck poured him two fingers of Cuervo in a paper cup and handed it over.

"Thanks," Ty muttered, still disgusted by the turn of his thoughts. He raised the cup and let the tequila slide down his throat. He was determined *not* to think about Jenna or about her sleepy son calling for his daddy.

DADDY...

Jenna opened her eyes and tensed. She could have sworn she'd heard Jay's voice. She glanced around her bedroom. Everything seemed familiar, normal. After listening for a few more moments, Jenna pushed the covers back and sat up.

Tiptoeing into Jay's room, she gazed down at her sleeping son. They'd both had a long day. He'd kicked the covers off, along with one of the pillows. But he was quiet, deeply asleep. The call she'd heard must have been her imagination.

Or the memory of his calling for his father while being held in Ty's capable arms.

Jenna ran a hand through her hair before bending over Jay and gingerly rearranging the sheets. There was no need for them both to be awake. She envied her son's ability to surrender completely to exhaustion. It seemed that for the longest time, she'd been unable to shut down completely and truly rest.

She supposed that came from suddenly becoming a single parent. Everything was up to her now. She'd become Jay's only source of safety and security, and as daunting as the prospect was, she was determined not to disappoint him.

Daddy...

She was also uncomfortably aware that there were some things she couldn't give him. Things only a father could understand and face with a son. Jenna sadly shook her head, then kissed Jay lightly on the forehead. "I'll do the best I can for you," she whispered as tears filled her eyes.

Returning to her room, Jenna sat on the side of her bed, reached for a tissue and looked at the green glow of the clock. Only ten. She'd barely slept an hour. No wonder she felt like a zombie. She dabbed her eyes and blew her nose. No wonder she was so quick to tears. She needed...someone to talk to. Someone to tell her that everything would be all right.

Jimmy. No, Jimmy couldn't help her now. Wherever he was, and she firmly believed he was in a better place, he couldn't comfort her. She needed a living, breathing person to put an arm around her and tell her that she—no, *they*—would be fine.

She thought of Ty, then dismissed the idea. She'd already called him late in the evening and woken him up once. She was determined not to bother him again. What would she say? What could Ty say about raising a son without a father? He had no children of his own.

Then one of his letters came to mind.

> By the time I was about ten years old, I'd decided I could do just fine without a father. I had my uncle and my granddaddy. But somewhere around twelve, I had a whole passel of questions that needed answering. Questions I would never ask my mother. So I just held them all in.
>
> Then one day, while we were out fishing my uncle asked *me* if I had the answers to some of those same questions. I think he saved my life. I thought I would surely explode without talking to someone.

Jenna felt close to exploding herself. Something inside her wanted to depend on Ty, perhaps because he'd been so close to Jimmy, but she knew that wouldn't be fair. There was only so much Jimmy's best friend could do for her and Jay, and Ty had already provided more than anyone could expect. Her son needed someone who would be there through the years. Ty would have a family of his own some day and be too busy to worry about Jay.

Jay needed a father.

Jenna shivered at the thought. Was that the way to help her son? Even after two years, it was difficult to picture falling in love and marrying again.

She had too many other things to preoccupy her. What if she couldn't love anyone? She thought of Rusty's parents just three houses down—in love and expecting a baby. Why would a man want to take on a widow and another man's son without the promise of love?

Ty's image rose in her mind as the only candidate, and she automatically pushed it away. It wouldn't be fair to depend on Ty when there could be no future for them. No matter how important he'd become to her and Jay, the fact remained that he was a lawman—a Texas Ranger. She'd lost one husband to his oath to protect and serve; she would not lose another. Jay already looked up to Ty, and she couldn't allow her son to be drawn to a profession that required carrying a gun.

Guilt rolled through her. She'd sworn to do whatever it took to provide for Jay's future. She couldn't discount the obvious. Whether she liked the idea or not, the best thing she could do for him would be to find him a new father. A father who would keep him safe and inspire him to a less dangerous career path.

Jenna crushed the tissue in her hand, then tossed it in the wastebasket. Out of old habit, she reached for the pad and pen she kept on the nightstand. She had to talk to someone. She could depend on Ty without his knowing.

I'm scared, Ty. I have to move on. I have to provide for my son. But I have no idea how to put our lives back together again. With Jimmy, everything seemed so easy. I knew exactly what I wanted and who I could depend on. But now even the smallest decision seems to stop me. I had hoped this confusion would pass, but it's been two years...and I'm still afraid.

Jenna put down the pen and shook her head. God, she hated sounding so weak. She still had her son and her health. And now she had a new business to get rolling. Things were certainly better than a year ago when she'd been so devastated.

She put the pad aside and straightened her spine. Soon, she promised as she stretched out on her bed and arranged the sheets. As soon as she and Sharon had the restaurant up and running and she felt some measure of financial stability, she'd start dating, looking for a—she grimaced at the word—husband.

"DID YOU HEAR old Randy Bond is gettin' married at the end of the month?" Sheriff Temple asked Ty. "Some little gal down Austin way. That only leaves you and Ray here as the sworn bachelors in the area."

Ray raised his beer to Ty. "Here's to us, hombre."

"I guess." Ty nodded and took a sip of his tequila.

"Took her less than six weeks to hogtie him,"

the sheriff continued. ''Either of you boys could be next.''

''I'd think she'd be too busy with Randy to worry about either of us,'' Ty said with a straight face.

Temple took the wisecrack in stride. ''Well, you know some women—they change their minds every ten minutes or so. You boys better lay low until after the weddin'.''

Ty thought of his own wedding to Mary Jo. All the time and preparation it took to say some simple vows, vows that M.J. hadn't seen fit to keep. He wouldn't go through that again, not for anything or anybody. If it took white gowns and limousines and a church full of people to get married, then he might end up like old Kirby, alone except for a mutt.

To head off those morose thoughts, he changed the subject. ''Either of you working on anything interesting?''

The sheriff rubbed his chin for a moment, then gave Ty a calculating look. ''I have a missing-person case that looks kind of fishy.'' He studied Ty a bit longer. ''Woman called in to report her husband missing—been gone about four days.''

''Why do you say it looks fishy?''

''Well, for one thing, the wife has been no help at all. She says she has no idea where he might have lit off to. She only called the police because her mother-in-law was concerned.''

''Another happy marriage, I guess,'' Ray interjected.

"More than that," the sheriff continued, looking at Ty. "When I drove out to talk to her about it, she had some fairly significant bruises on her face and arms. She's just a skinny little thing. When I asked her about it, she said she fell down the back steps, then clammed up. Shoot. You know that old dog don't hunt."

Temple shook his head, then leaned over to spit in the dust at his feet. "Now that I think about it, a Texas Ranger might be the perfect person to jog her memory and persuade her to help us out a little more. All you boys are so charming. After watching that Ranger TV show, I'd think she'd be anxious to answer any question you asked. Would you be willin' to go by and talk to her?"

Ty didn't hesitate. He had a lot of respect for Sheriff Temple, and hell, he'd take on a case of mistaken identity for Lucifer himself right now. The more he worked, the less he'd worry about Jenna Taylor. But he couldn't pass up the opportunity to provoke Temple a little. "Hell, I should have stayed with the highway patrol—I'd have less ground to cover."

The sheriff just grinned. "Maybe you should have come to work for me. But I guess I would have passed up a lot to be a bona fide Texas Ranger."

Ty went back to answer the original question. "Sure, I'd be glad to talk to her. I'll stop by your office tomorrow and pick up the file."

The conversation shifted then to war stories of

the outlaws versus the good guys. Ty knew the real reason these men were standing out in a field around a fire at ten o'clock at night. The same reason he was there. They needed somebody to talk to who would understand. Someone who wouldn't be traumatized or upset by the uglier side of human nature. You couldn't very well go home and discuss a double murder during a liquor-store robbery with your wife and kids.

"You know who I still miss?" Ray Guthrie said after a particularly comical description of a burglar who crawled through a hole in the roof of a convenience store, then got stuck on the way out because he'd downed so many beers. The officer on the scene had to call the fire department to get the man free before he could arrest him. "I miss old Jimmy Taylor. Ty, you remember that time Jimmy tried to help a woman catch an ostrich of hers that had gotten loose? He always had a soft spot for animals."

Ray sighed and chuckled. "Man, I nearly busted a gut when that bird turned on Jimmy. I thought we were gonna have to get animal control to shoot 'em both with a tranquilizer gun."

The vision of anyone shooting Jimmy stopped the conversation cold. Ty couldn't make his mouth move to a smile or a frown. The warm glow from the tequila suddenly faded.

"I'm sorry, I guess that wasn't the best way to put it," Ray backtracked. "But you know what I mean. I miss that old boy."

"Yeah," Ty managed to say as he tossed his empty cup into the back of the truck. "Me, too."

"Whatever happened to his wife and son?" the sheriff asked.

Ty cleared his throat. "Um, they went back east for a while, but they're in San Angelo now. Jenna, Jimmy's wife, is opening up a diner with a friend of hers. She seems to be gettin' along fine."

"They had a nice family. A real shame."

"Yeah." *A nice family.* Something Ty had never had. Ty looked at Ray. "I expect all you sheriff's department doughnut hounds to show up over there on Route 82 when they open up. The name is the Donut Wrangler—serving breakfast and lunch. It's the least we can do for Jimmy."

A chastened Ray nodded. "I'll pass the word."

CHAPTER SIX

JENNA WAS DRAGGING the last painter's cloth over a booth and had her back to the door when she heard Ty's voice. His low words sent a jolt of awareness through her. As she turned toward the sound, she told herself he'd just surprised her again—that's why her pulse had taken a leap. But when she looked up and saw him in the doorway, hat in hand, her heartbeat quickened rather than calmed.

She'd been depending on Ty as a friend. She'd filed the fact that he was a man in a don't-go-there section of her mind. When she saw him dressed in a plain white T-shirt and a pair of well-worn jeans that hugged every inch of his long legs, he seemed like a stranger. A good-looking and downright sexy *male* stranger. When he smiled at her, she had to swallow and pull her attention away from the view, all the time wondering why no woman had managed to steal his heart.

Maybe his wife had taken it with her as part of the divorce.

"Hey, Ty," Jenna said, reminding herself that Ty's love life was none of her business. For all she knew, he might have ten women lined up to apply for the position of heart thief.

"Jenna." He nodded, then replaced the ball cap he'd removed before extending his arms slightly. "I'm here to paint."

Sharon, entering the dining room from the kitchen, didn't waste any time taking him up on the offer. "Right this way," she said, then led him to the cans, pans and rollers set out on the linoleum. Jay was seated near the unopened cans. He stood as Ty approached.

Jenna watched Ty stoop to her son's level. "What are you up to, Jay?"

"Mama said I could help paint, too," Jay answered proudly.

Jenna crossed the room to her son, intending to keep him out of Ty's way. "Let us get things set up first, okay?" she said, coaxing him to stay back.

"Okay," Jay replied, looking disappointed.

Ty glanced up, and suddenly Jenna had a perfect view of his hazel eyes. He didn't smile, but the crinkles at the corners of his eyes reflected humor. "Don't you think we need a little workin' music?" he asked, still staring at Jenna instead of Jay. When she didn't answer, couldn't answer because her mind had gone blank as he held her with that playful look, he stood up slowly and shoved one hand into the front pocket of his jeans. Both she and Jay watched silently as Ty brought out a handful of change and began picking out quarters.

He extended the quarters to Jay. "How about we

plug in that old jukebox and you play us some songs?''

Jay didn't hesitate. He reached for the change and headed for the jukebox with Ty following.

Get a hold on yourself, Jenna muttered silently, surprised by her sudden awareness. Ty hadn't changed just because he was wearing different clothes, a different hat. He was still her husb—*her* friend. Why was she acting so foolish?

Sharon sidled up next to Jenna as Ty bent to lift Jay so he could reach the buttons. ''Mm-mm-mmm,'' she said under her breath. ''That man's backside could give a nun heart palpitations.''

''Sharon!'' Jenna hissed, and pushed her friend toward the painting paraphernalia. ''Hush!'' She could feel her own face warming, as if Sharon had read her thoughts.

Sharon moved where Jenna directed, but slowly. ''You know what I mean...don't deny it.''

''I'm not denying it. I just don't want to talk about it,'' Jenna said firmly. She wanted to put an end to that conversation in a hurry. *An end.* God, she was losing her mind.

As the first few notes of an old Tammy Wynette song echoed from the jukebox, the smell of frying chicken drifted from the kitchen and Ty glanced around.

Sharon answered his unspoken question. ''We hired a cook. He's making us lunch to try out the kitchen.''

''Well, then—'' Ty rubbed his palms together in

anticipation "—the sooner we get this place painted, the sooner we eat."

THREE HOURS LATER Ty decided that if he had to watch Jenna go up the ladder one more time, he might just gnaw off his tongue and have it for lunch. Damn! He wasn't sure how, but he'd become the official ladder steadier every time Jenna decided she wanted to touch up a spot near the ceiling. He should have told her to let *him* paint the trim. Then he wouldn't have had her shapely butt close enough to bite each time she went up the ladder.

He ruefully realized that it wasn't the work that had caused him to break out in a sweat. Each time he touched her, steadied her, took her hand to help her down, he felt the charge of sexual energy. Having her son in the same room buffered it slightly, but not enough for Ty to relax and just work.

When Sharon called them to lunch, it was with great relief that Ty busied himself closing paint cans and wrapping rollers—anything to keep his eyes and hands busy and away from Jenna.

He'd promised to be her friend and only her friend, for God's sake. No, for Jimmy's sake. A fist of guilt tightened inside him with a hold so strong that he had to take a deep breath. His own sainthood was being severely tested. It wasn't that he'd forgotten his best friend. It was just that Jenna… Jenna was… He closed his eyes and rubbed the back of his hand against his forehead. Being so close to

Jenna was driving him crazy. They'd been safe in the letters, at a distance. But now—

"Did the paint fumes give you a headache?" Jenna asked.

Ty looked up. Jenna stood over him, a glass of iced tea in her hand. "I brought you some tea. I think I have some aspirin in my purse if you need it."

"No. It's all right." Ty pushed to his feet and stepped back a bit. Of the many things he wanted at that moment, tea and aspirin weren't even on the list. The calm expression on her face did nothing to help. She wasn't affected by him in the least, felt none of the ragged, conscience-ridden heat that coursed under his skin. And why should she? She'd lost the man she loved. No one could take his place. A fact Ty knew better than anyone. She'd made it clear in her letters. That knowledge made him feel even worse.

"Let me wash up," he said. "You go ahead and sit down. I'll be there in a minute."

By the time Ty returned from the rest room, Jenna and Sharon had uncovered one of the booths by the windows and were helping the cook set out food for lunch. Jenna introduced him.

"Ty? This is Robert Ludlow, our new cook."

Ty extended his hand to the man as, out of habit, he studied him. On the thin side, Robert looked as if he could use a few steady meals himself.

"Robert, this is Ty Richardson, a friend of the family."

"He's a Texas Ranger," Jay added.

"Hello," Robert said.

The man had a solid handshake, but he'd pulled back slightly after Jay spoke. Ty didn't want to jump to any conclusions, but he wondered if Jenna and Sharon had checked the man's references.

"I thought we'd sit next to the window and watch the other painters for a while," Jenna continued.

Ty made a mental note to take a look at the cook's job application, then glanced out the window. The painters who'd been contracted to work on the outside of the diner had just begun painting the giant doughnut.

"Have some of this chicken," Sharon offered as Ty took the open seat across from Jenna. The table was laden with enough food to feed ten people: fried chicken, mashed potatoes, three different vegetables including his own personal favorite, squash casserole, finished off with biscuits and peach cobbler.

After tasting most of the dishes, Ty decided he didn't need to be in a hurry to check on Robert. Obviously the man could cook, and that's what Jenna and Sharon had hired him to do.

"This is real good," Ty said.

Robert, who was standing at the end of the booth after bringing out more hot biscuits, wiped his hands on the towel tucked into his apron and looked relieved. "Thank you."

''Where did you learn to cook like this?'' Ty asked.

Robert glanced nervously at Jenna before he spoke. ''Prison.''

The answer didn't surprise Ty very much. And judging by the expression on Jenna's face, Robert hadn't kept the information from his new employers. ''Which one?''

''Over in Florida. I had some trouble with alcohol and ended up with time to serve. I worked in the kitchen—paid my debt.''

''Well, you're a darned good cook,'' Ty said, and reached for another biscuit.

''Thank you.'' Robert looked at Sharon. ''What do you think about salt? Should I add more?''

As Jenna shook her head, Sharon said, ''No, this is perfect. We're here to feed 'em, not kill 'em. If the customers want to hike up their blood pressure, they can use the extra salt on the tables.''

''Why don't you ask the painters outside if they'd like a plate? We have plenty left over,'' Jenna added.

Robert excused himself to follow her suggestion, and Jenna breathed a sigh of relief when Ty brought his attention back to the food. She'd been worried about how to tell him they'd hired an ex-con. They'd been careful, called Robert's references and questioned him closely. Out of ten people who had applied for the position, Robert had the best qualifications. He'd moved around a lot, but all his former employers said they'd take him back in a heart-beat.

One hurdle down, one more to go. As she watched Ty dig into lunch, she decided it might have been a mistake sitting across from him. Trying to calmly eat and help her son with his lunch under Ty's watchful gaze made her feel as clumsy as a teenager. Sitting next to him in the small booth, however, would have been impossible. They'd already shared enough accidental touches for one day. And they still had a half day of work left.

"Look, the doughnut has icing on it," Jay said.

Outside, the painters had finished repainting one side of the doughnut.

"It does look like icing, honey," Jenna agreed. "That reminds me—" she glanced at Sharon "—what did you and Robert decide about the doughnuts?"

"He said he'd be willing to try, but he's never made them before. I scrounged up some recipes. Tomorrow might be a good time to work on them. We should be finished painting by then."

"I'm done, Mom. Can I go outside and watch 'em paint the doughnut?"

"All right," Jenna answered. "But stay out of the way. And remember, that paint isn't really icing so don't get any ideas." Jay decided to crawl under the booth to get out, and had the three of them laughing after having their feet stepped on and crawled over. As soon as Jay extricated himself and hurried out the front door, Jenna pushed her own plate away and sighed. ''I guess we should get back to work, too.''

''Well...'' Sharon looked around the mostly painted room. ''I'll finish in here if you two will get started on the rest rooms.''

For a moment neither Jenna nor Ty said anything. Jenna was picturing being in even closer proximity with Ty because of the size of the rooms. She didn't want to do anything to give herself away. Having spent lunch trying to keep her knees from touching his, she'd been hoping for a respite.

Finally Jenna offered a suggestion. ''I'll do the ladies' and you can do the men's,'' she said to Ty.

Ty shook his head, looking almost as uncomfortable as she felt. ''Won't work. We only have two ladders, and Sharon needs one.''

Puzzled, Sharon backtracked. ''I suppose I could work in the kitchen until you're done with the ladders, but I'd have to wait until Robert is finished in there.''

''Don't worry,'' Ty said to Sharon. ''We can share—we've been doing that all morning.''

Challenged by his steady gaze, Jenna swallowed once, then agreed. ''Right, no problem.'' She glanced out the window to find her son in the parking lot. He was well out of the way of the painters, but she knew he'd probably want a closer look as time went by. ''Uh, Sharon, will you keep an eye on Jay?''

''Sure,'' Sharon answered. ''I'm working near the windows.''

As Ty carried the ladder he and Jenna would share, he felt like swearing. There was no way he would let Jenna and Sharon know the battle he'd been waging since he'd walked in the door that morning. He'd spent hours in close proximity with people, in interviews, interrogations and depositions. None of them had unsettled his peace of mind like Jenna. None of them had made him question his honor or his loyalty to a friend. None of them had made him want to touch or taste a woman he couldn't have.

"Why don't I work on the lower walls in the ladies' room, so you can use the ladder on the upper walls of the men's?"

"Sounds like a plan," he heard himself say, glad for another reprieve. But then he stopped and looked at Jenna. Had she noticed something about his behavior that made her wary? That was all he needed to feel really disgusted. If he'd done something to make her worry about being around him... "Are you okay?" he asked, not knowing how else to inquire about the situation.

Her blue eyes widened slightly as he watched her choose an answer. "I'm fine. Just a little tired."

He held her gaze a moment longer before nodding. "Let's get this over with, then."

It only took about forty minutes to complete the men's room. Someone, probably Sharon with Jay's help, had cranked up the jukebox again in the dining room. True to the plan, and accompanied by country music's oldies but goodies, Ty painted the ceiling and upper walls before taking the ladder to Jenna. He'd offered to stay and hold the ladder steady, but she'd refused.

After putting the finishing touches to the baseboards, Ty bundled up the newspapers protecting the floor before checking on Jenna's progress. He stood frozen in the doorway, with his arms full of crumpled newspaper, as he watched. The first thing he noticed was that she was humming along with the jukebox. The second thing that registered was the unrestricted view of her backside. Unwilling to relinquish the unobserved pleasure of watching her, he remained silent.

Singing the last few words along with Emmylou Harris, she turned slightly to dip her roller in the paint pan and saw him. That didn't have quite the result he would have hoped for. Startled, she lost her balance, and the ladder rocked beneath her.

Ty dropped the papers and quickly grabbed for the ladder. But they had moved in different directions. Jenna's roller hit the paint and she watched, horrified, as the pan skidded over the step and fell...on Ty.

The ladder steadied just as the paint pan grazed Ty's head then hit his shoulder, spilling pale green paint as it went. In between songs the jukebox was silent as the paint pan hit the floor with a clatter. Then Jenna gasped and scrambled down from the ladder.

"Are you all right?" she asked.

Ty had seen what was coming and closed his

eyes. Now he held perfectly still. He could feel the wet paint running down his left arm and soaking into his T-shirt. He didn't want to even think about the rest of him. He opened his eyes and stared down at the offending pan and saw that his jeans and boots were covered with a nice mint green.

He raised his eyes to look at Jenna. With one hand pressed over her mouth, she looked ready to run.

"I'm sorry—you startled me," she said, and then, obviously unable to keep a straight face, she started laughing. "I'm so sor—sorry."

Ty attempted to remain dignified as he let go of the ladder. He tried to remember his stoicism as an officer of the law. But when Jenna continued to laugh, dabbing at the paint running down his arm and apologizing through her giggles, something relaxed inside of him.

He started laughing, too.

She was getting more paint on herself than on the paper, but he still couldn't let her off easily. "Who taught you how to paint on a ladder? You never just balance the pan—it has hooks to hold it steady!"

"I was almost finished and I—" Jenna continued to laugh, and he couldn't scold her when her blue eyes were filled with tears of mirth. He probably wouldn't have touched her if she hadn't said anything else. But she did.

As she pressed clean newspaper to his paint-soaked shoulder, she gazed up at him. "At least the color accents your eyes."

Right about then Ty lost his mind. Gazing down into her smiling features, Ty forgot about the paint, and the past. He shifted his attention to her mouth and with very little effort he closed the distance between them. He had to kiss her. He'd never felt a stronger need in his life.

Jenna wasn't sure just when she knew that Ty was going to kiss her. She'd like to say it was after it happened, but in the milliseconds before his mouth touched hers, time seemed to slow. She could have pulled away if she'd wanted to. But she didn't want to.

As his mouth touched hers, she breathed him in. She closed her eyes and let him kiss her. It seemed like the most natural thing in the world. The laughter that had risen inside left her. Suddenly the room quieted and in the silence a new feeling took hold. She wanted to be kissed. As she stepped toward him and his arms slid around her, Jenna felt suspended in a place with no past or future. No grief or responsibility, just laughter and kisses. It had been so long… And he tasted different, different from Jimmy—

"Mommy?" Jay's voice cut through the moment like a gunshot.

One second Ty's mouth was exploring hers; the next he had released her. She couldn't look at him; she turned to her son instead.

"Aunt Sharon sent me to ask if you fell off the ladder."

Jenna smoothed her hands down her thighs and formed a smile. "No, honey," she said, but spoiled her normal mommy voice by having to clear her throat. She could feel the troublesome heat gathering in her cheeks. She'd let Ty kiss her. Even now, his presence behind her felt solid yet looming. "Go tell Aunt Sharon that I'm fine."

"You have paint on you," Jay said, staring at her chest.

Jenna looked down at her blouse. The left side was colored with green paint. There would be no mystery as to where it came from since the right side of Ty's shirt was soaked.

"I know, sweetie," she said as soon as she could get the words around the embarrassed catch in her throat. "I dropped a pan of paint and we—" she shifted slightly toward Ty but still didn't look at him "—got splashed. Would you run and get me a roll of paper towels from the kitchen?"

Jay hesitated, staring at Ty. "You kissed my mommy," he said.

Jenna heard Ty clear his own throat before answering. "Well, yes, I did. It was sort of an accident."

His low, familiar voice sent a shiver of awareness through her. *Ty had kissed her.* "Everything is fine," Jenna said, hoping the statement held true. Everything *was* fine, but nothing would be the same.

CHAPTER SEVEN

NOW JENNA HAD TO FACE TY. She had no idea what to say, what to do. *Ty had kissed her.* Kissed her like a man, not like a friend.

He spoke first.

"Jenna, I—" He started to touch her, but must have thought better of it because he stopped and lowered his hand to his side again. "I'm sorry. I didn't mean—"

Jenna shook her head and tried to gather the words needed to bridge the uncomfortable situation. But she could still taste his kiss on her mouth and knew that she'd wordlessly asked for it. She certainly couldn't take him to task for something she'd participated in. It just couldn't happen again.

"It's okay, Ty. I—" An overwhelming sense of blame settled over her. The feeling that even one small, innocent kiss was some kind of betrayal of Jimmy. To prevent Ty from seeing her feelings in her eyes, she bent and picked up some of the wadded paper at their feet. Gingerly, and from a slightly greater distance, she rubbed the paper over the paint on his arm. "I'm sorry I laughed. I didn't mean to douse you in paint."

Ty didn't give up. "Jenna, please. It isn't your fault. I didn't mean to—for that to happen. It just did. What are you going to tell Jay?"

Still avoiding his eyes, she shrugged off the seriousness in his voice, and treated his question in a safer, more academic way. "Oh, I think he'll accept what you told him, although he's been asking questions lately about men and women. If he asks again, then I'll deal with it."

Ty put his strong hands on her shoulders, forcing her to look at him. "I'm talking about how he feels about me kissing his mother. I don't want him, or you, to get the wrong idea about me. I'm your friend, same as I've always been. I just forgot that for a minute."

Jenna gazed into Ty's solemn hazel eyes and wanted to agree that everything could be the same. But he was wrong; nothing was the same about him. Just the touch of his long fingers circling her arms made all the blood inside her sing with awareness...and wariness. She already knew she couldn't trust herself; now she knew she couldn't trust him. He wasn't a "safe" friend anymore. He'd kissed her and her body had responded. There was no way to go back and squash that genie back in the bottle.

Now she could only use her wishes. She wished—what? Was kissing him a terrible thing? Not in itself. But wanting to do it again...

"Ty," she sighed. "This would be so much easier if you were a stranger...."

"But we're *not* strangers," he said, his voice

bristling with intensity. ''Not since you wrote the first letter to me.''

Jenna's insides seemed to be slowly melting into jelly. He was right. They were more than friends. But where did that leave them?

''Ty, I—''

''Here's the paper towels, Mom,'' Jay interrupted.

Ty released her, and Jenna turned to find Jay and Sharon standing tentatively outside the door.

''What in the world happened in here?'' Sharon said with an evil grin. ''Looks like there was an explosion.''

Jenna could tell by the expression on Sharon's face that Jay must have told her about the kiss. With the finest air of calm she could muster, Jenna took the paper towels out of Jay's hands and rolled off a handful for Ty to use.

''We had a little accident,'' Jenna replied.

''Yeah. Ty got painted, then *ack*-cidentally kissed my mom.''

Helplessly Jenna met Sharon's eyes. Ty was suspiciously quiet. Taking the hint, Sharon herded Jay back toward the dining room.

''Well, let them clean up the mess. You know, accidents do happen,'' the older woman explained sagely. It didn't help that she winked at Jenna at the same time.

Ty bent all his attention on getting as much paint as possible off him and his clothes. He had to keep his hands busy or he'd grab Jenna again. He swore under his breath. Not to kiss her. He should never have kissed her. What had he been thinking?

That's the point, smart guy, you weren't thinking. Not with your brain, anyhow. He glanced at Jenna, but she didn't look up from her task of cleaning the floor. He could tell she didn't want to talk about it. He could also tell she was upset. The pinkness in her cheeks gave her away, no matter what she said. He shouldn't have mentioned the letters. What she'd written in those pages had remained as sort of an unspoken secret between them. He had no right to use them as an excuse for his behavior.

And she had a right to be upset. He'd kissed her without permission or provocation. He'd kissed Jimmy Taylor's wife. His friend had made him promise to comfort Jenna if anything happened to him. Kissing wasn't comfort, at least not the kind of kiss they'd shared. Kisses were meant to start things, not end them.

Jimmy's voice came to him out of the blue. "You know I'd kill the son of a bitch if he ever touched my wife." Ty and Jimmy had been talking about a certain co-worker of theirs who seemed to take great pride in seducing married women. They'd discussed how it would only be a matter of time until something bad happened. "You don't mess with family and walk away without paying the price sooner or later. If anything like that took place with Jenna, you'd be visiting *me* in prison," Jimmy had said soberly. "And I'd expect you, as my friend, to go by occasionally and spit on that man's grave for me.

"Jenna is the best thing that ever happened along in my life. Her and James Jr. You know, it's a little scary when you love somebody that much."

Sorry, buddy, Ty thought silently. *I didn't mean to kiss her. She was just so beautiful...standing there laughing at me and...*

"Jenna?" Sharon's voice sounded from the dining room loud enough to be heard over Patsy Cline's "Crazy."

"Coming," Jenna replied. They'd done all the cleaning they could do for now, so he followed her out.

Ty noticed an older woman talking to Jay, who'd been helped up on a stool. Jenna seemed to falter slightly, and he nearly walked into her, but then, she continued on. The woman looked them both up and down before concentrating on Jenna with a stern, forbidding expression. In Ty's opinion the woman appeared slightly ill, pale and not at all happy to see either him or Jenna.

"Hello, Barbara," Jenna said, and Ty could hear a slight quaver in her voice. Just that much discomfort on Jenna's part was enough to harden his attitude toward this stranger. Then Jenna turned to him.

"Ty, have you met? This is Jimmy's mother, Barbara Taylor. Barbara, this is Jimmy's—my friend, Ty Richardson."

"Ma'am." Ty touched his paint-splattered hat and did his best to look completely harmless.

Jimmy's mother. He'd been introduced briefly at the funeral, but all the time he'd known Jimmy, he'd never really known her. When he and Jimmy had been together, they'd usually been up to things a mother wouldn't approve of. Her identity tempered his sour attitude. But it was difficult to look dignified after being soaked with green paint.

With a stiff nod Mrs. Taylor acknowledged the introduction. Hard to tell if she remembered him or not. "What in heaven's name have you been doing? You look like you've been rolling in paint."

Jenna self-consciously brushed at her stained shirt and shrugged. "We had a little accident—"

"Mommy dropped a paint pan and—"

"Jay!" Both Sharon and Ty spoke at the same time.

After a few heartbeats of silence and a puzzled look from Jay, Sharon came to the rescue and stepped behind the counter. "Didn't I promise you a soda for helping us paint? What will it be, buddy?"

"Root beer, please." Jay changed directions, and Jenna's shoulders seemed to relax slightly.

"Could we turn that music down?" Barbara asked as Johnny Cash's "Jackson" followed Patsy.

Ty thought Jimmy's mother looked offended by the entire concept of music. "I'll take care of that," he said to Jenna, fighting the inclination to stay close and help Sharon protect her.

Jenna did her best not to look guilty. But she felt absolutely awful. Of all people to show up on the heels of being kissed by Ty, Jimmy's mother had to be the most unforgiving. Thank God Sharon had distracted Jay. Mrs. Taylor had already advised against Jenna going into business, she didn't need a lecture on how to act like a proper widow, too.

"So," Jenna said in as bright a tone as she could muster. "What do you think of the place?"

Barbara gave the dining room a cursory examination. "It's fine, I suppose. But it took me over forty minutes to drive over here. How do you expect to make any money out in the middle of nowhere?"

Caught up in her own guilt and confusion, Jenna couldn't think of anything to say for a moment. Again Sharon saved her. "Why, there's a big old manufacturing plant four miles down the road. Those men have to eat somewhere."

"How will you support yourself and your employees until those people notice you're open for business?" Barbara asked.

"Now, I'm glad you brought that up," Sharon said. "I'd been meaning to mention it to Jenna." Then she looked at her partner. "I've decided we need to go down to the factory and put up some flyers. Maybe hand them out when the workers change shifts. What do you think of that?"

Jenna forgot her mother-in-law for a moment and brought her panicked thoughts back to business. "That's a great idea. We can put together a flyer and get it copied." She ran one hand protectively through her son's dark hair. "You could help hand them out, couldn't you, Jay?"

"Sure," Jay answered.

"I could give them out to all the lawmen I know, too," Ty added.

His voice went up Jenna's spine and flashed her back to the moment she'd stood in his arms. Darn. The erratic change in her pulse made her feel warm and miserable, as if she were misbehaving all over again.

"Are you married, Mr. Richardson?" Barbara asked.

Jenna thought her heart might stop altogether. She swallowed nervously and waited for Ty's response. He'd have to be dumb as a post not to see what Barbara was really asking. And Ty could never be accused of being dumb.

"No, ma'am," Ty answered smoothly, leaving all the innuendos stranded in midair.

Barbara tried another tack. "Well, if you were, would you want your wife and son working in a restaurant out in the middle of nowhere?"

Ty seemed to think the question over for a moment. "I suppose if my wife thought it was something she really wanted to do, then I would support the idea."

Mrs. Taylor's mouth thinned. "I suppose you would, since you're here helping with this fiasco. If you were really James's friend, you'd know he wouldn't want this." She didn't give Ty time to reply. "Well, I can see you're busy and I need to start back home. It'll take me an hour to get there. I expect to see you on Sunday, Jenna.'' Then she leaned over and kissed Jay. ''You, too, James Jr.''

Softening, because she knew Barbara had lost her only son, Jenna held back any further comment. She put an arm around her own son and set him on his feet. ''Why don't you walk your grandmom to her car?'' Jenna said.

''Okay,'' Jay answered solemnly, looking older than his years. He held out his hand to Jimmy's mother. ''Come on, Grandmom.''

When they were safely out the door, Sharon was the first to break the tense silence. ''Whew. That woman could curdle every carton of milk in the place.''

''Now that's the truth,'' Ty agreed. He slid onto a stool. ''How about another glass of root beer, bartender?''

Jenna slumped down on the stool next to Ty. ''Well, at least we got past the first visit. I've been dreading it.''

''Don't let her get to you, girl,'' Sharon soothed as she plunked Ty's glass of root beer on the counter. ''We've got too much work to do to worry. Speaking of work—'' she glanced at Ty ''—I think I'll get back to the kitchen. I'm all done in here.''

And then, without warning, Jenna found herself alone with Ty once more. She slowly rotated on the stool until her knees were almost touching his.

''Ty—''

He looked so serious she wanted to reach out and

touch his arm, to smile—something to make her words more palatable. But she couldn't be too friendly, not now. She had to say what needed to be said and get it over with. It would have been so much easier to put the words in a letter the way she used to do. To regain the friendly distance they'd had for the past two years. In person, Ty could be a little unnerving.

"Ty, I'm not ready for anything beyond friendship right now and I don't know when I will be. And I need you as a friend...."

Ty ran a hand down his face and looked away before speaking. "I swear, it won't happen again. I know how you feel. Hell—I read your letters. All I can say is, I'm sorry."

Jenna did her best to fight the feeling that she'd just lost him, his friendship and anything else that might have occurred. It hurt more than she'd expected. When Jay returned from the parking lot, she knew they'd run out of time to talk. Acting normal seemed the safest course.

"Okay," she agreed. "I'm sorry, too. Let's start over then. I'll finish painting the bathroom. Why don't you help Sharon in the kitchen?"

TWO HOURS LATER, when Ty pulled into his own driveway, he felt as if his brain would detonate any second. He'd gone over the kiss fifty times in his mind and he still hadn't come up with any good excuses.

As he slammed shut his car door, he glanced toward the mailbox and sighed. This never would have happened if he'd just kept writing to her instead of jumping into her life, claiming to be her friend.

Well, dammit, he *was* her friend! Even if friends didn't kiss friends the way he'd kissed Jenna.

A memory came back of Jimmy, kissing his wife…kissing Jenna. Ty and Jimmy had been heading out at dawn on a fishing trip. The car was packed and they'd both gotten in when Jenna had come hurrying outside barefoot, still in her robe. She'd waved to Ty, but she'd kissed Jimmy. Not a wifely peck on the cheek, either. A toe-curling, y'all-come-back-now kiss. A kiss with the power to keep Jimmy quiet for at least five minutes after they'd pulled away. A world record, for sure. Ty himself had had some trouble getting his mind back on fish and bait.

Shifting back to the present before more guilt gutted him, Ty opened the mailbox, pulled out two bills and a coupon circular and realized that he missed Jenna's letters. Writing had been something just between the two of them—the part of her that belonged to him. No guilt required. He'd always gotten a little charge of exhilaration simply from holding the envelope in his hand. He never knew what she would say, whether she would be sad or hopeful, or talk about her dreams.

I dreamed I was flying last night. Over a city, at night. The lights were so beautiful—strung out like jewels in the darkness. That must be how it feels to be an angel. I hope Jimmy can look down and see us. I hope he's proud of his son and that he knows we will always love him.

Ty hoped Jimmy hadn't been looking down this afternoon, watching when his best friend kissed his wife. Ty couldn't even say he was sorry, because he wasn't, not really. He'd had to taste her laughter.

Determined to get his mind off past disasters, he unlocked his door and went inside. He needed to shower and change his paint-stained clothes. He looked down at his boots and shook his head. It would take some work to get the paint off, but that was fine. Work, he understood.

What he had to do was stay away from Jenna for a while, and he wanted her to understand why. But he also wanted her to understand what he was feeling. Now, there was a first. Wanting to explain his…feelings. The only way he could do that was in a letter. He picked up a pad and a pen and sat down at the kitchen table.

Jenna.

I've said I'm sorry for kissing you, and I meant it when I said it wouldn't happen again. I think it would be best if I stepped out of the picture for a bit. To allow some time to pass so we both won't feel…

Ty tore the page from the pad and crumpled it in his fist. Damn. He didn't know what to say except that he needed some time away from her, to let things calm down. But he didn't want to worry her.

Jenna.
I have to go out of town for a few days on a case. If you need me, call my pager number.
See you in a few days.

He hated to lie. As he sat there staring at his own scrawl, he realized his palms were sweating. He'd never been a good liar. Maybe that's why he could see through the criminals who tried to lie to him. Then it dawned on him that he could make this particular lie true. It was time to concentrate on his other obligations. Sheriff Temple had asked him to look into the case of a missing husband; that was something he could do.

Feeling lighter, more like himself, Ty addressed the envelope and put a stamp on it. He'd mail it on the way across town.

At four-thirty Ty knocked on the Mardells' front door. While he waited for someone to answer, he glanced around the unkempt front yard. Obviously Mr. Mardell hadn't been into yard work. More than half the grass had been worn down to dirt by car tracks and footprints. Several broken toys were scattered among the remaining weeds. The house itself could have used a coat of paint.

Ty already knew every legal detail there was to know about the missing man, Toolie Mardell. He'd been arrested three times for assault in the past ten years but had always gotten off, or in one case, received a suspended sentence. There hadn't been any official domestic-violence calls to the address, but that probably just meant nobody called the police when the Mardells had trouble.

The front door was opened by a young woman holding a toddler balanced on her hip. She looked barely legal—eighteen at the most.

"Mrs. Mardell?"

Her eyes, already too big in her thin face, seemed to grow larger as she saw the star pinned on his shirt. "Yes-s," she stuttered. "I'm Linda Mardell."

Ty tipped his hat. "I'm Ty Richardson. We spoke on the phone."

"Yes, sir," she said, then just stood there.

"May I come in?" he asked in his best nonthreatening voice. He was here to charm her, not scare her to death.

With a jerky movement she pushed the screen door open. "Sure. I mean, of course."

The interior of the house smelled like hot dogs and dirty diapers. Mrs. Mardell sat the toddler on the floor, then shoved a pile of clean clothes back into a basket, making room on the couch for him to sit. "Sit down," she said, then twisted her hands together as if she didn't know what to do with them. She'd been smart enough to wear long sleeves so he couldn't see the bruises. But one side of her face had a dark, slightly green cast that she'd attempted to cover with makeup.

Ty sat down and smiled an I'm-here-to-help-you smile.

The girl visibly relaxed. She pulled up a threadbare hassock and sat across from him. "You want to ask me about Toolie?"

"He's your husband, right? Toolie Mardell?"

"Yes, sir."

"Do you have a recent picture of him?"

The girl moved over to the end table and handed Ty one of those plastic picture blocks that held four pictures. One side was a picture of the toddler on the floor, the next had a newborn's squished and red face, the third side had a picture of a bass boat and the last held a photo of Toolie, he presumed, dressed in fatigues with a shotgun in one hand and a large, dead wild turkey in the other.

"How long have you two been married?" he asked. Long enough to have warranted a picture in the family cube, he figured.

"We got married about two years ago, but I been living here for five years."

"And you have two children together?"

"Yes, sir. Ruthy there." She smiled and pointed to the toddler on the floor. "And Thomas, he's the baby. He's in the other room asleep."

"Do you have any idea where your husband is, Mrs. Mardell?"

The question took away her slight smile. Her shoulders hunched as if she was used to having questions asked with a fist. "No, sir," she answered, and looked at her own bare feet. "He just took off."

"Were you two having problems?"

She looked at him then, some defiance back in her tone. "We had problems same as everybody else."

Ty leaned forward and gazed at her closely. Then he slowly reached out and touched her jaw enough to turn her head. "It looks like your problems were a little more violent than most folks. Did your husband hit you?"

She pulled away from his touch and covered her jaw with her hand. "I fell down, that's all."

"How did you fall?"

"What do you mean? I just fell."

"Did you stumble? Were you pushed?"

"I don't see how any of this has to do with Toolie."

"Well, Mrs. Mardell—Linda, I want to help you and to look for your husband. If you can trust me enough to tell me the truth, I'll help you any way I can. Do you have family in the area?"

"No, sir. I ran away from Ohio when I was fifteen. I don't suppose anyone looked for me for very long. My kids and Toolie are all I've got."

Ty spent a solid hour questioning and requestioning Linda Mardell. But he didn't get any further than the sheriff had. He ended the interview by giving her his card with his phone number circled. Then he went back to his office to work the computers and find out anything that might have been overlooked by the official search. He also planned to interview Toolie Mardell's mother, since she seemed to be the driving force behind the effort to find him. He hoped to find a few of the missing man's friends, as well. Tomorrow, while Linda Mardell was at work, he'd talk to a few of their neighbors.

There was usually one neighbor who watched everything that went on—at least on their own street. If he was lucky, he'd find someone who'd seen Toolie Mardell leave.

Then, having taken care of his official business, he pulled out the piece of paper he'd brought with him from the Donut Wrangler. Before he'd left, he'd talked Sharon into showing him Robert Ludlow's job application. He hadn't wanted to alarm Jenna, but Sharon had seemed to understand his need to check the man out.

It was nearing eight o'clock before he called it a night. On the drive home he congratulated himself for finding the perfect antidote to his attraction to Jenna—work. Even though a portion of that work had concerned her, he'd been able to concentrate on putting the pieces of Robert's background into perspective. Since Robert had gotten out of prison, the worst thing Ty could say about the man was that he'd moved around a lot. Not on account of trouble, either. There were no warrants, not even outstanding traffic tickets. It seemed Robert hadn't found the right place to call home.

Unfortunately, now that Ty had done all the work he could do for the day, he still had the evening to pass. Maybe he'd ride out to see Kirby.

Kirby and Buster were sitting on the porch when Ty drove up.

"Well, I'm surprised to see you tonight," Kirby said as Ty moved up his front steps. "Did you hear from Mary Jo?"

"No, sir," Ty said, and sighed.

Kirby paused for a moment, then went on. "How about those friends of yours who are opening the restaurant? They seemed real nice." The old man gave a chuckle. "Neither one of them is hard on the eyes, either. Did they get all that work finished?"

Ty's wayward thoughts flashed back to painting with Jenna. And kissing her. It was hard to admit that the smell of paint might be an aphrodisiac from now on. It would always flash him back to watching Jenna laugh. "They'll be having the grand opening next week," he answered. "You're invited."

Buster decided at that moment to walk over and rest his head on Ty's knee. As Ty gave him the pat he was looking for, he added, "Buster has to stay home, though."

"That's all right," Kirby said without missing a beat. "I can bring him home one of those doggie bags. He won't mind a bit."

Ty rocked without speaking, and Buster moved down the steps into the darkness. The evening air had cooled slightly from the daytime temperature, and the cicadas were singing. Kirby's place was just far enough from the main road to feel isolated.

"You ever think of movin' closer in to town?" Ty asked.

"Not for long years," Kirby answered. "Not since Sylvie was alive. She wasn't too crazy about being out here."

"But you didn't move?"

Kirby took some time to answer. "I woulda moved, but she up and died before we could make any plans."

Ty felt as if he'd intruded too far. "I'm sorry. I was just thinkin' that maybe you were tired of being out here all alone."

"I'm not alone," Kirby said. "I've got old Buster now. And you."

"That's not really what I meant. I was thinking about neighbors and such. And I'm going to be out of town for the next couple of days."

"Having neighbors isn't all it's cracked up to be." Kirby harrumphed. "They would probably have something to say about Buster getting into their garden or chasin' the cats. I'm happy the way I am. And you don't need to worry about me—I'll be fine if you have to go away. I'm content with being alone." Kirby turned to look at him in the gathering dark, and Ty could have sworn the old man was plotting something. "Besides, Mary Jo ought to be comin' back this way anytime now. Wouldn't that be a blessin'?"

Privately Ty thought the return of Mary Jo would be more like a curse, but he would never tell Kirby that.

THREE DAYS LATER Ty found Jenna in the center of the giant doughnut, stringing banners from the doughnut hole to the eaves of the building.

On the drive out he'd told himself over and over again that he had a good reason for visiting the restaurant. That his vow to stay away didn't include official business. But as he got out of the car and approached Jenna, all his excuses faded. It was damned good to see her.

"What in the world are you up to? If you fall out of there, you'll be on crutches for the grand opening," he said.

Jenna smiled, then gingerly lowered herself to a sitting position. "I'm almost done." She waved a hand toward the zigzags of fluttering silver-and-blue banners sparkling in the sunlight. "What do you think?"

He had to smile even though he shook his head. "Well, if you're aiming for attention, I think you've hit the bull's-eye. This place looks like a cross between a used-car lot and a UFO landing zone."

"I'll take that as a positive response," Jenna said. "We don't want to be ignored." She'd felt ignored for the past few days, even though she'd gotten his short note about going out of town. She knew his absence was for the best, but that didn't mean she hadn't missed him. Now he seemed more like a stranger than before. Picking up the roll of tape and a pair of scissors, she scooted toward the ladder.

"Hang on a second," Ty ordered, then circled the base to steady the ladder. "All right, come on down."

Jenna balanced herself and slowly descended. She was glad Ty had shown up when he did. Getting down was a little scarier than climbing up had been—especially with her hands full.

Two steps from the bottom, Jenna found herself eye to eye with Ty. His steady hazel gaze seemed determined to see into her thoughts, and for a moment she was mesmerized. As the seconds spun out into awkwardness, she pulled her gaze away and glanced down. She could feel her face warming and knew she should have been more careful about looking into his eyes. The last time she'd done that, he'd kissed her. *Don't think about it,* she chastised herself. She needed to start over where Ty was concerned.

"Whew," she said when she reached solid ground. "The sun nearly cooked me up there." She hoped that statement would account for the blush coloring her face.

Ty offered her an exaggerated frown. "Anybody ever mention that you ought to wear a hat to work out in the sun?"

"Anybody ever accuse you of sounding like my mother?"

Ty raised a hand in surrender. "Okay, I know.

You're a grown-up." He searched the parking lot. "Where's your little helper today?"

"Sharon had to go into town to pick up some things, and Jay went along for the ride." She shaded her eyes and looked into his. She couldn't tell him she'd missed him; that wasn't something you said to a man you were claiming to be only friends with. So she said the first thing that came to mind. "I—I got your letter. How was your trip?"

He looked away for a few seconds. If she hadn't known better, she would have thought he was squirming. "It went fine. I had to go down to San Antonio and interview someone about a missing-person case."

"Oh," she said, hoping he'd go on. But he didn't. Not knowing what else to ask, she offered, "Let's go inside and cool off."

Ty followed her into the restaurant, then stopped in amazement. "You two have done a great job with this place."

"Thank you," Jenna said as she placed the tape and her tools in the toolbox near the cashier's counter. With freshly painted walls and newly polished chrome, Jenna knew the diner sparkled like a new penny. That was the whole idea, to make it a place where anyone would feel comfortable having a meal.

She walked around behind the counter. "What can I get you to drink?"

"I'll have my usual," Ty said as he removed his hat and sat down. "Root beer."

"Comin' up," Jenna said, and reached for a clean glass to fill.

As she slid the glass of root beer toward him, Ty pulled out his wallet and put a dollar on the counter. "How much do I owe you?" he asked.

"Don't be silly, Ty. I'm not taking your money."

"Well, you'd better, 'cause I'm drinkin' your root beer," he replied. He pushed the dollar closer.

"We're not officially open yet—besides, I can't make change."

"I'd be proud to be your first paying customer," Ty insisted. "Keep the change as a tip. You better get used to that. Business is business."

"Okay, this will be our first dollar. We'll get one of those frames to put it on the wall." She smiled and placed the dollar bill on the counter near the cash register. Then she walked over to a glass case. "I want you to have something on the house, though," she said as she used a pair of tongs to put a large doughnut on a plate, then deposited it in front of him.

"We've been practicing. What do you think?"

Without any hesitation, Ty picked up the doughnut and bit into it. Jenna watched him with worried eyes.

Ty didn't exactly know what to do. After he took a big bite of the alleged doughnut, it seemed to swell in his mouth. He tried to swallow, but the "dough" in the "nut" was lodged in his throat. He had to take a swig of root beer to force it down.

"Well?" Jenna asked, as if his opinion really meant something.

"It's a—" he had to clear his throat "—a little dry," he said finally.

Jenna looked deflated.

"It wasn't bad," he said, searching for the right words.

"It wasn't good, either." Jenna picked up the plate and tossed the remains in the trash. "I don't know what we're going to do. We've tried all kinds of recipes." She sighed. "We can't open the Donut Wrangler Diner without doughnuts."

Ty didn't know what to say. She was right. In a restaurant with a giant doughnut out front, they needed to have at the very least "good" doughnuts. These were—well—these were... These doughnuts could choke a horse. Then he remembered he'd told every lawman he knew to visit the diner and eat lots of doughnuts. He wondered for a moment if they would actually lynch him or merely hold it against him for the next few years.

"Robert is going to try one more recipe, but if that doesn't work...I guess we'll cater the doughnuts for the grand opening."

"Sounds like a good backup," Ty responded, trying not to sound too eager.

Jenna smiled as if she knew he was doing his damnedest to remain diplomatic. She picked up a damp rag and wiped down the already pristine countertop. "I've been going on about doughnuts—did you have a reason for stopping by?" she asked.

Other than wanting to see her? That's what he couldn't say. "To be honest, I wanted to have a little talk with Robert. Is he around?"

Jenna looked surprised. "Well...yes, he is. He's back in the kitchen. What do you want to talk about?"

At least she didn't take a swing at him right off, he thought. He'd been bracing for a fight. Maybe she'd understand that he had her own good in mind.

"I just wanted to ask his intentions," Ty said.

"His what?"

"His plans for the future, is all. I checked him out, and he's been keeping out of trouble as far as the law is concerned. I just want to ask him about his connections in San Angelo. If he has family or friends to keep him on the straight path." He offered her a friendly smile. "The kind of things policemen usually ask ex-cons."

"That's what I was afraid of. I wish you wouldn't do that, Ty."

He held her gaze and shook his head. "I'm sorry, Jenna. I don't want to upset you. But I couldn't live with myself if I didn't at least look the man in the eye and get his word that there won't be any trouble as far as you and this restaurant are concerned." He reluctantly dropped his trump card into the conversation. "You know Jimmy would do the same thing if he was here."

That stopped her. She stared at him a full minute before dropping her gaze. "All right," she agreed. "But don't scare him off. We need him."

"I won't, I promise. I've put a lot of men in jail, but I've learned that even though a man like Robert has made a mistake, he usually deserves a second chance. As long as he's paid his debt to society and stays on the up-and-up, I'll help him any way I can."

"Do you want me to call him out here?"

"No, that's okay." Ty drank down another gulp of soda, then reached for his hat. "I'd rather go back there and talk to him. Thanks for the root beer."

Jenna watched him walk toward the kitchen and tried to calm her jumping nerves. Ty was all Texas Ranger today. Wearing his gun, his badge and his hat, he looked more intimidating than she remembered. It seemed as if she'd known him forever. How did he manage to keep surprising her?

The day he'd kissed her, he'd been different. For a few hours she'd forgotten he was a Ranger, forgotten that he had been Jimmy's best friend. He'd just been Ty. The man who'd answered her letters and kept her sane for the past two years.

And now he was acting as if the kiss had never happened. As a friend he was keeping her safe. She had no doubt that he would put the fear of God and the Texas Rangers into Robert. She'd seen Jimmy do that once—with a group of boys he'd caught vandalizing an old lady's fence. Jimmy had been all sheriff's department serious, scarier than Clint Eastwood, and those boys had done everything he'd told them to do after that. Needless to say, there wasn't any more vandalism or even reckless bicycle riding on their street.

Unable to resist, Jenna walked over to the kitchen door and glanced in. But she wasn't going to be able to eavesdrop; Robert and Ty had stepped out the door. From the back window Jenna could see Ty waiting while Robert lit a cigarette.

TY KNEW ROBERT WAS NERVOUS. That was a good thing. It might make him think twice about any lingering ideas of getting up to somethin'.

"Now," Ty began, "I'm not here to get on your case about the past."

Robert looked at him, then took another drag on his cigarette.

"I just want to make sure you know the story here. In case no one mentioned it, Jenna Taylor's husband was a deputy sheriff. He was killed during an armed robbery two years ago."

The color seemed to drain out of Robert's face, and he glanced away for a few seconds. Then he looked at Ty again with steady eyes. "She never asked me why I was in prison. She only asked if I'd hurt anybody."

"Well, I know you didn't." Ty faced him with his hands planted firmly on his hips, right above his gun belt. He wanted Robert to understand that he was serious as a heart attack. "You obviously can do this job. You're a damned good cook and they need you. I'm not going to tell her why you were in prison, but I am going to ask for your word concerning this job, this restaurant and this woman,'' he said. ''Are you being straight with Jenna?''

''Yes, sir,'' Robert said. ''I don't mean her any harm. I want to work. I'm not going back to jail.''

His words had the ring of truth. ''Do you have friends in San Angelo? People to look out for you?'' Ty asked.

Robert drew another lungful of smoke from the cigarette. ''I go to meetings. I've met a few people there.''

''AA?''

''Yeah. They help when things get shaky.''

''That's good.'' He pulled one of his cards from his pocket and handed it to Robert. ''If you've got problems, call me,'' Ty said. ''I'll help if I can. But understand this—if you do anything illegal or put either of these women in danger, I'll come looking for you.'' He lowered his chin to make sure the man was paying attention. ''And I won't stop till I find you. You got it?''

''I got it,'' Robert said. He shoved the card into his back pocket, dropped his cigarette on the ground and stubbed it out with his shoe. ''She's a nice lady,'' he said. ''I'm sorry about her husband. I won't cause any trouble.''

Ty looked up and saw Jenna watching them from the window. ''I guess I've kept you away from work long enough.''

Robert nodded and moved toward the back door. As he approached, Jenna disappeared. Not wanting Robert to see her, Ty supposed. He decided he needed to be on his way, as well. He'd done what he came to do. Anything further and he'd be accused of hanging around just to be near Jenna—which was closer to the truth than he wanted to admit.

CHAPTER EIGHT

THE MORNING of the grand opening, Jenna thought about pinching herself. A huge congratulatory arrangement of flowers from her parents and two sisters in North Carolina had arrived and now decorated the counter opposite the cash register. The diner had been cleaned and polished, ceiling to floor. From supplies on the storeroom shelves, to the salt and pepper shakers on the tables, to the smell of frying bacon—they were ready. Seeing the fruits of their hard labor alternately filled Jenna with power and amazement. They'd done it. She and Sharon, with a little help from their friends, like…Ty. They'd made what Jimmy's mother had called their "pipe dream" a reality.

She wondered what Jimmy would think about it, then frowned. She hoped he'd be proud, but his mother's words were hard to ignore.

Jimmy wouldn't have wanted this.

Jenna remembered the disagreement—she hesitated to call it an argument—between her and Jimmy when she'd taken a part-time job at a department store one Christmas. The job wasn't demanding, but it did require a lot of evening hours.

She'd wanted to make extra money to spend on gifts, but the hours were long and the logistics of making sure one of them was home for Jay became a problem.

Jimmy, having just come off his own eleven-hour shift, decided that he wanted a homemaker, not a working wife.

"If we can't afford a couple of extra gifts, then we don't need 'em," he'd said. "James and I need you. I promise, I'll work a few more hours and try to get some overtime."

But she hadn't wanted *him* to work more. He was right, though, a few more gifts weren't worth it. So she'd quit her job.

A shiver of contrition drifted through her. Barbara Taylor's statement was probably accurate. Other than Jenna's semiserious dream of working with children, maybe being a teacher, she had never looked at herself as a career woman. She'd had her family; she and Jimmy had intended to have more children. And his job had been so demanding, her presence in their home had seemed doubly important. A job, especially a business of her own, would have taken her away from Jimmy and Jay. That was one of the reasons she wanted Jay with her now. She had to remain the constant in his life since his father was gone.

Out of the blue she remembered Ty's answer to Barbara's hypothetical question: "If my wife thought it was something she really wanted to do, then I would support the idea."

Just then, Sharon came through the kitchen door followed by her ex-husband. ''I told you, making doughnuts is more difficult than you think,'' Dean said. ''Those aren't bad, but people aren't going to pay good money for them.''

Sharon rolled her eyes at Jenna. ''All right, I give up. We'll buy our doughnuts—at least until Robert and I find a recipe that works.''

Instead of arguing further, Dean looked thoughtful for a moment. ''You know, I sold an insurance policy to the guy who runs the local Royal Doughnut franchise. I wonder if I could get any secrets out of him.''

Sharon seemed so shocked Jenna smiled in spite of earlier thoughts.

''And I wonder if I can believe my ears.'' She looked at Jenna. ''Did you just hear this man actually make a helpful suggestion?''

Jenna held up her hand and declared, ''I'm a witness.''

Sharon crossed her arms and gazed shrewdly at Dean. ''You get us a recipe that works, and we might just make you an honorary customer for a year.''

''If you don't learn how to make doughnuts, you won't be in business in a year,'' he replied, looking pleased but unwilling to jump at her offer.

Sharon shrugged and tossed a towel onto the counter. ''There he goes again. Mr. Negative. I knew it couldn't last.''

"Now who's being negative?" Dean grumbled under his breath.

"Mom? Is it time to make the doughnuts yet?" Jay asked. He'd taken up residence in the back booth with several of his favorite toys. But now he was getting down and moving toward her, a hopeful gleam in his eyes.

"We're gonna let Robert make the doughnuts today, remember?" Jenna explained. "You can help sometime when things aren't so hectic. Okay?"

Jay looked at Dean to see if *he* was going to get to help. Dean noticed.

"That's right, partner," Dean said. "You and I have been thrown out of the kitchen for the time bein'. You want to show me what you're up to over there? Maybe I can give you a hand." He followed Jay back to the booth where he'd left the toys.

Sharon shook her head. "Must be a man thing. If we can just keep them busy with lots of toys, they might just stay out of the way."

Jenna chuckled as she walked over to unlock the front door of the restaurant. "We're ready as we can be. Let the grand opening begin," she said. Together she and Sharon flipped over the sign that read Open.

THEIR FIRST CUSTOMER for the grand opening ended up being an astonished trucker who'd stopped for a cup of coffee. By showing up before any of the invited guests, the man earned a complete breakfast and a cup of coffee to go, on the house. He also received a very warm invitation from Sharon to "stop by again," which left Dean frowning.

By ten o'clock Jenna didn't have time to worry. She and Sharon were busy greeting every friend and acquaintance the two of them had thought to invite, and several of the men from the Everhardt plant. Nearly all the seats in the diner were filled. Several deputies from the sheriff's office had taken up the stools at the counter, making Jenna feel good. Jimmy's buddies hadn't forgotten him or his family.

The only obvious no-shows were her mother-in-law and Ty. She knew Barbara was absent out of protest, but Ty had surprised her. She'd assumed he'd be here. Maybe she should have called to remind him, but she'd been sure he wouldn't forget. He'd been distant lately, since the day he'd kissed her, and that was probably for the best, she decided. But today would be one of the most important days of her life, and she'd hoped to share it with him. As a friend, of course. Again the feeling that she'd lost something came over her. She'd missed his letters, his unqualified support. So much so that she'd continued writing to him even though she never intended to mail the letters. Last night she'd written:

Ty,

Tomorrow is the big day. The day Sharon and I will always remember. Whether that's because it's the first day of a successful partnership, or the day we both lost our minds and all our money, remains to be seen. Whatever happens, I'm so excited. I wish I could tell you how much this enterprise has helped me move on. Helped soften the pain of losing Jimmy. I hope he's proud of me. I hope you are, too.

Determined not to let Ty's absence take the polish off an otherwise sterling day, Jenna smiled at one of the deputies as she poured him more coffee. "Would you like to try one of our homemade doughnuts?" she asked.

"Yes, ma'am," the deputy answered.

TY PULLED into the crowded parking lot and felt a sense of pride. The Donut Wrangler looked prosperous, and he was sure Jenna would be happy with the turnout. True to his plan of staying away from Jenna, he'd put off his arrival as long as possible. He'd even gone out to pick up Kirby. As the two of them got out of the car, Kirby rubbed his hands together.

"I sure hope those girls put my pancakes on the menu. I can almost taste 'em."

"Yes, sir." Ty smiled and nodded, hoping the pancakes were better than the doughnuts. As he opened the glass door for Kirby, the smells of fresh coffee and bacon hit him, and his stomach growled. He'd skipped breakfast so he'd be able to do justice to whatever they served him at the Donut Wrangler.

He intended to make Jenna feel confident in the diner's success.

"Why, hello, Ranger," Sharon said as she sashayed by with a half-empty coffeepot in her hand. "Y'all have a seat anywhere you like." Then she winked at Kirby. "I'll put in your order for pecan pancakes."

As Kirby slid into a booth, he nodded toward Sharon. "I think I'm gonna like it here," he said.

Ty felt the same way as Jenna came walking out of the kitchen balancing plates of eggs and hash browns for the customers in the next booth. It seemed as if weeks had passed since he'd seen her, so he took his time watching her work. Then he noticed that two of the deputies seated at the counter also followed her progress with their eyes. He wasn't sure he liked it.

"Good morning, Ty," Jenna said, sounding out of breath. "I thought you'd forgotten us. Hello, Kirby."

"Not likely," Ty said. *Not a chance in hell.* "I've still got green paint in the creases of my boots." Painting brought back the memory of kissing Jenna, and he flinched. Maybe he shouldn't have said it, but something unfamiliar was driving him. In this roomful of people, his protective instincts had gone on alert.

Instead of frowning, she playfully nudged his arm, and grinned. She looked happier than he'd seen her in a long time. He was glad to see it, but he wished he'd played more of a part in the cause. "If business picks up, I'll buy you a new pair."

He had a hard time concentrating when she smiled that way. She certainly didn't appear upset with him. The uncomfortable thought that she'd already put the kiss behind her troubled him. But he wasn't about to rain on her happy day. "Not unless you're gonna wear 'em and break 'em in for me," he countered.

She laughed and shook her head before she went on. "What can I get for you?" Leaning over them, she plucked two menus from behind the napkin holder. The stretch of her waitress uniform across her breasts and the flash of shapely thigh nearly made Ty's breath stop. If he'd been chewing gum, he'd have swallowed it.

Get a grip, he cautioned silently as Jenna pulled out a pad and pencil to take their order. Thankfully she seemed too busy to notice his reaction. He focused on the menu. "Uh, eggs, over easy, with sausage and biscuits will do me fine."

"I'll have those pecan pancakes Sharon promised me," Kirby added. "And some coffee."

Sharon appeared with cups and a coffeepot as if Kirby had uttered the magic words.

"Seems like the opening is going pretty well," Ty said as Sharon poured his coffee.

"It's great," Jenna said.

"It sure is. If we had any more customers, we wouldn't know what to do," Sharon agreed.

"Thanks for all your help, Ty," Jenna said with

a sweet smile. Then, waving the order slip, she added, ''Let me get this in to Robert.''

''You two want to try some doughnuts while you're waitin'?'' Sharon asked.

Both Kirby and Ty answered at the same time.

''No.''

''Yes.''

Sharon gave Ty a wicked grin since he'd been the one who'd declined. ''Well, I'll just bring some over and you can decide then.''

There wasn't much time after that to talk to Jenna. She worked the dining room like a pro, taking orders, serving food, delivering condiments, cleaning tables and pouring coffee. Ty supposed that being a mom and a wife had prepared her. But he could also see Sharon coaching her occasionally. The only sign of her nervousness was the way she pushed back one strand of hair that seemed determined to fall in her eyes.

Ty frowned and returned his attention to his breakfast. If she worked this hard every day, she'd be worn out. He had no business worrying about her, but he did, anyway. He'd help her all she'd let him, but this was her choice. His mind wandered to the image of her exhausted, falling into bed....

''Hey, Ty,'' a male voice said.

Ty turned and found Ray Guthrie grinning down at him. ''We showed up.'' He indicated the three deputies standing behind him. Then he glanced toward Jenna. ''The view is nice,'' he said slyly. ''But take my advice—don't eat the doughnuts.''

Amid a rumble of male laughter, the deputies walked out.

AN HOUR LATER Jenna looked up to see Ty standing at the cash register ready to pay his check. *He's leaving.* Her heart responded with several disappointed beats before she caught herself. For the twentieth time she pushed back the strand of hair that kept getting in her eyes. First she'd been worried because he hadn't shown up. Then when he did show up, she hadn't had any spare moments to really talk to him. She couldn't expect him to hang around all day, could she? She gave the table she was cleaning a final swipe, then headed in his direction.

"I'm sorry I didn't have more time to visit," she said as she took the bill and money from him. She smiled at Kirby. "So, how did you like the pancakes?"

Kirby made a show of patting his stomach. "Perfect. Miz Sharon even got me a doggie bag to take to my dog, Buster. You ladies have made me a happy man."

Jenna laughed as she handed Ty his change. "How about you?" she asked him. "Are you a happy man?" Ty seemed to freeze at her question, as if he didn't know what she'd asked or how to reply. She let him off the hook. "Was your breakfast all right?"

"Just fine," Ty answered, then he glanced around the half-filled diner. "You've had a crowd of people in here this morning. I'm glad it's working out for you."

Jenna heard the words but couldn't tell from his expression if he was sincerely impressed by the crowd or not. "Thank you," she said.

His gaze came back to her face. Held by his attention, Jenna felt the wayward strand of her hair fall forward again. "How's the littlest partner doing?" he asked, watching as she pushed the hair back behind her ear.

Something in his eyes made every nerve she owned come to attention at once. As if it had been his hand touching her hair. She realized her own hand was trembling, so she lowered it to the counter to steady herself. *How does he do that? All he has to do is look at me and I get as silly as a teenager. It's a good thing he hasn't been around much.*

"Jay's fine," she said, barely managing to get the words out. Her reaction had to be the result of the kiss. If he'd never kissed her, she wouldn't be spellbound by his eyes, or the way his mouth moved when he spoke. She wouldn't wonder... Clearing her throat in an effort to get back to the subject, she went on, "He's in the office with Dean, Sharon's ex-husband."

Ty settled his Stetson on his head, then nodded. "Tell him I said hello." Then he turned to leave.

"Ty?" His name was out of her mouth before she knew what she wanted to say. She only knew she wasn't ready for him to walk out the door.

He pivoted and leveled his serious gaze on her once more.

For a few seconds Jenna could only stare at him, every thought drained from her brain—lost in space. Something told her it was for the best that there was a high Formica counter between the two of them. It felt so awkward, being surrounded by strangers and treating Ty like a regular customer—not like her closest living friend. Not like the man who had kept her from falling off a ladder, then surprised her with a spine-melting kiss.

Hello? Earth to Jenna!

Suddenly she remembered what she'd intended to say. "Look," she said, and pointed to the framed dollar bill prominently displayed on the wall. "Our first dollar, from our first customer." She smiled. "That would be you. Thanks for everything…for being such a good friend."

She had to hand it to Ty; when he smiled, which was seldom, he could brighten any female's day. She was no exception.

"You're welcome," he said, and between his low, familiar voice and the unfamiliar sultriness of his smile, Jenna felt singed.

Sharon appeared to the left of the cash register. Peripherally Jenna saw her grin at Ty and Kirby. "Y'all come back now, you hear?"

"You bet," Kirby said. Ty touched his hat in reply, then pushed open the door for Kirby.

"I'm tellin' you, that man looks like he knows what he wants without ever looking at the menu," she said on a sigh, before shoving Jenna's shoulder. "And I'm not talking about food," she added as she walked away.

"Sharon!"

Undaunted, Sharon laughed and went to check on her customers.

Knows what he wants. As Jenna poured more coffee, then handed out menus to three new customers, she thought about what Ty wanted. She realized she'd never asked him. And he'd certainly never volunteered the information.

As for herself, she'd gotten what she wanted, hadn't she? Opening day of the Donut Wrangler was an unqualified success. Except, of course, for the doughnuts. But they would work on that. One part of the near future was settled. It looked as though she would have enough work, and enough worrying to do without borrowing trouble.

After taking two orders, she walked into the kitchen rather than sliding them over the warming counter. She gave the orders to Robert, then peeked in the door of the office to check on Jay. He and Dean were watching *Sesame Street* on a small TV Dean had brought along. Rather than interrupt, since they both seemed totally involved in the letter *M,* Jenna got back to business.

Her gratitude to Sharon's ex-husband for watching Jay on their opening day brought her promise to find Jay a father back full force. She needed a partner more than ever if she wanted to have a business and raise her son. But she didn't know where to get one. She'd met Jimmy shortly before graduating high school, and they'd married two years later. It had seemed so easy back then, to believe in love and the future.

Now, older and wiser and with a child to worry about, the idea of finding a husband seemed much more daunting than risking her life savings on the Donut Wrangler. The only available man she knew and trusted was Ty. Jimmy's friend, her friend... and a Texas Ranger. She knew she could ask his help with anything; he'd offered often enough. But she couldn't ask him to help find her a husband. Somehow that seemed above and beyond the call of duty.

Returning to the dining room after picking up a plate of pancakes and eggs, Jenna nearly collided with Sharon and her coffeepot. She needed to get her head out of the clouds and pay attention to her work.

Sharon laughed and stepped around her. "How are your feet holding out?" she asked.

Jenna had been so busy, she hadn't had time to think of her feet. "I guess they're fine," she answered. "I can't feel them anymore."

"Trust me. You'll feel them by closing time."

AS THEY COUNTED UP the day's receipts at two-thirty, Jenna had to admit she was glad to have time to sit down.

"You were right about my feet," Jenna said as she lowered herself into the booth across from

Sharon and propped her feet—her brand-new waitress shoes—on the opposite seat. "In these new shoes, they feel like chicken-fried steak without the gravy."

Sharon offered a tired smile. "You should trade off. Wear some tennis shoes tomorrow and give your toes a rest."

Jenna sighed. "It's a good thing both of us were here today to handle this instead of taking shifts. I couldn't have done it on my own. Be sure to thank Dean again for me, too. He was a lifesaver with Jay."

"Yeah, he can be great when he isn't moaning about how old he is. I'll tell him next time I see him."

"I'm beginning to realize how hard this is going to be," Jenna continued.

"You mean running a restaurant?"

"No, not that. I'm not afraid of hard work. I'm talking about trying to look after Jay and this place at the same time."

"Well, little boys his age do get bored pretty fast. But don't worry too much yet. Every day won't be like today in here, and if it is—" she grimaced as she stretched her lower back "—we're going to hire more help."

"I've been thinking of a different solution," Jenna confessed, hoping Sharon would understand.

"What's that?"

"I've decided that once we get this business off

the ground and running, I'm going to start dating. To try to find someone who—''

''A husband?'' Sharon looked surprised but covered it quickly. ''Hmm. You know, you may be on the right track about that. Seems to me that Texas Ranger would be a fine candidate.''

Jenna's pulse leaped in panic. ''No, it can't be Ty,'' she said quickly. There, she'd spoken the words out loud. She'd convinced herself that she couldn't consider Ty for a hundred reasons, yet the one that always remained in the back of her mind was the biggest.

Sharon stared at her for a long moment. ''Why? On a scale of one to ten, I'd put him right up there at ten and a half. He's good-lookin', he's responsible and helpful—''

''He's a police officer.'' Jenna fought to ignore the physical evidence that he was also a man. A man who had reached past her defenses and touched something inside her with a kiss. ''I won't marry another man who carries a gun for a living. I lost Jimmy. I don't want to take the chance of losing someone else.''

Dismissing that argument with a wave of her hand, Sharon said, ''Well, any kind of gambler would tell you the odds of you losing another man in a gunfight are practically nil.''

''It's not just that. Look at Jay and how much he admires Ty. What are the odds that my son, whose father was a sheriff's deputy, will grow up and want to be a police officer, too? How much would those odds increase if Jay's stepfather was in the same profession?''

Sharon shook her head slowly. ''I hadn't thought of that.''

''I think about it all the time. It would be so easy to depend on Ty, to...care about him. But I won't take advantage of his friendship. Besides, Ty has never talked about wanting to get married again. Why would he want to marry me?'' *Just because he kissed me?* ''He was Jimmy's friend and now he's my friend. We've both decided to keep it that way.''

Sharon looked as if she wanted to argue the point but instead she took a deep breath and kept her thoughts to herself. ''All right, then. We'll just have to find you someone who—''

''Mom?'' Jay skipped out of the kitchen followed by Robert. ''Can we go home now?'' he asked when he reached the booth.

''We're almost ready,'' Jenna answered. Then she glanced at Sharon and remembered the reason for their marriage conversation—keeping one step ahead of a six-year-old. Jay was ready to leave, whether she'd finished work or not. ''See what I mean?''

Sharon nodded.

''Everything is squared away in the kitchen,'' Robert said as he reached them. He'd removed his apron and had his keys in his hand.

''Okay, thanks, Robert,'' Sharon said.

''You did great today,'' Jenna added. Then she

ruffled her son's hair. "You did, too, mister." Jay laughed and squirmed when she hugged him.

"See you in the morning," Robert said.

Sharon pushed up from her seat. "Let's get out of here, too. Tomorrow will come soon enough."

CHAPTER NINE

THE RESTAURANT HAD BEEN open nearly a week when Sunday rolled around, and Jenna made her weekly visit to her mother-in-law's house. Sitting in the kitchen watching Jay play outside with the dog, Jenna decided to open the subject weighing on her mind.

''We missed you at the grand opening,'' Jenna said as Barbara poured her a cup of coffee.

Without acknowledging her words, Barbara returned the coffeepot to the warmer. ''Are you still determined to keep James Jr. with you while you work?''

''It hasn't been easy,'' Jenna admitted. All week it had taken both her and Sharon, along with occasional help from Robert, to keep Jay occupied and out of trouble. And beginning on Monday, Jenna would be by herself in the afternoons. Sharon would be taking the early-morning shift, and Jenna the later one. ''He's getting used to it.'' She hoped her reassurance was true.

Barbara shook her head in disbelief, then went on. ''What are you planning for his birthday?''

Jenna inwardly cringed, anticipating her mother-in-law's reaction. Jay's birthday would fall on a weekday this year. When Jenna had mentioned it to Sharon, she had suggested having a party at the Donut Wrangler after closing. That way Sharon could help, and Jenna wouldn't have to rush home from work to host a party. Plus there was plenty of room for the kids to play games, and the jukebox would provide some extra noise. Her neighbors, Rusty's parents, had promised to come up with enough kids to make it fun for Jay.

"We're going to have a party for him at the restaurant. I'll invite some of the kids from the neighborhood. You're invited, too." She rushed on, "I hope you'll come."

Barbara frowned. "That's a long way for me to drive and for the parents of the other children."

Fighting her own exasperation, Jenna chose her words carefully. "All we need are three parents to drive their cars. The kids can ride together. It'll be an adventure." There was nothing to say about Barbara's long drive, but Jenna hoped it wouldn't be the deciding factor in her decision not to come.

"I still think you should let me keep him rather than dragging him to that restaurant every day. I could have a perfectly good party here."

Jenna didn't know how to explain why she wanted Jay with her. It wasn't that she didn't trust Barbara. She was Jay's grandmother and entitled to spend some time with him. But on a daily basis, Jenna didn't think it would be good for him. Barbara was still so mired in her grief over losing

Jimmy, and she expected Jenna and Jay to feel the same. Jenna had learned the hard way that life had to go on. Maybe Barbara could afford to spend her future looking back, but Jenna couldn't.

"Maybe he can stay with you a few days a week," Jenna suggested. "But I've already told him we're having the party at the diner, and he's looking forward to it."

DRIVING HOME two hours later, Jenna felt drained; even Jay had fallen asleep in the back seat. It seemed as if every visit with Barbara was an endurance test. Jimmy's mother might mean well, but her questions and opinions were nonstop. And they almost always challenged Jenna's.

It hadn't been that way when Jimmy was alive. He'd told his mother early on that he was the head of his family. She was welcome to be a part of that, but he and Jenna would make the important decisions together. But now Jimmy was gone, and obviously Barbara didn't trust Jenna's judgment.

Barbara had even asked about Ty.

Jenna heard herself explain again how Ty was only a friend. And that Barbara didn't have to worry about losing Jay to another family, to a stepfather. The entire time she was talking, she realized there was no way for her to make Jimmy's mother happy. It seemed as though Barbara remained stuck, like a butterfly in amber, frozen in place by her grief. If she took one step into the future, she would lose the memory of her son altogether. Jenna could understand how that had happened. Barbara was alone; her husband had passed away from lung cancer ten years before. If Jenna hadn't had Jay to anchor her firmly in daily life, she might have closed her mind and her heart. As it was, she *had* to go on or Jay would suffer.

Besides, she'd found she wanted to go on, to have a normal life, a whole family like her new friends, Rich and Nancy. Maybe have another child.

She didn't want to contemplate what Barbara might say about Jenna's plan to find Jay a new father. One step at a time, she reminded herself. Barbara was still getting used to Jenna's decision to open the restaurant. No need to introduce the idea before she actually had a candidate for stepfather.

Ty's face drifted through her thoughts again. What would *he* think about her remarrying? Surely he'd be happy for her and Jay. Would she be happy if she found out that Ty was engaged?

Her hands tightened on the wheel. What if Ty stepped out of their lives before she and Jay were ready? Guilt rolled through her. *Talk about selfish!* her conscience scolded. *Ty doesn't belong to you. He doesn't owe you a thing. As a matter of fact, he's done more for you than everyone else combined.*

There was no doubt about it. Ty had been her truest friend since the night Jimmy had been shot. He'd probably be happy to have the responsibility of a widow and a fatherless boy off his hands. Jenna swallowed against the lump of apprehension in her throat. Her eyes began to sting and fill with tears.

It was only a matter of time until Ty went on with his own life. Jenna needed to find a husband before that happened, or she and Jay would be totally alone once again.

''HE SHOULDA NEVER MARRIED that girl,'' Mrs. Mardell, the missing Toolie's mother, said emphatically. ''She's been nothin' but trouble.''

Toolie had been missing for almost two weeks now, and Ty had learned much more than he wanted to know about the man. A few of his friends had called him a hell of a guy; the others had several different ways of saying that Toolie was one mean son of a—

''Why do you say he shouldn't have married her, Mrs. Mardell?''

''Because she spends his money and causes all kinds of problems. Toolie is always havin' to borrow extra from me to get through the month.'' Mrs. Mardell's face scrunched up like she'd smelled something bad. ''And who knows if those kids are really his?''

Ty thought of the pictures he'd seen in the house, of Toolie hunting and of his flashy bass boat, and decided it was rather unlikely that Toolie's wife had been in control of his money. The couple had only one checking account, and there was very little money in it. The bank had informed Ty there had been no major withdrawals in the past several weeks.

"What kind of problems does she cause?" Ty asked.

"She's always following him around, callin' to check on him. He told me once she even came down to the lake to find his truck, the nosy tramp. Then she goes out and buys those kids expensive toys, or so she says. She's probably givin' Toolie's money to some other man."

Now, that was odd, Ty thought. At a time when Toolie seemed to be truly lost, his "nosy" wife wasn't looking for him. "Did you ever actually see her with another man? Or did Toolie tell you about anyone particular?"

"No. He always said not to worry—he could handle her."

"I see."

"But now he's missing, and I bet she killed him for the insurance money." Mrs. Mardell sniffed then blew her nose on the tissue she'd been crushing in her hand.

"Well, that can't be the case, Mrs. Mardell. I checked. There is no insurance policy."

Like a growling mama dog who'd just been poked, she snapped, "You go and check again, then. I'm sure she killed him. It's your job to find out why."

"My job right now is to find your son. Is there anything else you can tell me that might help? Places he might go? Friends out of state?"

"I've told you all you need to know. Toolie wouldn't run off. You go arrest that girl. She killed Toolie as sure as I'm sittin' here. I told him not to marry her."

ON THE WAY BACK to his office, Ty pondered the women in the missing Toolie's life. If he was a bettin' man, he'd put good money on the theory that Mardell was the troublemaker in that marriage. Ty had never understood women who stayed with men who hit them or covered for abusive husbands when people asked questions. But, even after being beaten, Toolie's wife should at least want to track him down, if for nothing else than to get court-ordered child support.

Ty shook his head at the complications of marriage. But then again, his personal understanding of women and marriage was limited. Maybe Toolie's wife had taken her vows a little more seriously than say, someone like Mary Jo. To Mary Jo, marriage was in the same realm as buying a new car. If the vehicle didn't meet her needs, she could trade it in for another model. And then there was Jenna, a woman who'd married the man she loved and made a good life with him. Until, through no fault of her own, that life had ended. Jenna *wasn't* Jimmy's wife anymore. Why did Ty still see her that way? *Because that's the only way you've known her,* his mind whispered. And yet, when he'd touched her, kissed her, he'd only been thinking about Jenna. About Jenna and Ty. Besides feeling really lousy about it, his attraction wasn't even what Jenna wanted.

So be it, he decided. She said she needed him to be her friend and nothing else. He wouldn't step over the line again.

RIGHT AT SEVEN O'CLOCK Monday morning, Ty drove into the parking lot of the Donut Wrangler. It was his first visit since the grand opening. He'd stayed away for a week, kept busy with the Mardell case and finishing up the paperwork on his last closed file. But this morning he had to go into Austin for a policy meeting, and he'd decided to stop for a cup of coffee and biscuits—no doughnuts. He'd managed to warn most of the men he'd told about the restaurant, but a few of them had beat him to the punch and attached a note to one of the flyers he'd put up on the bulletin board at the sheriff's office. The note said, "WARNING! Don't eat the doughnuts."

As Ty pulled open the front door and stepped inside, Sharon greeted him with a smile. "Hey, Ranger. You're out bright and early this morning."

Ty took his Stetson off and nodded. "That's me, the early bird."

"Well, roost yourself on a stool and I'll get you some coffee."

Ty glanced around the diner as he sat down. Two booths and several of the stools at the counter were occupied, mostly by working men. Not bad for this early in the morning. But there was one thing missing. Jenna was nowhere to be seen.

"Where's your partner?" Ty asked as Sharon poured his coffee.

"We're splitting the shifts now. I come in at six-thirty and leave at one-thirty. Jenna comes in at eight-thirty and leaves at three-thirty. It makes it easier on us, and on Jay."

"And how is Jay handlin' this whole arrangement?"

Sharon frowned and put the coffeepot back on the warmer. "He's doing okay so far. It's still fairly new to him. If he can make it through the last of the summer until school starts, then Jenna and I will switch shifts so she can be home in the afternoons."

"Sounds as if you have everything under control," Ty said, taking a sip of his coffee.

"Well, almost..." Sharon gave him a shrewd look. "We haven't found Jenna a husband yet."

Ty almost choked on the hot coffee. He gingerly set the cup back in the saucer and tried to sound disinterested. "A what?"

"A *husband.* You know, the 'I do' kind of man." When Ty couldn't scrape up an answer, Sharon kept rolling. "Know anybody like that?"

He could tell Sharon was workin' on getting a reaction from him, but he had no idea what reaction she was after. "I suppose I could give it some thought," he said finally. "When did she decide she needed a husband?"

"Sometime right after you kissed her."

Ty could feel his neck getting warm and felt like cursing. He hadn't blushed in years. He couldn't tell whether Sharon was blaming or complimenting him. Had he scared Jenna into this?

"I told her you would be the best candidate," Sharon said, watching his face.

"I don't believe she feels the same way," Ty replied.

Sharon sighed and braced her arms on the counter. "I know, and I'm sorry to hear it. She's scared to get involved with another lawman, and she's got a good point. There's nothing either of us can do about that. The best we can do for her as friends is to get her what she wants."

Before he could reply, Sharon walked away to wait on another customer, leaving Ty feeling as if he'd just been kicked in the chest by a two-thousand-pound mule.

He was supposed to help find Jenna a husband?

Just the thought made his blood pressure rise. Why in the hell would he want to find her a husband, when just the idea pushed all his protective instincts into overload? He did his best to keep a neutral expression on his face when Sharon came back to take his order. He decided to play along.

"So, what kind of man are we lookin' for?"

"Oh, let's see." Sharon raised one hand and counted off the fingers as she named requirements. "Someone sensible, responsible... Someone with a *regular* job. It wouldn't hurt for him to be good-lookin', either.

"Not that I'm an expert on husbands," she added, and waved one hand to indicate a customer sitting on the last stool at the counter. "That's my former choice over there." She frowned in his direction. "You see how that turned out."

"I don't know," Ty said, thinking of his own poor choice. "At least yours stayed in the same state."

Sharon smiled. "That's true for sure. I can hardly get rid of the man."

Dean must have known he was being talked about. He nodded in their direction, then seeming unconcerned, continued eating his breakfast.

"I suppose it wouldn't hurt for Jenna to find someone like Dean. He was great for the first twenty years."

Twenty years?

Ty wondered how long it took before you could call a marriage a success. He thought of his own marriage and then Jenna's, which had ended in tragedy. Even the missing Toolie Mardell's marriage looked like a huge mistake. The whole institution seemed destined to hit bad luck or hard times, once it was official. Might as well place a bet in Las Vegas—the odds of winning were probably about the same.

Unable to voice his own feelings, he asked Sharon about hers. "You still love him?" Once it was out of his mouth, Ty couldn't believe he'd actually asked her.

Sharon seemed surprised, too. She glanced at her

ex again, then sighed. "I suppose I do. But sometimes love isn't enough."

"Amen," Ty agreed. His thoughts turned to Jenna and the way she made him feel. Was that love? Or was it just friendship and responsibility—an offshoot of his kinship with her dead husband? Whatever it was, he'd vowed to put it away. And what better way to take care of the problem than to help get Jenna married off? She'd be taken care of, and he'd never been attracted to married women.

Before he could force himself to volunteer for the husband hunt, Sharon turned to capture the plate of biscuits he'd ordered from the warming counter. "Here comes my partner now," she said.

Ty looked beyond Sharon and saw Jenna, her arms full of Jay's toys, cutting through the kitchen toward the office. A sleepy-looking Jay shuffled in front of her. She smiled and shrugged instead of waving. Ty's heart took several hard beats. He was supposed to find Jenna a husband? The idea again set off a confusing mix of emotions inside him. Then the objective part of his mind took over. Jimmy wouldn't want her to be alone—not if it meant she'd be harried and unhappy trying to raise their son. And she'd made it clear that Ty wasn't a candidate.

"Don't forget what I said about a husband. Keep your eyes peeled," Sharon whispered. Then she left him to his breakfast.

FIFTEEN MINUTES LATER, after getting Jay settled on the couch in the office, Jenna straightened her apron, checked her order pad and pencil, then stepped into the dining room. Her gaze went directly to Ty. She'd been half-asleep driving out, but just seeing him brought her to total awareness. It was worrisome. Why did the mere sight of him set her pulse pounding? Besides the obvious, that is. He was an attractive man who'd seen fit to kiss her. She shook her head. That kissing part should have worn off by now. He'd done exactly what she'd asked; he'd backed off. Heck, they'd barely seen him since he'd apologized.

But whatever it was between them, friendship or misplaced attraction, it wasn't over yet. The best thing for both of them would be for her to find someone else to distract her from the memories. Unable to resist his presence, she walked along the counter until she stood in front of him.

''Hey, Ty,'' she said. He'd taken his hat off and placed it on the next stool, leaving his hair slightly rumpled. Jenna's hand itched with the desire to comb it back into place. She chalked up the urge to the motherhood thing...she'd run her hand through Jay's hair often enough.

Liar, she chided herself. The urge rushing under her skin had nothing to do with mothering.

''Jenna.'' Ty nodded. Then he simply stared at her.

Jenna had the uncomfortable feeling that he'd just read her mind. She stumbled on. ''How's your breakfast?''

Ty glanced down at his half-eaten biscuit before answering. "Good. Don't take offense, but Robert's biscuits are better than his doughnuts."

Jenna shrugged but felt better, on firmer ground, discussing food rather than feelings. "I know. We're working on it." She stopped to wave at Dean. "Sharon's ex—I mean, Dean is trying to get a recipe from the Royal Doughnut store in town."

"Well, I hope he doesn't get arrested for breaking and entering."

"Me, too," Jenna said. "But we need that recipe, bad." She took the opportunity to refill his coffee cup. "How have you been? Jay and I have missed you."

Ty held her gaze for a moment, chewing and apparently thinking. "I've been pretty busy with work." He didn't comment on the missing part.

"I know how that is," Jenna said. "I feel like I spend twenty-four hours a day here for one reason or another."

Two new customers entered the front door, bringing Jenna's attention back to business. She handed them two menus. "Sit anywhere you like."

"Is Sharon here?" one of the men asked.

Jenna smiled. Sharon had taken customer service to a new level. She felt it was her duty to flirt with every man who walked through the door. When Jenna teased her about it, she said it wouldn't hurt anything. She wasn't plannin' on getting cozy with any of them, and a little flirting might brighten their day enough for them to come back.

"She'll be out in just a minute," Jenna said. "Sit over in the back booth—that's her section." Then she noticed the other man was staring at her.

"Where's your section?" he asked.

Before she could stop herself, her gaze slipped to Ty. For some reason it felt awkward, flirting in front of him. She dragged her attention back to the man. "You only get one waitress at a time. I'll wait on you the next time you come in."

The man smiled, tipped his ball cap and then followed his friend to the booth in the back.

After giving the man a hard measuring look, Ty pushed his plate away and wiped his mouth with a napkin. "I guess I better be gettin' on the road."

"You haven't finished your coffee yet," Jenna said. She'd just arrived and Ty was leaving. They'd hardly had time to talk.

"That's my third cup," he answered, and reached for his hat. "I have to drive into Austin."

Feeling suddenly deflated, Jenna cleared the counter in front of him. She couldn't think of a thing to say other than "Drive safely, then."

Ty stood and shoved one hand in his pocket, withdrawing a five-dollar bill. He placed it on the counter with the check. "I will. You take care."

Suddenly Jenna's mind unfroze. "Ty?"

He waited.

"I forgot to invite you—we're having a little party for Jay's birthday, next Wednesday at three-thirty. It'll be here. Do you think you can come? I'm sure he'd like that. We'll have cake and..."

Jenna knew she was babbling, and finally closed her mouth, while Ty simply stood and watched her make a complete fool of herself.

He didn't seem too put off by it, though. He nodded and said, "I don't see why not. I'll let you know one way or the other."

"Oh, and bring Kirby if he can stand about ten seven-year-olds."

"I'll ask him."

As Jenna watched him leave, Sharon waltzed past her. "Remember, that Ranger's not even on the list, honey. Now come over here and meet the local trucking distributor."

THAT EVENING, after driving into Austin and spending most of the day in meetings, Ty felt exhausted. So why couldn't he sleep?

Because the thought of Jenna actively looking for a husband had thrown him for a loop. He remembered one of her letters:

> I can't even imagine wanting to marry again. Jimmy was my first love, my first lover. I don't know how to be that innocent…that hopeful again. Not to mention courageous. The thought of trying to date scares me spitless. I don't know how to be with anyone but Jimmy.

Ty rubbed the back of his neck and sighed. Determined to get past his preoccupation, he picked up the remote and leisurely ran through the channels. With any luck he'd find something to take his mind off Jenna. He caught the end of the newscast and watched the highlights of the baseball game.

"You should find yourself a woman like Jenna and get married again." The memory of Jimmy's voice came out of nowhere. "That way our sons could grow up and play baseball together." Jimmy had laughed and slapped Ty on the back. "Can you imagine the two of us as Little League coaches? We'd be deadly."

As the news ended, Ty wondered if Jenna would marry a coach good enough for Jimmy's son.

JENNA SAT DOWN at the kitchen table with her pad and pen. Jay was in bed and the news had just finished, but she wasn't sleepy. She knew from past experience when she felt this way, there was no use in lying down. Might as well do *something*. Falling back on old habits, she decided to write a letter.

Ty,
I know you probably don't understand this. Heck, I don't really understand it myself. But I have to get married again. It's the most positive thing I can think of for Jay. He needs a whole family.

You've been so good to us. And the thought of losing you, of not having you stop by or of even never seeing you again hurts. More than I can tell you. I wish… I wish I could…

Jenna put down the pen and reached for a paper towel. She didn't know what she wished anymore concerning Ty. He was alternately a beacon of friendship and an enticing temptation. And since Jimmy's death, he'd been the only man in her life. Her rush to find a husband meant that sooner than later, she'd have to get along without him.

She dabbed at her eyes and blew her nose. Then she looked at the phone. Even now, the person she really wanted to talk to about the whole husband-hunting thing was Ty. But she couldn't depend on his equanimity on the subject. And to be truthful, she was afraid that he might just say, "Leave me alone. I can't help you."

And he couldn't help her. Not with this.

She picked up the pad and pen and headed for her bedroom. The room and bed she'd shared with Jimmy. Neither of the men she cared about the most could help her tonight.

CHAPTER TEN

"HAPPY BIRTHDAY TO YOU..."

As the guests sang to her son, Jenna drew in a shaky but relieved breath. By the look on Jay's face, Jenna could tell having the party at the restaurant had been the right decision. He'd already given the children a tour from the perspective of a seven-year-old co-owner. He'd proudly shown them things like the line Robert had taped on the floor three feet from the deep fryers that no one under thirty was allowed to cross. Then he'd moved on to his personal play table, which had been set up in the kitchen near the television so he and Robert could watch cartoons while they played fish.

"...Happy birthday, dear Jay. Happy birthday to you."

As Jay leaned forward to blow out the candles on his cake, Jenna remembered his last birthday. She and her family had done their best, but because it was Jay's first birthday after his father's death, there had been little real happiness. Especially when he'd confessed that his birthday wish had been to see his father again.

As the applause faded, Sharon made an announcement, bringing Jenna back to the present. "All right. I want all of you to line up in front of me." She pulled a roll of quarters from the pocket of her apron and stripped off the paper on one end. The children stumbled into a line as she continued, "Now, while we cut the cake, I'm gonna give each of you a quarter. I want you to go over and pick out some songs on the jukebox." She handed the first two children in line their quarters. "I want you to take turns over there. Let everybody get a choice."

Jenna slid the cake off the booth table and placed it on the counter where the paper plates and plastic forks were arranged.

"Why in the world do we have to crank that music up? Isn't there enough noise in here?" Barbara asked as Ray Stevens started singing about Ahab the Arab.

Barbara had taken up residence on the first stool at the counter when she'd come in earlier. Jenna couldn't help but notice that she'd chosen the stool closest to the front door. In case she needed to make a quick exit, Jenna supposed.

After searching behind the counter for a knife to cut the cake, she raised her gaze and saw Ty and Kirby getting out of Ty's car.

Her heart did a little hop, skip and a jump before she got herself under control. She'd been so busy, she hadn't had time to worry about whether Ty would come to the party or not. Now, however, she realized how happy she was to see him. Relieved.

She'd wanted him to be here. Not wanting to think about Barbara's reaction to his presence, she kept her mind on the party and moved past her mother-in-law.

"Hi, Ty. Hi, Kirby," she called as she delivered the first table of squirming children pieces of cake and cups of punch. "You're just in time for cake."

"Looks like you might be havin' a party," Kirby said as he surveyed the chaos. Then he presented Jenna with a wrapped box. "This is for the birthday boy, from me and Ty."

Jenna took the box and smiled at Kirby, then at Ty. "Well, thank you. You didn't need to do that, but I'm glad you could come," she said.

"Wouldn't miss it," Ty replied as he removed his hat.

She'd *missed* him. As hard as it was to admit. On the heels of that thought, she realized she'd spent more time lately missing Ty than thinking about Jimmy. Before the guilt took root and ruined her day, she pushed it away.

"Well, find a seat if you can and I'll bring you some cake," she said.

An hour and a half later, after Jenna had introduced Ty and Kirby to Rusty's mom, Nancy, and once more to her mother-in-law as "her friends," and after the kids had played musical chairs using the stools at the counter, everyone moved outside to see who could break the piñata hung from the giant doughnut. Now the kids had settled down to sort through the candy they'd grabbed outside and watch Jay open his presents.

Everyone oohed and aahed over his growing stack of books and games. The adults were more impressed by the expensive jeans and tennis shoes Jay's grandmother had given him than Jay seemed to be. Jenna's parents had called him the night before and sent two Disney videos along with a chemistry set complete with formulas for invisible ink and baking-soda propulsion. By the time Jay got to Kirby and Ty's gift, he was already ecstatic and running on pure sugar. Jay ripped open the paper and pried the top off the box. Then he reverently pushed the paper aside and removed a red cowboy hat complete with a string to go under his chin. "Look, Mom," he said as he held up the hat.

Jenna laughed and moved over to help him. "Put it on, cowboy," she said as she adjusted the string under his chin. She was just thinking that she needed to get him a pair of boots when he reached in the box and brought out a tooled holster with a kid-sized six-shooter nestled in place. Everything seemed to stop for Jenna.

"Oh, boy! A real gun," Jay said, and stood up to strap on the holster. When he had trouble with the buckle, he looked to Jenna. "Help me, Mom."

Jenna felt as though someone had her by the throat. She couldn't breathe, certainly couldn't speak. And there was no way she could help Jay put a gun around his waist. She knew everyone was watching, but the scene around her seemed to move in slow motion. She found herself staring at Ty.

''Come here. I'll help you with that, son,'' Kirby offered, looking pleased.

Jay walked past her to Kirby, and Jenna managed to push herself up from the floor. She had to leave the room before she did something completely crazy, like take the gun, run out the door and throw it as far as all her strength would send it.

By herself in the kitchen, she took several calming breaths and did her best not to cry. How could Ty give Jay a gun? He, of all people, should understand that she never wanted a gun in the house—not a toy, not a real one.

''Jenna? Are you okay?'' Ty's voice startled her, but only because her insides were already doing back flips. She tried to get control of herself as she turned to face him, but the words came out just the same.

''How could you?''

''How could I what?''

She took another deep breath and felt her eyes fill with tears. ''How could you give Jay a gun?''

He looked confused. ''It's a toy. The whole set came togeth—''

''He can't keep it.''

Ty ran a hand through his hair and sighed. ''Jenna… I know that a gun took your husband—took Jimmy. But this gun is just—''

''When did you start playing with guns, Ty?''

''Every little boy plays cowboy, Jenna.''

''Not mine,'' she said emphatically.

Ty put his hands on her shoulders and spoke calmly, while her pulse pounded in her ears. ''Don't you think you're taking this a little too far? I know how much Jimmy's death hurt you, but you've got to stop this.''

''Stop what?''

''You've got to stop coddling Jay. If you don't let him have a toy gun, he'll make one out of a stick or a carrot. It's something all little boys do.''

''How many of those boys grow up to be policemen?'' She gazed at him unflinchingly, daring him to refute her. ''Or Texas Rangers?''

Ty seemed to lose his own temper momentarily. ''Not nearly enough, if you want to know the truth.''

''My son is *not* going to be one of them.''

They stared at each other in a test of wills, until someone pushed open the swinging door to the kitchen and leaned through it. Both Ty and Jenna turned, and his hands dropped away from her shoulders.

Barbara stood in the doorway. ''We've opened the rest of the presents. It's time to say goodbye to the kids.'' She looked as if she had more to say but thought better of it. She shrugged and let the door swing closed.

''We'll talk about this later—'' Ty began.

''No, we won't. As soon as everyone leaves, I'm going to take that gun away from Jay. You can return it and get your money back.''

"Jenna—"

Unable to convince him or to change her own position, she turned and left him standing in the kitchen alone.

"DID YOU EVER SHOOT ANYBODY?" Jay asked.

He and Ty were sitting on the back steps of the diner while Jenna and Sharon cleaned up inside. It had come down to Ty's explaining to Jay why his mother wouldn't let him have a gun. He didn't agree with her, but as in everything else, he would follow her wishes when he could. He'd made a promise to Jimmy. That promise included telling the truth, although he wasn't sure how to discuss the subject with a child.

"Well, yes, I have," Ty answered.

"My daddy got shot and he died," Jay said. He looked down at his six-shooter, then back up at Ty. "If I had a real gun, I'd shoot the man who hurt my dad." Ty had to swallow to clear the strangled feeling in his throat. Gazing into Jay's determined brown eyes was like stepping back in time and seeing his father.

Look after Jenna and my son....

Ty put his hand on Jay's shoulder. "Your dad wouldn't want you to do that. Shooting somebody isn't always the answer. It can't bring your dad back and it makes *you* the bad guy then. It would only hurt you and your mother even more." He couldn't explain about the law and prison. He'd have to save that for a later conversation. Jenna had been right about one thing; he hadn't realized how the simple gift of a cowboy outfit could become an emotional battlefield. If she believed Ty had some ulterior motive, she was wrong, but he couldn't fault her logic. He'd just remembered being a boy playing the Lone Ranger and thought Jay might like to be a cowboy, too.

"You know what your dad told me once? He told me he hoped you'd grow up to be a baseball player." It wasn't strictly true, but Ty said it anyway, hoping he could ease the blow of losing the new gun.

Jay turned the gun over in his hand, handling it like a treasure. His eyes filled with tears. "Can't I keep it?" he asked.

Ty heard the door close behind him but he didn't move. Jenna's voice made him want to swear. She sounded so sad. "Honey." She sat down beside Jay and put her arm around him. "You have so many other presents...."

"But I want to be a cowboy." He sniffed.

Ty was beginning to feel lower than a slug under a slimy rock for ruining Jay's birthday. "I can take it back and get you something else. You can even pick it out. How about a new baseball glove?" He didn't know what else to offer; the damage had been done.

Jay pulled the gun to his chest, then turned his face into his mother's side. "I want to keep this one. Mr. Kirby said it was lucky."

Ty saw Jenna blink back tears, then watched as

she sighed and squeezed her son close. ''All right. I guess you can keep it.''

Jay brightened immediately. ''I promise I won't do anything bad with it,'' he said earnestly.

''I know you won't,'' Jenna replied. ''Now, why don't you go help Aunt Sharon pack up your other presents?''

''Okay. Thanks, Mom.''

''You're welcome. Don't forget to thank Sharon and say goodbye to your grandmom.''

Believing he deserved whatever Jenna had to say to him, Ty stayed where he was. When the door behind them closed, she shifted her gaze to him but didn't speak.

''I'm sorry, Jenna.''

She sighed and propped her elbows on her knees. ''Oh, it's all right. I know I overreacted....'' She glanced toward the horizon for a moment. ''I should probably apologize to you. I just lost it there for a while.''

Unable to stop himself, Ty reached for her hand and held it between both of his. That brought her attention back to him. ''I should have mentioned it to you first. I didn't know how you felt. Kirby and I just went and bought boy stuff. I never meant to cause you any pain.''

''And I jumped all over you without even saying thank-you.'' Her hand squeezed his. ''Thank you for talking to him. I know it wasn't easy.'' She smiled slightly. ''Now you know how hard it is to be a mom.''

Or a dad, he thought.

She let her hand rest in his. "Everything I do is for him, for his future. I don't want any more unpleasant surprises for him or me."

Ty thought of what Sharon had said about Jenna's looking for a husband. Was that part of the plan? Even as he asked the question, he knew it was true. She wanted to put her family back together again. Jay needed a father.

"I understand." When she didn't answer, he added, "I really do." Thinking of her wishes, rather than his own, he said, "I hope you find what you're looking for."

Jenna didn't move or answer. He could feel her pulse. At that moment it seemed as if the two of them were suspended in time, sitting side by side looking into the future. The worst heat of the day was over. The late-afternoon sun sparkled through the leaves of the trees, and a slight haze of dust drifted in the air. A cricket chirped in the bushes near the steps. Ty realized he was content with the simple companionship, with holding Jenna's hand and feeling her trust.

He silently vowed one more time not to screw it up. He gave her hand a final squeeze before he let it go.

"Well, I guess I better find old Kirby and get on the road," he said. Brushing his palms down his thighs, he pushed to his feet, then held out a hand to help her up.

A deep pleasure spread through him as she took

his hand, without hesitation, and allowed him to help. He wished every offer of his help could be so natural and straightforward. For the first time since he'd kissed her, he felt back on firmer ground. He could do this; he could be her friend without strings.

But then she brushed a kiss against his cheek and whispered, "Thanks, Ty, and thank Kirby for me, too," before moving up the stairs. Every nerve ending from his neck to his knees jumped at the brief contact, and all his good intentions burned right out of him.

CHAPTER ELEVEN

THE NEXT DAY, after yet another night of tossin' and cussin' instead of sleepin', Ty sat at his desk and did what every "friend" would do in his position. He began making a list of potential husbands for Jenna.

The evening before, he'd gotten a call from Deputy Ray Guthrie—the supposed bachelor for life. It seemed as if Ray was willing to reconsider his status after seeing Jenna at the diner. He'd wanted to know if Ty would be bothered if he asked her out.

Bothered didn't begin to describe how Ty felt. He was furious. As a public service he'd told Ray not to waste his time, that Jenna had distinctly singled out police officers as her "least likely to date."

Now he racked his brain for names. If he could put together a respectable list of single men, he could weigh one against the other and evaluate them as husband material.

The plan was sound. The main problem with the idea cropped up after an hour. He'd only thought of two names: Garland Peters, his insurance man who'd briefly commiserated about divorce the last time he'd updated Ty's policy, and Ronald Cluett, one of the clerks of the court who had mentioned to Ty that his parents were all over him about not producing any grandkids.

This might be harder than he thought. Garland Peters seemed suitable, but Ronald looked a little like Barney Fife, and Ty couldn't picture Jenna married to a man who still lived with his mother. He shook his head in disgust. All the other single men he knew were police officers.

From this day on he needed to remember to ask the men he met whether they were married or not. The sooner Jenna found a husband, the easier it would be for Ty to be the friend she wanted him to be. At the moment he was the kind of friend who refused to even contemplate a stranger putting his hands on Jenna. He had to stop thinking and get on with it. He decided he could at least get started by calling Garland.

But after dialing the insurance agent's office, he'd been told that Garland was on another line and would have to return Ty's call. Left waiting, Ty realized that he didn't really know what kind of person Garland was. He only knew he had a regular job, wore a suit instead of a gun and he didn't have a police record. That wasn't saying a whole lot about a man's qualifications as a husband.

What did Jenna want in a man? Jimmy had been playful, with a wicked sense of humor, but he'd had a hot temper when someone tried to push him. He'd also been head over heels in love with his wife and crazy about his son. Ty didn't know if Garland had it in him to be what Jenna needed or wanted. He'd have to let her decide.

The phone rang and Ty picked it up.

"Howdy, Ty," Garland said. "I'm surprised to catch you in your office."

"Well, you know there just isn't that much crime happening around this building. So I usually have to go out and find it."

"I see what you mean." Garland laughed. "What can I do for you?"

"Did you ever get remarried?"

"Ex-cuse me?"

Ty tapped the pencil he'd been using to make his list against his knee and searched for inner strength. The image of another man kissing Jenna—besides Jimmy…besides himself—and her possible reaction to it, ran under his skin, raising his hackles. His grip tightened on the pencil, and it broke in half.

"Bear with me," he said to Garland as he tossed the pencil pieces in the trash. He *really* didn't want to do this. But he had to. "I have something I want to talk to you about, but I need to know if you're married or not."

"Uh, no. I have a couple of women I go out with occasionally, but we aren't talking marriage."

"Good. There's a woman I want you to meet."

"HOW ABOUT HIM?" Sharon whispered in Jenna's ear as she passed her behind the counter.

"Who?" Jenna's attention had been on the ketchup and mustard she'd promised to deliver to booth three.

Sharon used her shoulder to turn Jenna in the correct direction. "That one over there with the blue plaid shirt. He's a manager at the Everhardt plant and has the prettiest blue eyes."

"Sharon!" Jenna hissed under her breath as she tried to casually check the guy out without being noticed. "How do you find out so much about everyone?"

With an arch of her eyebrow, Sharon said, "I ask them, silly. How else do you find out things about strangers?"

When the man in the booth turned and almost caught her staring, Jenna lowered her eyes and picked up the ketchup. She was about to congratulate her partner on her nerve when Sharon added, "It helps when I tell them I'm husband hunting for a friend."

Jenna's breath seemed to leave her body in one rush. "You tell them what?"

Sharon laughed and headed for the kitchen. "Don't worry, I don't tell them it's you."

After nearly dropping the ketchup bottle, Jenna made the mistake of glancing at the man in the blue plaid shirt again. He smiled at her. This time the bottle slid out of her fingers. She winced when it bounced off the top of her left shoe. At least it didn't break, she thought as she quickly stooped to pick it up. She wished she could stay hidden behind the counter until the table of men, who were now laughing at something, finished their lunches and left. She was sure her face was as red as the ketchup.

When she'd told Sharon she was going to look for a husband, she hadn't meant an all-out cattle call. Especially not in the restaurant. How could she work when she was being evaluated by every man in the room? As she straightened up, she was grateful to find a man sitting down on the stool between her and the man in the plaid shirt. At least she could pretend to be distracted by her job.

"Hi," she said. Of medium build, and wearing a suit and tie, the guy stood out from the other men who were dressed in work clothes. She handed him a menu and said, "I'll be right back for your order." She held up the ketchup she'd rescued. "As soon as I deliver this to booth three."

The man didn't look at the menu, he kept his eyes on her. "Are you Jenna Taylor?"

Something in the tone of his voice stopped her. "Yes?"

He extended his hand. "I'm Garland Peters."

Jenna shook his hand. "Nice to meet you." She waited as he checked her out from head to toe. Just as her patience had had all the mystery it could stand, he spoke again.

"Ty Richardson sent me."

LATER THAT AFTERNOON, when business had slowed, Jenna cornered Sharon in the office. Busy counting the day's receipts, Sharon didn't look up until Jenna closed the office door.

"Why did you tell Ty I was looking for a husband?" she asked, trying to keep her voice calm and level. After struggling all afternoon with the question, she was afraid it would come out as a screech.

Sharon still didn't raise her eyes, and Jenna wished she could be so easily distracted. But when her partner did look up, she had a thoughtful expression on her face.

"Why shouldn't I tell him? He's your friend. Doesn't he want you to be happy?"

"I can't believe you did that," Jenna continued. "It makes me sound calculating or desperate. I just wanted to try dating again." Suddenly all her energy had seeped into the ground through the soles of her shoes. She flopped down on the worn couch that faced the desk. "He actually sent a man in here to meet me."

Again Sharon watched her intently. "He *is* just your friend, right?"

Doing her best to get herself under control, Jenna pushed her hair back and gazed at her partner. "Of course he's my friend. You know that. But—"

"But what?" Sharon asked. She leaned back in the office chair and crossed her arms, waiting. "I think you should pay attention to any man Ty sends you. That Ranger has a good head on his shoulders."

"It just doesn't seem right somehow," Jenna said.

Now Sharon looked surprised. "Really? Why?"

"Well, the man was fine. He seemed very nice, but Ty—" Losing her train of thought, Jenna fell silent.

"Seems like Ty is doing his best for you. Maybe you should just accept his help and say thank-you."

Jenna knew she sounded ungrateful. She'd told Sharon she wanted to find a husband. So why was she feeling put out because her friends had pitched in to help?

"I guess I didn't expect things to happen so fast," Jenna confessed, although she knew that wasn't all there was to it. "I need some time to get used to the idea."

"As my mother used to say, there's no time like the present. Add that to, God helps those who help themselves, and you'll see, you need to stop thinkin' so much. Jump in the water and start swimmin'."

Jenna smiled despite her confusion. "You sure you don't have something from Confucius you'd like to add?"

Sharon grinned, unfazed. "No, but I'll go to the library and look somethin' up, if it'll help." Sharon leaned forward eagerly. "All right. Which one was he?"

Jenna didn't bother acting as if she didn't know whom they were talking about. "The one in the suit who sat at the counter. He's an insurance salesman."

"Hmm." Sharon thought about it for a moment. "I guess that wouldn't be bad. Dean's been into insurance for years. He's made a good living. Not too exciting but...regular. So when's the date?"

"Whoa," Jenna said, laughing. "He gave me his card. Said he'd let me decide whether I wanted to call him or not."

"No pressure—I like him already." Sharon shifted her attention to the calendar. "Okay, it's already Friday. You'll have to wait till Monday to call."

"Is that some kind of rule?"

"It is," Sharon answered. "You heard about that book of rules about dating?" Before Jenna could answer, Sharon raised one hand in a dismissive gesture. "You just forget about *those* rules—you're going to follow *mine*. You're my partner and I intend to see you settled and happy. We'll do this together."

"Together?" Somehow that didn't make Jenna feel more at ease.

"I'm talking strategy." Sharon winked at Jenna's skeptical look. "Hey, it's working so far with the diner, isn't it?"

Why did you send him to me, Ty? Does this mean you're tired of us? Of Jay, and me?

JENNA STARED DOWN at her own handwriting, wishing things were the way they used to be. How they'd been in the past, when she could be honest with Ty about her feelings. She'd had a lot to think about today and needed to talk about it. Though part of her confusion, a *big* part of it, had to do with Ty himself. She didn't know how to write him about that.

She'd rather hear his voice, have him tell her what he was really thinking. But could she return the favor? Could she tell him all the confused messages she sorted through each and every time he walked into the room?

Jenna rested her chin on her palm. Could she tell him that every man Sharon introduced her to would automatically be compared to him whether she meant to or not? Could she tell him that since her husband had died, the closest she'd been to having that crazy, dizzying feeling of wanting someone, was when she'd been in his arms and covered in paint?

No. She couldn't confess any of that. So how could she expect him to settle things? Especially if she happened to be the only one who was confused. What if he told her he *was* tired of being her friend?

It didn't matter. She had to see what he'd say. She moved across the room, picked up the receiver and dialed.

TY HAD BEEN DROWNING his sorrows in his biggest vice—milk and chocolate-chip cookies—when the phone rang. He swallowed again to clear his throat as his heart worked harder than it needed to. ''Hey, Ty.''

''Jenna? How are you?''

''I'm—'' she faltered slightly ''—I'm fine.''

She didn't sound fine. Ty sat up straighter and slid his feet from the coffee table to the floor. ''Well, good. Uh, is there a problem?''

After a pause she answered. ''No. Not really.'' A few more seconds of silence went by before she added, ''I wanted to ask you a question.''

Ty could feel the blood rushing through his veins as he waited. She'd called him; he was determined to let her talk.

''What do you think of me getting married again?''

Damn. Ty's pulse took an unwanted leap, and he felt a suspicious tightness in his chest. He hoped he was having a heart attack since the alternative was that he wanted to tell her getting remarried was a bad idea. And he knew she didn't need to hear that. He also knew he had no right to make her feel badly about going on with her life. He'd encouraged her to do just that in his letters.

''I want you to be happy,'' he said diplomatically. He *did* want her to be happy, didn't he? He just didn't think rushing into another marriage would necessarily cause that.

''The man—Garland—who you sent to the restaurant. He, uh...''

''He seems like a good person,'' Ty finished for

her. *God,* he begged, *please don't make me have to talk her into going out with him.*

"And he's not a lawman," she added.

"There is that."

"I guess I'm going to call him next week."

Ty's fingers gripped the phone a little tighter. "That's good." Terrific. Wonderful. He thought he heard a rumble of thunder in the distance. He hoped lightning would strike and knock him off the phone, out of this conversation.

"Are you sure? I mean, is that how you really feel about it?" she persisted.

There was that word—*feel.* What did it matter how he felt about it? She wanted to find a husband and he was helping her do it. Why did he have to feel anything?

Because he did. And it made him want to kick the coffee table. Every cell in his body screamed at him to tell her to forget her plan and to forget Peters, but he'd made a promise and, by damn, he intended to keep it. He swallowed to keep his "feelings" out of his voice.

"I think it's great, Jenna. He may or may not be the one, but I'm happy to see you moving on."

There, he'd said the right thing. If he could just get off the phone before his gut made him spill the truth, he'd be forever grateful. "I'll stop by the diner every once in a while to see how you're doing. And you know you can call me if you need me."

"Yes, I know." She didn't sound very happy or

excited to Ty. But then again, maybe he was hearing what he wanted to hear.

"I'll see you later," he said. "Good night, Jenna."

"Night, Ty."

Ty hung up the receiver and looked toward the ceiling. "Well, Jimmy. I hope you're up there somewhere enjoying this torture. 'Cause my promise to you is killin' me."

The only answer was another distant rumble of thunder. Ty picked up his half-empty glass and kicked the coffee table on the way to the kitchen.

CHAPTER TWELVE

THE NIGHT OF THE BIG DATE had finally rolled around, and Jenna wouldn't admit she was nervous, because in truth, her mental condition hovered closer to petrified. Instead of being frozen like an ancient tree in the desert, however, she'd become a whirlwind.

After being coached all morning by Sharon on the pleasures and pitfalls of first dates, Jenna had rushed home, gathered up Jay's overnight gear and delivered him to her mother-in-law's for the night. That would relieve Jenna of having to find and worry about a baby-sitter, or of having to come home earlier than planned. And it would also stave off any criticism by giving Barbara what she wanted—more time with Jay.

Then she'd returned home and ransacked her closet, wondering why she hadn't gone shopping for something new to wear. By the time she'd finished, she still had at least six possible date outfits scattered over the bed. Unable to choose, she changed course and headed for the shower. Finally, after she'd scrubbed, shampooed and shaved her legs, her thoughts seemed a little clearer. She'd wear the blue dress, not too sexy but, on the other hand, not too mommyish.

Unfortunately, as she stood in front of the mirror combing her wet hair, there was a lull in her panic. That's when she thought of Ty.

She wondered what he'd be doing tonight, while she and Garland were at the Bar W steak house. Ty had stopped by the diner once since she'd called him and made a fool of herself. He'd been polite and friendly, when she'd told him about the date. Then, after two cups of coffee, he'd said he had to go back to work.

A strange kind of sadness moved through her as she stared at her own reflection. Tonight was the start of her new life, the setting in motion of her plan to find a husband. She should be excited; at least that's what Sharon had told her. Instead, she felt more alone than ever. She sighed and picked up the blow dryer. Maybe the aloneness came from Jay's not being home. They hadn't spent a night apart since she'd moved back to Texas.

Ty's image came back to haunt her. She recalled his face the day he'd laughed with her over spilled paint, then kissed her. She set the dryer on the counter and brought her fingers up to touch her lips. She wondered if Garland would kiss her tonight. Her panic returned at the thought. Then her wayward inner voice taunted, *You'd be more excited if your date happened to be with Ty Richardson.*

It was true; she'd be more comfortable with Ty even though something about him made her as nervous as a schoolgirl. A part of her wanted to find out why.

Jenna closed her eyes and willed her mind back to what she and Garland might talk about later, at dinner. *Garland, Garland, Garland.* If she kept repeating his name, maybe she wouldn't think about Ty.

TY TURNED INTO THE DRIVEWAY of the Casa Blanco Apartments and found a parking space. He knew who was waiting behind door number 10, his date for the evening, Marcie Wright. He'd met her at the Caballero the night Jenna had called to ask him about Garland. He'd called and asked Marcie out the day after seeing Jenna at the diner and hearing her talk about Garland and their planned date.

He wasn't doing this for spite. He had to do something about his own life before he went ballistic. He needed to be with another woman so he could get past his preoccupation with Jenna. And he would. He was determined—and a realist.

In his line of work there was no room for second guessing. Jenna had her life, and he had his. No use wishing it was otherwise.

As he walked to apartment 10 he searched for his sense of humor. He didn't want to intimidate Marcie. She was young and friendly and, unlike some people he knew, she didn't have a problem with what he did for a living. In fact, she was fairly impressed by it.

That was as good a place as any to start. He

straightened his back, settled his Stetson over his eyes and knocked on the door. Seconds later the door opened and on a whiff of sweet-smelling perfume, Marcie said, "Hello, Ty. Come on in."

DINNER SEEMED TO BE TAKING a long time to find its way to their table, Jenna thought as she casually scanned the room for their waitress. Then she smiled at Garland. They'd run out of casual conversation a few minutes ago, and after two glasses of wine, Jenna still didn't feel very relaxed. She decided that in the future, she really needed to learn how to calm down.

"So, what do you like to do for fun, Jenna?"

Fun? "Well… I haven't really had much time for fun. Opening the diner and all…"

Garland smiled before he took another sip from his vodka and tonic. "Now, that's something we'll just have to change," he said, looking friendlier than before. "You need to get out, kick up your heels some." He clinked his glass to hers. "A good-lookin' woman like you needs to loosen up."

He winked as he put his drink down, letting her know that he was the man who intended to help with the process, and Jenna felt a stirring of unease. It had been so long since she'd been faced with unabashed male attention she wasn't sure how to react. Was he being too friendly? Or had she simply forgotten how to flirt?

"Well," she said, trying to slow things down, "you know I have my son to think about."

Garland's gaze drifted off as a waitress walked by; he seemed to enjoy the view. Returning his attention to her, he picked up his drink again. "That's right. You have a son. But you shouldn't let him hold you back. That's what baby-sitters are for."

Hold me back? Okay, now he'd hit a nerve. Jenna immediately thought of three ways to tell him how to mind his own business, but then the waitress arrived with their food. Saved from making a comment, she decided to give him the benefit of the doubt. People without children usually didn't understand how hard it was to leave them. And Garland had had three drinks while they'd been waiting for their meal. Maybe he'd be different with a little food in him to counteract the alcohol.

"I take it you don't have any children, then," Jenna said as she cut into her steak.

"Oh, yeah, I've got two. They live with my ex-wife. I get them every other weekend." He took a bite of his steak and chewed. "That's what I mean. I had to switch weekends so I could go out with you tonight. The kids understand."

I bet they do, Jenna thought. But she smiled and continued eating. Better to eat than say something she'd regret.

AFTER TWO LONG-NECK BEERS, Ty had a pounding headache. When Marcie leaned over and asked him to dance, he winced. But he couldn't deny that he knew how to two-step. As the music was cranked up, he led Marcie onto the floor.

He knew he should lighten up. Marcie was doing her best to have a good time, and he needed to at least smile once in a while. As he swung her out, then back under his arm, she laughed and slid her palm along his back. He had to admit Marcie was a good dancer. And he'd heard it said that women who were free spirits on the dance floor might also have other talents behind closed doors. Probably had something to do with being athletic, he decided in a detached sort of way. Mary Jo had loved to dance, but it hadn't spilled over into their love life. By the time they got home, she'd be suddenly "too tired."

Then he thought of Jenna and wondered if she could dance. Ty's hands automatically tightened on Marcie, and she reciprocated.

Now he'd done it. But just as he was bemoaning how to straighten out mixed signals, he realized he was free, out with an attractive woman and over twenty-one. In other words, the warmer part of his libido whispered, *Why not?*

Why the hell not? his pride added. *It's a sure way to get rid of that headache.*

JENNA'S FEET HURT. After she worked a shift in the restaurant, then wore heels for the first time in months, her toes were rebelling. She wished she could slip her shoes off under the table but knew better. Once they were off, there would be no getting them back on for the trip home.

And she was beginning to worry about getting

home at all. After dinner Garland had ordered two more drinks. She'd switched to water with lemon because drinking more had seemed foolish. Especially with her date drinking enough for both of them.

When Garland asked if she was ready to leave, she decided to visit the ladies' room first. When he stood to help her from her chair, he staggered against a person passing behind them. Jenna's concern kicked up several notches.

On the way to the ladies' room she glanced back and watched Garland's effort to sit back down. He'd definitely had too much to drink. What should she do now? Would he be able to drive home safely?

She took her time in the rest room, washed her hands, refreshed her lipstick. Then it hit her. She couldn't allow Garland to drive. Not just for their own safety but for Jay's. Her dinner suddenly felt like lead in her stomach. If, heaven forbid, she was injured or killed in an accident, who would take care of her son?

She passed a telephone in the hall on her way back to the table and hesitated. What if she asked Sharon to pick her up?

No. She would offer to drive them both home and explain to Garland that she couldn't take a chance with her future. Bolstered by her decision, she resumed her seat across from Garland and made the offer.

"I think it would be better if I drove us home," she said.

His face seemed to go completely blank for a second before he waved a hand in dismissal. "I'm fine. I had a few drinks, but I can drive."

Jenna persisted. "I would really feel better if you didn't."

Garland's features soured. "What's wrong with you? I told you I could drive. What part of that do you *not* understand?"

Jenna wanted to duck. Several people at the tables around them had turned to look. Mortified, she couldn't think of a thing to say.

"Here's the deal, then," Garland said, pushing to his feet as if he'd been challenged to a sparring match. He accidentally knocked his unused coffee spoon off the table, and it hit the floor with a clang. He didn't even blink. "You can find your own way home if you don't come with me now."

His ultimatum only strengthened her resolve. There was no way Jenna would get in a car with him in his present condition. "Good night, Garland. I hope you get home safely," Jenna countered. And she meant it. The thought of his causing an accident made her blood go cold. She remained seated as he bullied his way to the exit.

"Do you need some help, ma'am?"

Jenna jumped, not realizing she'd been braced for a fight, then turned to find one of the waiters had stopped. He looked concerned.

"No, I'm fine," she said as she took a sustaining breath. "I'll just call a friend to come and get me."

SO MUCH FOR TAKING CARE of his headache, Ty thought as he drove out of Marcie's apartment complex. Oh, he'd had a reasonably good time this evenin', and Marcie had seemed willing to explore a few more possibilities, but his heart—not to mention other things—hadn't been into it.

"Maybe next time," she'd said.

Maybe, he thought in answer. *But not tonight.*

He'd just made the turn onto Bryant Boulevard when his beeper went off. He held it up to the light to see the number but didn't recognize it. He pulled into a gas station to answer the call.

JENNA WAS DETERMINED not to cry, even though her feet hurt and she'd been technically dumped by her date. She'd experienced one more blow when she'd called Sharon for a ride and got the answering machine. Not home. It had taken her ten long minutes of debate before she called Ty. When he'd answered the page, she'd had to fight back tears once more. His voice had sounded strange and his abrupt "I'll be there in fifteen minutes" hadn't calmed her nerves. When he pushed through the doors of the restaurant, he looked fit to be tied.

Jenna rose on sore feet and shaky knees as he approached her. She was so glad to see him, she almost hugged him. Her own guilt and the undercurrent of anger she sensed in him, however, made her keep her distance. She apologized instead. "I'm so sorry for having to call you. Sharon isn't home and I—"

"Let's go," Ty said, taking her arm and guiding her toward the doors. He acted as if they needed to get out of there before something else happened.

"I hope I didn't ruin your Saturday night," she said as they walked toward his car. She felt humiliated. *Poor Jenna, couldn't even get through one date without disaster.*

Ty stopped at the passenger's side of his car, then turned and searched her eyes. "Did he hurt you?"

Surprised by the taut anger in his voice, Jenna shook her head. "No. This whole thing is embarrassing, but I'm fine."

He nodded and relaxed slightly before he opened the car door. After settling her in the seat, he leaned one arm on the roof of the car and looked down at her. "You shouldn't be apologizing to me. I'm the one who sent him over to meet you." His expression hardened once more. "If he's lucky, he won't cross my path again."

He shut the door and went around to the driver's side. He started the car and maneuvered it onto the street, then said, "Now, I want you to tell me exactly what happened."

Jenna related the facts of the evening to him without embellishment or emotion. She was past the embarrassment and relieved to be driving with someone she trusted.

"At least he didn't leave me with the check,"

she added, trying to find a little humor in an otherwise disastrous evening.

Ty was quiet for a minute. Jenna could tell some of the tenseness had drained out of him, but he still looked lethal. "I'm glad you called me," he said finally, "for two reasons. The thought of you driving with a drunk makes me so mad I could spit nails. Secondly the fact that I put you in the situation makes me want to commit murder or at least aggravated assault on Garland Peters." He glanced over at her. "You've got to believe I had no idea he would treat you like this. He certainly never drank too much around me. Of course, we don't actually socialize."

"I don't hold you responsible, Ty," Jenna said as she eased one of her shoes off. She couldn't hold back a sigh of relief as she levered off the other. "I think I might be going about this dating thing all wrong anyway." She shook her head and smiled slightly. "I told Sharon I wasn't good at it. I still feel like a married woman."

Ty studied her sad smile. Then, forced by driving to pull his gaze away, he frowned at the oncoming traffic. "This isn't your fault, Jenna. None of us knows how to pick up our lives and go on—we just do the best we can."

"I know," Jenna answered, sounding defeated.

As they turned onto the road leading to Jenna's house, Ty searched for the words to reassure her that everything would be all right. That she would find the right man. But something deep inside him resisted. He still thought of her as Jimmy's wife. If not Jimmy's, then...

"What were you doing when I called?" Jenna asked.

He slowed the car, and chose his words. "I was on my way home." He stopped there. It wasn't a lie, exactly. He *had* been on his way home. He didn't need to fill in the blanks of where he'd been and with whom. "Speaking of home," he added as he turned into the driveway, "here we are."

Ty shut the engine off and got out to open the passenger's door for Jenna. She was looking down, slipping her shoes back on for the walk to the house, and Ty's breath nearly stopped at the view. Her blue dress had hiked up slightly, showing more leg than he was sure she'd intended to reveal. A gentleman would have looked away, but Ty found that his manners had limits. He waited and watched until she glanced up and caught him. She gave him a puzzled look before taking the hand he held out to her.

They were halfway to the front door when Ty noticed the house was dark except for the front porch light. "Where's Jay?" he asked as Jenna dug in her purse for her keys.

"He's spending the night with his grandmom," she answered. "I haven't had time to find a good baby-sitter in the neighborhood." She turned the key in the lock, and Ty swung the door open for her. Jenna walked through, but Ty remained on the threshold. She immediately kicked off her shoes again, dropped her keys into her purse, then switched on a light. Turning in his direction, she smiled and said, "Come on in."

Ty had heard those exact words from Marcie earlier in the evening, but that invitation hadn't interested him. With Jenna, however, he found his fatigue and his headache had evaporated. He stepped through the door and closed it before his conscience could sort through his conflicting feelings. He told himself he only wanted to make sure she was home safe and sound. That he somehow had to smooth over the unpleasant evening he'd had a hand in causing. But he knew there was more to it.

"Want some coffee?" she asked as she walked down the hall to the kitchen.

Something about the sight of her almost bare feet combined with the dressy blue dress made his throat go dry. He could barely answer. "Sure, I'll have a cup," he said. He dragged his hat off and followed her down the hall as far as the kitchen door.

Jenna kept herself busy setting up the coffeemaker while Ty leaned against the door frame, watching. She'd felt tired, defeated and embarrassed since he'd arrived at the restaurant. But all of that had changed when he'd helped her out of the car. Something about the way he'd looked at her made her go shivery inside, as though he'd whispered in her ear or run a hand along her thigh. A pure man-woman communication that even the darkness couldn't conceal. And she could still feel it, like electricity in the room.

The aroma of fresh-brewed coffee filled the kitchen as Jenna got out cream and sugar. Not wanting him to notice her sudden nervousness, she turned into the perfect hostess. ''Why don't you have a seat in the living room? I'll bring the coffee in.''

Suddenly Ty was standing next to her.

''You shouldn't have to wait on me like you're still at work,'' he said. He placed his hat on the table, then put his hands on her shoulders and gave her a little push. ''You go sit down. *I'll* bring your coffee.''

One glimpse of his face told her there was no use arguing. And his touch had set off those exhilarating sensations inside her again.

''Okay,'' she agreed. ''I take a little cream and one spoon of sugar.''

He nodded but his gaze held her immobile. The fact that this was the first time she and Ty had been alone together since they'd painted the bathroom at the diner occurred to her. The day Ty had kissed her. She realized she'd rather stay in the kitchen with him than rest on the couch. The air seemed warmer in his vicinity. ''I'll be in the living room, then,'' she said unnecessarily. *Move,* her mind ordered. But he was still watching her and the corners of his mouth had quirked up, almost into a smile.

''Don't you trust me with the coffeepot?''

A wave of embarrassment swept through her, but

she ignored it, determined to act like an adult. "Of course I do. I'm just not used to being waited on."

"Well, I can manage this." He made a point of glancing at her feet. "Go put your feet up."

Without further argument she left him in the kitchen. She passed a mirror in the hallway and stopped briefly to check her makeup and hair. She hoped she didn't look as frazzled as she felt. She ran one finger along her bottom lip to even out a smudge of lipstick. She remembered wondering earlier if Garland would kiss her and how that possibility had brought Ty's kiss to mind. The difference now was that she *wanted* to be kissed...by Ty.

Unnerved by the old adage "Be careful what you wish for," she quickly left the mirror and found a seat on one end of the couch. She pulled one foot underneath her and did her best to think of anything besides Ty Richardson's serious eyes and his warm, teasing mouth. She had no right to have those kinds of thoughts, she reminded herself. She needed Ty as a friend, not as a date. She folded her hands in her lap and tried to look as prim as a nun.

Ty entered the room a few minutes later carrying two cups. "I think I got it right," he said as he set the cup on the coffee table in front of her.

He glanced from the couch to the chair opposite Jenna but she made the decision for him. She patted the couch and said, "Sit here."

Ty sat down, then let his gaze wander around the room. "It's funny, this place looks so different from the way I remember it," he said.

Jenna almost said, ''For one thing, Jimmy isn't here anymore,'' but she stopped herself. They both knew that—there was no use going back over it again. ''I— When Jay and I moved back, I rearranged the old furniture and bought a few new things,'' she answered. She'd also put away many of the pictures and all of Jimmy's certificates and commendations. She'd save them for Jay, but seeing them every day had only reminded her of why her husband had died—because he couldn't help being a hero.

''I remember when you and Jimmy moved into this house,'' he said, smiling slightly. ''He worked us like a drill sergeant and paid us in barbecue and beer.'' Ty fell silent for a long moment. Then he shook his head and looked at her, his eyes bright with unshed tears. ''I miss the hell out of him,'' he said simply.

Jenna met his gaze and felt her own eyes sting with emotion at his honesty. Ty had never mentioned his own grief before, not even in the letters. ''Me, too,'' she said.

He blinked and his wistful look turned hard. ''It seems like my life has been divided into two sections, the time before Jimmy was killed and the time after. Guess it must be the same for you.'' His look held her immobile. ''It should have been me that died, not him. That would have saved you and Jay a whole lot of pain. Nobody depended on me.''

Jenna didn't have the words to agree or disagree. She said the first thing that came to mind. ''Jay and

I depend on you now. Probably more than we should. You've helped us so much."

He shrugged off her declaration. "It's not the same. I just did what any friend would do."

Memories of all the times he'd been there for them to help and comfort rushed back to Jenna. His strong arm practically holding her up at the funeral. His taking the time and trouble to answer her letters. His steady strength carrying her son. He'd done more than would be required of any friend. Without warning, she had a sobering thought that until now hadn't even occurred to her.

"Who comforted you?" she asked.

He looked surprised. "What do you mean?"

"All those times when you were strong for us and for Jimmy...who comforted you for your loss of a friend?"

He glanced away. "I'm not the one who needs comforting," he said brusquely.

She touched his arm, bringing his gaze back to her. The naked emotion she saw in his eyes made her heart hurt. It seemed only natural to pull him into her arms, to offer him the only comfort she knew. He held himself away from her for a minute, then he gave in. His arms went around her, tight, holding her so close it seemed as if his heartbeat became hers. He buried his face in her hair and drew in a deep, steadying breath.

They remained that way for several long moments, two people sharing past pain and present consolation. Then, like a shift in barometric pressure, the atmosphere between them changed. Ty stirred slightly, opened his fingers and slid them across her back. Jenna's mind and body began to catalog an array of sensations: the firm muscles of his chest; the faint smell of shaving cream and something indefinably male on his skin; the time-honored attraction between male and female. Jenna's pulse quickened. She wasn't sure if she wanted him to pull away, and if he did, whether she could let him go.

Ty had intended to pull away. The rush of old grief battering him was too unfamiliar, too raw. Jimmy's death had left a hole inside him that he'd just as soon not fall into. But then there was Jimmy's wife comforting *him* for *his* loss. He had no right to accept her comfort as a friend, because his body wasn't thinking friendly thoughts. His body wanted to be as close as possible for as long as he could. Guilt caused him to fight against the attraction.

But when he eased back and looked into Jenna's wide and questioning eyes, his mind froze. He wanted to kiss her more than he wanted his next breath. His gaze dropped to her parted lips, and his heart pounded in his temples like a symphony of thunder.

"Ty?" Jenna whispered.

He couldn't answer, could barely breathe. He needed to let her go. *Right now.*

Then he watched as her eyes fluttered shut and she brought her mouth to his.

Heaven and hell. He held back for as long as he could, thinking she surely meant to kiss him like a friend. A lukewarm peck on the lips to make him feel better. But her lips parted, and he had to taste them, to taste her. He might never have another chance.

He kissed her, like a man offered his last glimpse of light and joy before being plunged into darkness. She sucked in a little surprised breath as his tongue coaxed hers, then one of her hands dug into his back, fingers twisting into his shirt, and he forgot any form of the word *stop*.

Her mouth was soft and wet and tasted like coffee, familiar yet exotic. They'd been circling this attraction for weeks, months maybe, and now the truth arced between them. He couldn't let her go. Each time he eased back, teasing her lips as a prelude to ending the kiss, he'd go back for more. When Jenna arched up to meet him and made a small sound of pleasure, he took her mouth again, harder, deeper, feeling out of control.

Finally—it could have been seconds or minutes later—Ty found his equilibrium and relinquished her mouth. He had to stop now or go further, and he was sure that Jenna—

"Don't think, Ty," Jenna pleaded. Reclining against the cushions where the weight of his body, the force of his need had pushed her, she gazed up at him with half-closed eyes. She raised one arm and caressed the back of his neck before pulling him downward. "Don't make *me* think."

CHAPTER THIRTEEN

TY FELT THE BURDEN of grief lift off his shoulders. *Don't make me think.* On the heels of her plea, he mentally slammed the door on the past and his mouth sank into hers as though he had every right to kiss her, as though in that moment she belonged to him. As if she'd *always* been his.

Jenna, his mind whispered.

She whimpered, moving to meet him with each touch of his lips, his tongue, and Ty's grasp on friendship and honor melted. He wouldn't be noble, couldn't stop unless she stopped him. Maybe not even then.

That thought scared him. He wasn't used to being out of control. He left her mesmerizing mouth to nuzzle along her cheek, her neck and downward, kissing, tasting. When her hands tightened on his biceps, he drew back and looked down at her flushed features framed by tousled blond hair. The expression on her face nearly gave him a heart attack. So much longing, so much heat. Then, out of nowhere, a disastrous thought nearly gutted him. What if she was looking at him, but remembering

Jimmy? Surely her husband had been the only man who'd seen her this vulnerable, this undone.

"It's been so long," she sighed. "Please, Ty, don't stop."

She'd said his name, not Jimmy's, and she'd given him permission. He offered her one last chance. "Are you sure?"

Jenna felt as if she were poised on a precipice being driven by an unrelenting wind. Ty's touch had brought her to this place. She couldn't move, couldn't stop what was about to happen. And some eager stranger inside her wanted it to happen. Wanted Ty to give in to whatever was building between them. She nodded. "Yes, I'm sure." Whether from grief or gratitude, she couldn't deny the physical heat between her and the man who was now much more than just her husband's best friend. He'd become part of her, and she had to give in to the surge of delirious fire generated by his touch, his kiss.

His hesitation disappeared. If she'd thought Ty was intriguing before, the man in her arms was even more complex. He persistently stroked his hands over her skin, yet held her as if she might break into pieces any moment. His mouth was hotter and more demanding than his hands, but his whispered murmurs of encouragement soothed and coaxed. Giving herself over to his kiss, she felt his warm palm slide along her thigh, and thought she might just die of the pleasure.

It had been too long.

She wanted him to hurry. She needed him to—Jenna forced her own hands to move, gripping his shirt and pulling upward. She had to feel his skin, a desire expanding to urgency. As she dragged his shirttail free and splayed her fingers across his bare chest, she felt more than heard him groan. *Yes.*

''Wait a second,'' he said through clenched teeth. Then he shifted. The thump of one of his boots hitting the floor was soon followed by the second. He twisted and brought them both up to a sitting position. Watching her reaction, he slid one hand along the nape of her neck. She took a quick breath as a shiver of response skittered down her spine. He held her gaze as his fingers slowly lowered the zipper of her dress.

Ty had to see her, was trying not to rush it, but worry hung over him. He felt as if he'd waited most of his life for this moment of completion and that at any time Jenna could be snatched away from him, by the past or the future.

When the zipper reached the small of her back, Ty insinuated his hand inside the fabric to stroke her soft skin. She arched her spine in reaction, then shrugged, allowing the top of the dress to fall away from her shoulders. He dragged the dress from beneath her and draped it over the back of the couch. It took one twist of his fingers to unfasten the lacy white bra.

Her breasts felt like warm silk in his hands. Her nipples, already aroused, begged for his attention. He wanted to take his time, to investigate the weight and shape of each one, but Jenna had closed her eyes. He could tell by the dazed, dreamy expression on her face that she needed to be kissed.

All over.

As his mouth closed over one pebbled nipple, Jenna's restless fingers combed through his hair. She curled toward him and held him close. The soft mewling sound she made sent a message that went straight through him. It was more than any mortal man could resist. By the time he'd paid sufficient dedication to her other nipple, she was twisting beneath him. And he knew he couldn't, *they* couldn't, wait much longer.

Jenna helped shove her panty hose down, but it was Ty's honor to remove her panties. He kissed her belly as he pulled them down her hips and intended to go lower, but he had to sit up to release her in order to get her naked. After accomplishing that goal, he unfastened his jeans and kicked them off as Jenna shoved at his shirt.

The sight of her naked, waiting for *him*...caused something in his chest to clench. A feeling of privilege, of responsibility, ran through him.

Jenna trusted him.

He wouldn't do anything to jeopardize that faith. He found his wallet in the pocket of his jeans and extracted protection. He tore the package open with his teeth and lived up to his own code of ethics. That was the last meaningful thought in his head, however, because in the next heartbeat, his body took over.

With a sigh of welcome, Jenna arched up to meet him and wrapped her legs around his hips. He found her mouth with his and coaxed her into his rhythm, their rhythm, the slow sultry dance of male and female. Of Jenna and Ty. He wanted to take his time. To move inside her until she was breathless and pleading. But she'd already reached breathless, and soon he'd be the one pleading.

Jenna.

As the layers of sensation in Jenna's body built toward climax, she felt her normal lonely, rational self fall away. A naked, yearning, untamed and untouched part of her seemed to take over. She couldn't stop the wild woman inside her from pushing, from answering Ty's thrusts with her own stronger ones, from digging her nails into his back to keep him inside, deeper, longer. Her body coiled and clenched, and she couldn't remain silent or docile. The wildness inside her screamed, and Ty's reaction reverberated deep within her.

Ty.

After Ty's groan of completion, the only sound Jenna could hear was the pounding of her own pulse and gasping breaths. Ty's weight held her immobile, and a fine sheen of sweat coated their skin, proof of their exertion. Except for leisurely stroking along Ty's back with one hand, Jenna felt no inclination to move. For the first time in a very long time she felt relaxed and renewed. Ty had given her that.

Then she thought of Jimmy. She'd just allowed

Ty to touch a part of her that only her husband had shared. And if the truth be told, Ty had brought something out in her that even Jimmy had never seen. The wildness. Slightly shocked by the unexpected reaction Ty had so effortlessly kindled in her, she wondered if everything in her life would be a discovery from now on. Just as everything in the past two years had been a measure of her grief.

The man in her arms, who'd been her friend from the beginning, had now become her lover. And he'd taken her further than she would have imagined. If Jimmy had been her first love in the spring of her life, then Ty had definitely brought along the summer.

And it was hot.

Ty moved his head close to her ear. "Are you okay?" he asked between labored breaths. He felt as if he'd just raced the Kentucky Derby, on foot. But along with that heart-pounding, breath-stealing ache in his chest was happiness. If he'd just run the race, then he'd come out a winner.

"I'm good," she murmured.

He resisted the urge to agree with her. She was incredible, and right then he had to be the luckiest man wearing boots. Or not wearing boots, since his were on the floor somewhere. He didn't want to move and spoil the moment but he knew his weight must be suffocating her. He put one hand on the floor, then gingerly turned and coaxed her to turn on her side facing him. It would have been accomplished much more easily if they'd been in a bed.

In any case he wasn't ready to let her get too far away just yet. It felt too good to finally be holding her.

He found himself staring into her eyes. He wasn't sure what he'd expected, but Jenna seemed calm and, for want of a better word, satisfied. A purely male rush of accomplishment suffused him. He cradled her cheek with his palm and lightly kissed her lips. She looked so damned beautiful his heart took several pounding beats. He had no idea how to tell her, and she didn't seem to expect words. He struggled with the silence for a moment, anyway. Then he gently ran his thumb along her cheek bone. "Thank you," he managed to say, and kissed her nose.

She smiled as sweetly as any angel. "No. Thank *you,*" she said, then brought one hand up to her mouth to cover a huge yawn. "Sorry," she added before her eyes fluttered shut.

"Do we need to talk about this?" he asked, dreading her answer.

"Probably," she answered, her voice hazy with lethargy. Her arm slid around him as if she were settling in for the night. "But not now." She blinked her eyes open. "Okay? I don't think I'd make much sense." Another yawn interrupted her, and she covered it by pushing her face against his neck. "We'll talk…later."

For at least ten minutes, Ty remained still, holding Jenna as her breathing slipped into the regular rhythms of sleep. Again the enormity of her trust hit him. She hadn't trusted Garland Peters to drive her home, yet here she was sleeping naked in Ty's arms without a care.

It was then he knew he loved her. He'd fallen in love with Jimmy Taylor's wife.

Damn.

Earlier she'd said she still felt like a married woman. No one knew better than him how easy it would be for her to live in her memories of past happiness, rather than taking a chance on an uncertain future. She'd told him as much already. But now Ty had touched her, loved her. Nothing would ever be the same again between them. Whether she felt married or not, she'd invited him into her arms, her body. He didn't intend to let it begin and end here.

Moving slowly so as not to wake her, he got off the couch and stood. He kept his gaze on her as he slipped on his jeans and zipped them up. The tenderness and protectiveness he felt was stronger, deeper than he'd experienced before. Mary Jo had never wanted or needed his care. She'd been too busy with her own agenda. He didn't miss Mary Jo, but something inside him knew he'd always miss Jenna, no matter what took place between them after this night. Tucking that realization away someplace safe, Ty walked into Jenna's bedroom and pulled down the covers on the bed.

Jenna murmured when he picked her up. He wasn't about to leave her naked on the couch. And he knew he couldn't stay. Not until they'd both discussed what happened and decided what to do next. He'd see her safe in bed, then see himself out.

She sighed as she stretched out on the sheets, and Ty's resolution immediately went to war with his libido. His good sense regained the upper hand, and reluctantly he drew the covers over temptation. In the dim light he saw a picture on the nightstand. A picture of Jenna, Jimmy and Jay, taken at a baseball game, reminding him that this was Jimmy's house, his bed...his wife.

I'm sorry, old buddy. But now I know why you loved her.

Then his own name, written in Jenna's handwriting on a pad near the clock, caught his eye. He picked up the pad and read:

> I'm scared, Ty. I know I have to move on. I have to provide for my son. But I don't know how to start. I have no idea how to put our lives back together again. Before, with Jimmy, everything seemed so easy. I knew exactly what I wanted and who I could depend on.

Ty felt uneasy about reading what Jenna had written, but that didn't stop him. Only Jenna could have stopped him and she'd fallen sound asleep. He took the pad out into the light, intending to read every line she'd written to him but never mailed. He knew how she felt. Hadn't he sat down to write her himself?

You kissed me. I wish you hadn't done that. I wanted to keep everything the same, to keep you at a distance. I need you as my friend. But now, after kissing you back, I can't look at you without remembering…your mouth…your taste. Why did you have to do that? How can we be friends now? When all I want is for you to kiss me again?

After he finished, before he could determine the significance of her words about fear and confusion, of wanting to be kissed, he flipped to the next page.

I wish I could just sit down and talk to you, like we did in the letters. I miss them. You were the only one I could open my heart to and not be afraid that you'd think I was a coward, or just plain crazy. Somehow, in moving back to Texas, in being face-to-face, I've lost you.

The next page was empty. Ty wrote a short message to Jenna, replaced the pad, turned out the lights and locked the door behind him.

Face-to-face. He'd get better at it, or die tryin'.

JENNA ROLLED OVER the next morning and sighed, feeling weightless and rested. Without opening her eyes, she stretched languorously and shifted her legs beneath the covers. That's when she realized she was naked.

The events of the evening before came back to her in a rush. She opened her eyes. The house was quiet; she was alone in her bed.

Ty. Warmth ran under her skin and heated her face. She and Ty had— what? Had sex? Made love? Gotten naked on the living-room couch? She glanced toward the living room as if the couch could tell her what had really gone on the previous evening. She was glad she hadn't had to see Ty first thing this morning.

She brought a hand up, pushed her hair back out of her eyes and sighed. Ty had made love to her, hot and urgent, fueled by her response. She searched around inside for the voice of her conscience but found only silence and a wonderful lethargy. For better or worse—and right now she felt better–she and Ty had shared their most intimate secrets and passions.

She remembered telling him not to make her think, and he'd obliged. Determined not spoil her first night of truly restful sleep, Jenna decided to go with the no-thinking policy for as long as she could.

Sitting up, she angled her legs to the side of the bed and looked at the clock. Eight. She had plenty of time to shower, have some coffee and not think before she had to pick up Jay. That's when she saw the note written on the yellow paper of her legal pad. As she read the words, her insides did a funny little flip-flop of desire and anticipation.

Jenna,

You were sleeping so soundly, I couldn't bring myself to wake you to say good-night. It was an amazing night, actually, and I'm not finished talking or thinking about it. I'll call you.

Ty

"HEY, SWEETIE," Jenna said as Jay rushed to hug her. "Did you have a good time with Grandmom?"

He nodded yes with his head pressed against her hip. Then he looked up at her. "Grandmom made me brownies for dinner."

"For dinner!" Jenna said in mock surprise, then squeezed him again until he squirmed.

"Now, James," Barbara said, "you know we had chicken for dinner. The brownies were for dessert." She sounded scandalized that anyone might find out she'd fed Jay brownies for dinner.

Jenna smiled at her mother-in-law. "I bet he wanted to have them for breakfast, too."

Barbara relaxed. "Well, we did have a discussion about it."

"She said I could bring them home with me," Jay added.

"Uh-huh," Jenna said. "Do you have all your stuff packed and ready to go?"

He shook his head.

Jenna leaned down and patted him on the seat of his jeans. "Go gather up your things while I visit with Barbara," she said.

"I've got some coffee made," Barbara offered.

Jay made a beeline for the living room, and Jenna followed Barbara into the kitchen. As soon as they were alone, Barbara seemed to shift her complete attention to setting out a coffee cup and filling it for Jenna. But, after giving it to her, she got to the point.

"How was the date last night?"

Jenna had prepared herself for Barbara's questions. She'd gone over the events of the evening and decided she couldn't tell Barbara *any* of what happened for a variety of reasons. The main one being the certainty of a lecture from her mother-in-law with a few I-told-you-so's mixed in. And she wasn't ready to talk about Ty, especially not to Jimmy's mother. So Jenna had decided to boldly go where she hadn't gone before. She'd decided to lie, bald faced and with embellishment if any occurred to her.

"Everything went well. We had a nice steak dinner and I got home around ten. I was asleep by ten-thirty."

Jenna almost flubbed the last part because her mind had shifted to being naked on the couch with Ty—no embellishment needed. And she'd been asleep by ten-thirty because Ty had carried her to bed. She fought to remain calm and believable, but her pulse raced at the mere memory of Ty's touch.

Barbara spent a moment stirring her coffee, watching Jenna. "Do you intend to see him again?" she asked casually.

"You mean Garland?" she said before thinking.

Then she remembered Barbara didn't know about Ty.

Relief washed through Jenna. No need to lie about that answer, except for the reason behind it. "No, I don't think so. He's nice but we don't seem to have much in common."

Jenna could tell that information pleased Barbara, although she was polite enough not to say it. "Well, I enjoyed having James Jr. here. He reminds me so much of his father. Thank you for letting me keep him."

Guilt made Jenna's throat tighten. She took a sip of coffee to ease the sensation. Jimmy's mother would be scandalized if she knew what had really taken place the evening before. Especially if she found out Jenna had lied to her. Jenna's conscience seemed to be waking up after a short but action-packed dream. What would Jimmy think of this new face of hers? What would everyone else think?

Just then Jay came bounding into the room with an armful of toys and derailed Jenna's thoughts.

"I got all my stuff," he announced, and dropped his cargo at Jenna's feet.

Jenna surveyed the pile. She'd made sure Jay had left his new toy gun at the diner. "I don't see your backpack or your toothbrush."

"Oh, that's upstairs," he answered, then sighed as if he were absolutely too worn out to go up to find them.

"We'll go up and get them before we leave," Jenna said. Released from bondage, Jay's energy level suddenly returned and he dropped down on the floor to play with his big-wheel monster truck.

Jenna returned her attention to Barbara and swore to herself that she would spend some quality time with her, not just bide her time until she could leave. Oppressive or not, Jimmy's mother was a part of her and Jay's life. If Jenna couldn't offer Barbara the whole truth and nothing but the truth, she could at least share the part of her life that held them together—Jay.

Two hours later Jenna unlocked the front door of her house and heard the phone ringing.

"I'll get it," Jay called, and after dropping his toys on the living-room rug, he raced for the telephone.

Jenna heard him say hello as she deposited her purse and his backpack on the couch.

"Mom? It's Mr. Ty."

Jenna's insides seemed to roll into a somersault. *Ty.* She'd been alternately dreading and anticipating the moment they'd have to talk about what had happened between them. She'd known he would call or come by. He wasn't the type of man to put things off.

She took the phone from Jay's hand, swallowed to ease her dry throat, then spoke. "Hey, Ty."

AT THE SOUND OF HER VOICE, something inside Ty relaxed. He'd called at least four times during the morning, and there had been no answer. He'd just about been ready to get in his car and drive over when Jay had picked up the phone. He did his best to keep the worry out of his response.

"Hey, Jenna. Are you okay?"

"Sure. I'm fine."

"I called earlier but you didn't answer."

"Oh, I drove out to pick up Jay from his grandmom's. Remember, I told you she was keeping him for the night."

The oblique reference to the night before was enough to set Ty's pulse into an uneven rhythm. "Yeah, I remember." The image of her naked and waiting for him blocked out most rational thought. "Did you sleep all right?" He felt like an inquisitor but he needed to know he hadn't hurt her in any way when they'd made love. The thought of her regretting what had happened between them made his jaw tight.

After a slight hesitation, Jenna answered. "I slept great. I'm sorry I conked out. I, um, got your note. Thanks."

Ty heard Jay's voice in the background. Then Jenna said, "Just a minute, Jay. I'm on the phone."

Ty realized that he wasn't going to be able to really talk to her.

"Don't apologize for falling asleep," he said. "You were awake for the important stuff." His body reacted warmly at the memory. "I want to come by and talk to you. When could I do that?"

"I promised Jay we'd watch *The Lion King* again after supper." He heard a little huff of laughter in her voice. "I won't ask you to suffer through that. Why don't you stop by the diner tomorrow?"

Ty thought for a moment. The diner was neutral territory—not like Jenna's house. He wanted to see her alone, but if they were lucky, business might be slow after lunch and they'd be able sit outside. Or if worse came to worst, he could follow Jenna and Jay home after the diner closed.

"Okay," he agreed. "But be ready, 'cause I want to talk—face-to-face."

CHAPTER FOURTEEN

SHARON AMBUSHED JENNA before she even got in the door the next morning.

"Well? How did it go?" she asked impatiently.

Jenna ushered Jay through the kitchen and grimaced. "Awful. I think we need to seriously rethink this husband-hunting plan of yours."

"Awful? What in the world happened? Did he stand you up?"

"Worse," Jenna answered as she settled Jay on the couch in the office. He was still half-asleep, but she didn't intend to go into details in front of him.

"Worse..." Sharon's words trailed off as she watched Jenna. Then, when she'd finished with Jay, Sharon took her arm and pulled her out into the kitchen. "Tell me what went on," she demanded.

After Jenna told Sharon about the big date with Garland, her partner seemed ready to instigate World War III. It took Jenna's repeated assurances that everything had turned out all right to calm her down.

"Hon, I am so sorry, about the date, and about not—" she began. "How in the world *did* you get home?"

Jenna couldn't head off a smile. "I called Ty," she answered.

"Has murder been committed?"

Jenna laughed. "What are you talking about?"

"Well, I can see how Ty looks at you. I figured if he thought another man had been rude or mean to you he'd probably unpin that badge he wears and take the law into his own hands, if you know what I mean."

Jenna hadn't thought of that. Ty had seemed angry but he'd gotten over it fast enough. He'd been distracted. They'd both forgotten about Garland after their first kiss. Jenna would like to forget about Garland altogether, but that was another thing she and Ty needed to discuss.

Just then, Robert put two plates under the warming lights and said, "Sharon, breakfast for number three is up."

Sharon guiltily glanced through the ordering window toward her waiting customers, then reluctantly pushed through the swinging door to the dining room. She looked back through the window as she balanced the plates. "I intend to hear the whole story later."

Jenna nodded, although she wasn't sure how much of the story she wanted to tell Sharon. She didn't mind talking about Garland; as far as she was concerned, he was history. But Ty was a different matter. The problem was, her partner had an almost psychic sense when it came to Ty. Sharon seemed to see the truth before Jenna did. She wondered how in the world she could explain what had happened on her own couch the night before last without pleading temporary insanity.

"Good morning, Robert," Jenna belatedly greeted the cook.

"Mornin'" he answered. "Can I fix you something?"

"I'll take a fried-egg sandwich," she said as she followed Sharon into the dining room. As part of their morning ritual, Robert handed her his coffee cup through the order window and she filled it along with one for herself. When she turned to glance around the dining room, she noticed Dean sitting in his usual spot at the end of the counter.

"We've got to stop meeting like this," she said as she refreshed his cup of coffee.

"Shh." He glanced at his ex-wife. "Don't tell Sharon." He winked. "Wouldn't want to hurt her feelings."

"Hurt my feelings about what?" Sharon asked as she took the coffeepot out of Jenna's hand and went back to her customers.

"The woman has ears like a bat." Dean chuckled. "It's a good thing I'm not prone to keeping secrets."

"I know what you mean," Jenna commiserated. "I don't even have to say things out loud. She's already read my mind."

"That comes from living with three men," Sharon said as she sat on the stool next to Dean. "Self-preservation."

"What are you talking about?" Dean asked in mock surprise. "You were the queen of the house. You said jump, and I made sure those boys left the ground."

In a rare amiable moment, Sharon patted Dean's hand. "That's true. I can't take all the credit."

A laugh rumbled from Dean. "Look out, she's being sweet. That means she wants something."

Sharon looked thoughtful for a moment. "As a matter of fact, I do. I want you to kill someone. His name is Garland Peters."

"Sharon!" Jenna nervously glanced around to see if the closest customers were paying attention.

Dean didn't seem fazed. "I don't think killin' the customers can possibly be good for business. What did the man do to get on your list?"

"He was rude to Jenna and left her in a restaurant on Saturday night."

Jenna, feeling as if everyone already knew waaaay too much about her personal dating debacle, tried to steer the conversation in a different direction.

"By the way, Sharon, where were *you* on Saturday night when I called you to come and save me?"

Jenna watched in amazement as Sharon actually blushed. Her partner pulled her hand away from her ex-husband, and they both looked at each other. For a moment Jenna thought she'd made the largest faux pas in her short life. Had Sharon been out with another man?

"I was on a date," Sharon answered rather stiffly.

"Oh! Well..." Jenna wished the linoleum would open up and swallow her.

Dean stared at his ex-wife in a rather affronted way. But Sharon had suddenly gone silent. "She was on a date with me," he informed Jenna. Just then Sharon excused herself, and Robert set Jenna's egg sandwich under the warming light.

"Your breakfast is up."

Jenna couldn't help but smile. So, after all of Sharon's talk about not wanting Dean around, she'd gone out with him. Returning Dean's earlier wink, she said, "I, for one, am glad to hear it." She was also glad to finally *not* be the one on the hot seat for a change. She intended to keep Sharon on the defensive as much as possible. That was the only way her partner might not put two and two together and come up with Jenna and Ty.

Jenna grabbed her sandwich and coffee, thanked Robert and grinned as she passed Sharon on the way to the kitchen. "I'm sure we'll talk about this more later," she said. Then, chuckling at Sharon's blank face, she went to eat her breakfast before starting her shift.

TY WAITED until one o'clock before he drove out to the diner. The first thing he'd done that morning was call Garland Peters. He knew if he went to see him in person, things might get ugly, and assault would look bad on his record. But even short of rearranging Garland's face, after their little chat he figured he didn't have to worry about the insurance man bothering Jenna again. After all, as he'd explained to Garland, Ty's patience wasn't what it used to be, and he did wear a gun for a livin'. And just to reinforce his point, he'd canceled his insurance policy with Garland's company.

Feeling a little more satisfied with the day, he'd done some phone work from his office and stopped by the courthouse to file some paperwork a judge had asked for, then he'd waited. He didn't know whether it was a blessin' or a curse that things in the law-enforcement business seemed to be slow at the moment. It was good because it gave him plenty of time to think of what he wanted to say to Jenna. Then again, he had too much time to worry he might say the wrong thing.

He was in love with her, but he knew he couldn't say that. The taste and feel of her still shimmered in his mind, moved under his skin. He wanted her, everything about her, yet he knew if he pushed he'd scare her off. Could he talk her into hooking up with another lawman? He wasn't sure. She had good reason to be worried about being a Ranger's wife. There, he'd said it, or he'd thought it anyway. That's what he really wanted—for her to be his, to let him look after her and Jay, to love them the best he could. And until Saturday night, he'd pushed that thought so far back in his mind it would've needed a road map to find its way back.

Then he'd made love to Jenna. Now all bets were

off. He'd do whatever it took to convince her. And the first thing that had to be changed was her new version of the dating game. He'd never liked the idea to begin with, and now he felt as if they'd dodged a bullet with old Garland. What if some man they fixed Jenna up with really hurt her? The thought didn't stand contemplation.

There were still several cars in the parking lot when he pulled in. He smiled to himself. He had to hand it to the two Donut Wrangler partners; even in the short time the diner had been open, it looked as though it would be a success. As he slammed his car door shut and walked toward the building, an unexpected sense of pride filled him. Pride in Jenna. She'd overcome her fears, rolled up her sleeves and gone to work on her future. Now if he could just convince her to let him be a part of that future, the world would be a brighter place for one Texas Ranger.

She was standing near the cash register when he walked in the door. Almost as if she'd been waiting for him, and that idea made his smile widen. He dragged his hat off and nodded.

"Jenna."

Then she did something that completely set him off kilter. She walked around the counter, reached up and hugged him. He hugged her back in a friendly, automatic way. When she stepped back from him, his heart was beating so hard, he was speechless.

Before either of them could say anything, Sharon moved closer behind the counter.

"Ah, the cavalry," she said.

Jenna, her face a few shades pinker than it had been a few moments before, moved away from him, and he had to try to act normal.

"Except for the horse, I suppose," he said to Sharon as he took a stool at the counter and placed his hat on the stool next to him.

"I mean on Saturday night. I hear you had to save a lady in distress," Sharon continued.

Ty looked at Jenna before replying. She seemed as nervous as he felt.

"Well, if she'd called me earlier, you'd probably be reading about it in the morning newspaper."

Sharon looked pleased. "He better not show his face in here again," she warned.

Ty gave her his best imitation of Clint Eastwood. "I don't think you ladies have to worry about that happening."

Sharon laughed and poked Jenna in the arm. "I knew it." Then she looked at Ty. "Lunch is on the house—what would you like?"

Jenna was the one who delivered his fried chicken a few moments later. Sharon had thanked him again before leaving to take care of her customers. The chicken Jenna set in front of him smelled delicious, but he was more interested in the waitress.

"Are you okay?" he asked.

Jenna nodded. She could barely bring herself to

look him in the eye. Every time she did, she remembered his hot mouth, his urgent hands and the wild woman they'd both discovered hiding inside her. She was a little embarrassed, but most of all she wanted to touch him again and that scared her.

She used a damp towel to wipe down the already pristine cooler behind the counter as Ty picked up his knife and fork.

"I want to talk to you," he said. "Alone."

The intimacy in his voice sent a shiver of heat through her. *Alone.* She knew what would happen the next time they were alone if the wild woman had any say in it. But she also knew he wasn't talking about that kind of alone.

"I know. We do have to talk." Although talking seemed more dangerous to her peace of mind than touching. When he'd touched her, she'd forgotten everything but Ty. If they talked, she'd have to remember.

Ty had taken a bite of chicken and was chewing when she added, "I don't regret anything, though." Jenna watched him swallow, watched color rise above his collar and knew he was remembering. Her heartbeat quickened and she had to look away.

At that moment a boy's voice said, "Hold it right there, mister."

Both she and Ty turned toward the sound. Jay had sneaked around the counter with his toy gun drawn and now had the drop on Ty.

"Take it easy there, partner," Ty said, raising

his hands, which held silverware. "I'm on your side."

That didn't seem to faze Jay. He clicked the gun and made several shooting noises. "I got you," he proclaimed, and ran behind the counter.

"Hey," Ty complained, "you don't shoot a man when he's eating."

Jenna corralled her son. "And we don't play cowboys in the dining room, do we?" she asked.

All the spunk went out of him. "No, ma'am," he said, dejected.

"Go back in the kitchen, okay?"

Jay looked hopefully at Ty, like a con hoping for a pardon. "Your mom's the law around here, buddy. I'll come back and visit you after I finish lunch."

"Okay," he answered, and trudged toward the kitchen.

It was an hour and a half later before Jenna had to face Ty alone. Sharon had left for the day, and there were only a couple of customers in the dining room. Robert was busy cleaning up the kitchen, and Jay had settled in to watch television and have a snack after Ty had chased him around the parking lot in an abbreviated game of tag.

When Ty stepped into the office and closed the door behind him, Jenna's heart began to flutter the way it had earlier. Every time he walked into a room she was in, she felt instantly more alive and aware. Dangerously aware now that she had more than her imagination for fuel.

He simply stood there, looking at her, and suddenly Jenna couldn't remain still. She pushed up from her chair and moved around the desk. Before she realized what she'd been after, she was in his arms, his mouth hovering over hers.

"Jenna—"

Unable to resist, she closed the distance. She needed him to kiss her, right now.

He took his time. The kiss was long, slow and wet. Instead of ending it, he'd relax, tease her lips, then delve in again. By the time he stopped, her fingers were gripping the back of his shirt, her breathing was ragged and her knees felt wobbly.

"Whew," she said in a shaky voice, and pushed back slightly. He let her go but only so far.

"Well, that answers one of my questions," Ty said, looking a little surprised but pleased just the same. "Now I know you feel fine." He smiled. "Taste good, too."

Embarrassed, but without regret, Jenna managed an answering smile. She didn't know what to say so she waited.

"Jenna I—I'm not gonna say I'm sorry for what's happening between us, because I'm not. But I need to know how you feel about it."

Jenna took a deep breath, reluctantly stepped back from him and indicated he should have a seat on the couch. She sat close, but not touching. It was the only way she could keep her mind on talking.

"I'm not sure how I feel about it." She looked

him in the eye. "All I know is that whenever you touch me or kiss me, I get crazy. I guess you figured out that much already," she added with a laugh.

"I wasn't asking about what happens between us. Physically we seem to spontaneously combust, and I'm not putting that down. As a matter of fact, I'm enjoying the hell out of it." Ty reached over and took her hand. "But I don't want to take advantage of that...of you. God knows I want you, but you have to want me, too.

"I know you're lonely and vulnerable and I don't want you to think you owe me something because I've been your friend. It would kill me if you felt you couldn't say no to me because of that."

Jenna couldn't do anything other than tell him the truth. "Oh, Ty, if I was just lonely, I could have let Garland take me home on Saturday night. I don't know how to explain you and me. I just know that when you kissed me, I— Something inside me wanted more. More from you, not just because you happened to be there. Does that make sense?"

Ty nodded. "Where does that leave us now? I want to see you, be with you."

Looking into Ty's steady gaze, Jenna felt hot moisture forming in her eyes. "I want that, too, but I can't make any promises and I can't tell you how it'll turn out. We'd have to take it one day, one night at a time. Can you handle that?"

"As long as you're not saying no, I can handle anything." Ty stared at her for a long moment.

"You'll have to call off the husband hunt for a while."

Jenna made a gesture of dismissal. "I already did. Sharon's under strict orders to cease and desist."

"Does she know about us? About Saturday night?" Ty asked.

"No. I think I've had enough of everyone knowing my—I mean, our business."

Ty nodded in agreement before continuing, "There's one more thing you need to know. I read your letters."

"What?"

"The letters you wrote and didn't send—on your night table."

Jenna felt an immediate stab of discomfort. She remembered writing letters to Ty; she just couldn't remember exactly what she'd written in them. Probably the truth. That was a scary thought.

"I didn't mean to snoop," Ty continued. "I just saw my name and went from there. I wish you'd sent them to me. I've missed your letters."

"I'd made writing to you a habit. It was hard to give that up when I moved back," Jenna confessed. "Now you know all my secrets."

"Not quite all of them." He squeezed her hand. "Are you mad at me?"

"Not yet."

"Not yet?"

"I have to go home and see what you read before I can be mad," Jenna said.

Ty smiled and pulled her closer. ''You confessed that you liked it when I kissed you.''

Jenna pushed her face against his shoulder and groaned. ''That's what I mean. No fair.''

His fingers nudged her chin up so he could look into her eyes. ''I can see why you don't want everyone to know that, but you can tell me.'' He lowered his mouth to hers. ''You can always tell me. I won't get tired of hearing it.''

Then he was kissing her, slowly and so gently it made Jenna's heart swell in her chest. She felt like a woman who'd been out in the cold for longer than she could remember, and now she was being enfolded, warmed and cherished. She didn't want to do anything to disrupt the moment or the wonderful, hopeful tingle of comfort seeping into her bones. Even the sigh of relief hovering in the back of her consciousness would be a distraction. Right now she only wanted Ty.

A knock at the door and a plaintive ''Mom?'' ended the kiss. But even as Jenna left Ty to open the door for her son, the warmth went with her. It was the first time she'd felt whole in a long, long time.

''Can Mr. Ty play fish with me?'' Jay asked.

Jenna glanced at her watch, then at Ty. The least she could do was get him off the hook. ''I think it's about time for Mr. Ty to get back to work.''

Ty pushed to his feet and agreed. ''Truthfully, if I don't, somebody might send a posse out lookin' for me.''

Jay looked disappointed. Ty squatted in front of him. "Tell you what—next time I see you, we'll practice hitting those baseballs I've been promising you."

"When?"

"Why don't you come over for dinner later?" Jenna suggested.

Ty shifted his attention to her for a long moment, as if to see if she really meant it. "How about if I come over later and take you two *out* to dinner. You've been working all day, you deserve a break."

"Can we, Mom?" Jay asked. It seemed that going out to eat would be an acceptable trade for a game of fish.

"Okay. How about six o'clock, and you two can hit baseballs when we get back?"

"Yea!" Jay agreed excitedly.

Ty stood and gave Jenna a slow smile. "I'll see you at six, then."

JENNA'S FRAGILE sense of peace lasted through dinner and all the way up until she was putting her son to bed.

"Mom? Can Mr. Ty be my new dad?" Jay asked, and Jenna's soaring outlook made an abrupt crash landing.

"I don't know, honey," Jenna answered, working to keep her voice normal and momlike. "Do you want him to be?"

Jay nodded. "He knows how to play baseball and

he's a real Texas Ranger.'' Jay had only seen the television show *Walker, Texas Ranger* once or twice, but obviously he'd come away with a dose of hero worship. Exactly what Jenna had been worried about all along. And now, here she was, involved up to her chin with the one man she'd decided would be the worst influence on her son's future.

She gave Jay the only answer she could put together on such short notice. The answer parents had been giving their children for centuries. ''I don't know. We'll see.''

''Don't you like him, Mom? I know he likes you.''

Jenna snuggled her son and made him giggle. ''How do you know that?''

Breathless with laughter, Jay looked up at her with his father's eyes and answered, '''Cause he told me.''

Jenna felt a little breathless herself. Since getting her nerve up for her date on Saturday night, her life seemed to have broken out of control like a herd of mustangs in a tornado. ''He did? Did he?''

''Uh-huh. And he said he was my dad's friend.''

''He was your dad's very best friend,'' Jenna said. ''That's why he's around to help us so much.''

Jay twisted the sheet around one of his fingers. ''If he was my new dad, he could live with us all the time.''

The thought of having Ty around all the time felt inexplicably right—for her. As a friend she trusted him completely; as a lover she'd found uninhibited satisfaction in his arms. The concern she had about Jay and the choices he'd make when he grew up overrode any considerations of her own, however. The memory of Jay's birthday party and Ty's gift rose to blot out the happy picture of putting her broken family back together again.

She suddenly wondered what Jimmy would think about her and Ty. Not about the fact that they'd been intimate, but about Ty taking his place with her *and* with Jay. She knew her husband would disagree with her fears for Jay's future. Jimmy would have been proud to see his son go into law enforcement. Of course, that was before any of them knew the price Jimmy's commitment would exact from their family.

"Like I said—" she kissed Jay good-night "—we'll see."

Ty was waiting for her in the living room when she finished with Jay. Jenna tried to keep up the facade of her earlier good mood, but Ty seemed to see through it.

"You look like you stubbed your toe between here and the bedroom," he said jokingly, but he didn't smile. "Everything okay?"

Jenna realized she had sort of stubbed her toe—on reality. "Guess I'm a little tired," she answered.

He seemed about to disagree with her pat answer, but then he tapped the couch next to him. "Sit down. I'll rub your feet."

Staring at Ty's long-fingered hand resting on the

couch cushion brought back the memories of Saturday night like a lightning flash. She could barely look him in the eye because her body was reacting to the memory of being touched by him. She nodded and sat down but a little farther away than he'd indicated. That didn't slow him down, however. He bent and pulled her feet into his lap.

As Ty pulled off Jenna's shoes, his heartbeat went into overdrive. Her feet were warm in his hands, and he forced his fingers to dig in and ignore the rest of her body stretched out on the couch in front of him. He wanted to kiss her, but he knew if he ever started, it would take an earthquake or an act of Congress to stop him.

Jenna groaned slightly, and Ty eased up a little on his massage. No need to take his frustration out on her toes. When she closed her eyes and put her head back to rest against the pillows behind her, Ty let his gaze run over her relaxed features. As long as her eyes were closed, she wouldn't be able to see the naked need in his.

"What am I going to do with you?" she said, without opening her eyes.

"I can work up a list of things if you like," Ty quipped, trying to keep it light.

"You know what I mean," she continued. And he was afraid he did.

"I thought we said we'd take this one day at a time."

"We did." Jenna sighed. "But I forgot about Jay."

Ty placed his thumbs at the top of her arch and dragged them downward. Her toes curled and she flexed her foot. "What about him?"

She remained silent as he moved to her other foot. Just when he thought she might not answer, she said, "I don't want him to grow up wanting to be a Texas Ranger."

Ty's grip tightened slightly, but he made himself relax. "We talked about that."

Jenna opened her eyes then and stared at him with such longing he thought she was about to say goodbye.

"I don't know what to do. He's crazy about you already." She looked down for a second, then met his gaze. "I'm sort of fond of you myself."

Ty felt as if the sun had just come out after forty days of rain. He got up, placed her feet where he'd been sitting, then sat next to her hip and took her hands in his. "Then let's just play it out. I can't quit, but I promise not to make my job look glamorous to him."

Jenna gave him a sad, enigmatic smile. A smile that he couldn't decipher or resist. As he bent to kiss her, she met his mouth with hers and he stopped thinking altogether.

SEVERAL HOURS LATER, at 4:00 a.m. to be exact, Ty's beeper went off. He'd been dreaming about Jenna so his first thought was to call her. But the number on the pager wasn't Jenna's.

"Hello? This is Ty Richardson," he said after dialing.

"Hello, Ranger. This is Robert Ludlow. You know, the cook at the Donut Wrangler."

"What's going on, Robert?"

"I'm really sorry to wake you...but I wanted to tell somebody and I figured you'd be best. I need you to tell Miz Kellerman and Miz Taylor that I can't work for them anymore."

"Are you in trouble?"

"Well, yes and no. Not with the law," Robert said quickly, then stopped. Ty could hear a semi's brakes in the background. "I'm out here at the truck stop on the Interstate on my way out of town. Will you tell them I'm sorry? But I have to go."

"Why don't you wait and tell them yourself in the morning?"

"I'm afraid if I stay till mornin' I'll change my mind. I liked it here and I liked my job."

"Isn't there some way we can help you work it out?"

"No, sir. I know me and I know when I start driftin' off the path. I need to move on."

"Well, I appreciate your honesty, Robert. But, you know, some day you're gonna have to face those demons."

"Yep, I know. Please tell them I was grateful for the chance they gave me. Sorry I didn't live up to it."

"All right. You keep my card. Call if you get in a corner."

"Thank you, Ranger. Goodbye."

CHAPTER FIFTEEN

"I STILL NEED an order of pancakes for table three," Sharon said as she picked up the two plates of eggs Jenna had placed under the warmer.

"Comin' up." Dean sounded completely unperturbed. He flipped the uneven group of pancakes on the grill and waited for them to brown. The kitchen looked like a disaster area, but between Dean and Jenna the orders were being filled.

"Robert always made this look so easy," Jenna said. She was in charge of setup and finish while Dean did the actual cooking. "Thanks for helping out."

"No problem." Dean wiped his wrist band across his forehead. "I used to cook when Sharon and I first went into the restaurant business. The secret is getting organized." He ruefully shrugged toward the utter chaos in the kitchen. "We've got a ways to go yet."

Later, after the initial morning rush had settled down, Jenna and Sharon had a chance to discuss their lack of a cook.

"We could put another ad in, or call back a couple of the applicants we passed up the first time,'' Jenna suggested.

''I just can't believe Robert would let us down like this,'' Sharon muttered.

''Ty said he didn't sound happy about it. Leaving town was just something he had to do.'' Ty had called her at 5:00 a.m. and told her the news. She'd contacted Sharon and they'd gone into emergency mode. Jenna had even dropped Jay off at his grand-mom's for the day. Somebody had to cook, and they wouldn't have time to watch Jay, as well. ''I hope we can find someone as good as he was.''

''They don't have to be as good if they'll promise to stick around and not leave us without warning.'' Sharon eyed her partner. ''So how do you like the restaurant business so far?''

Jenna had to smile. ''We'll do fine.'' She wasn't sure where that confidence came from, but she had a sneaking suspicion Ty's faith in her had something to do with it. ''Dean said he'd help out until we get another cook.''

Dean left the stove and moved over to join the conversation. He looked more jovial than she'd ever seen him. ''I'll be glad to fill in. And as soon as things settle down a bit, I'll try to find a doughnut recipe. See if we can come up with some edible doughnuts in here.''

Sharon's gaze softened as she studied her ex-husband. ''Thank you, Dean,'' she said simply.

Dean's eyes sparkled. ''You are quite welcome,'' he said, grinning.

His grin seemed to fluster Sharon. She abruptly said, "I've got to check on my two in the back." A few seconds later she'd disappeared through the dining-room door.

"Robert may have done me a favor by leavin' when he did," Dean said. Then he winked at Jenna and started whistling as he went back to the stove.

TY SHOWED UP right around closing time. He'd called midmorning to see how they were faring without a cook and promised to stop by.

"Well, the doors are still open—I guess that's a good sign," he said as he sat down. Jenna was refilling the salt and pepper shakers while Sharon cleaned the pie cabinet.

"I wish you'd gone and dragged Robert back here by his ears," Sharon said. "He's got no business running out on us."

"I can't arrest the man for dereliction of duty. And I got the feeling he didn't have a choice," Ty said. "There must be a good reason why he's moved around so much. You might want to take that into consideration when you're hiring next time."

"Now I know why all his references said they'd take him back. We'd be happy to see him if he changed his mind," Jenna said. "Wouldn't we, Sharon?"

"Yes," Sharon agreed reluctantly. "We all worked so well together, I hate to have to start over again."

"How *did* it go today?" Ty asked.

"As well as can be expected," Sharon said.

Jenna glanced at her, puzzled, then she added, "Dean did a fine job filling in. I don't know what we'd have done without him."

"That's true," Sharon admitted. "And now he's got it in his head to make doughnuts." She sounded miffed.

"I'd say that sounds like a good deal. At least you know where to find him if he doesn't show up," Ty countered.

"I don't suppose *you* know how to cook?" Sharon asked, changing the subject.

Ty shook his head, then smiled. "I'm the good customer. The one who orders the food and eats it. Cooking is out of my realm of expertise unless you want to change this to a barbecue restaurant."

"Sharon, where'd you say you put that new grill scraper?" Dean asked through the ordering window. "Howdy, Ranger," he added when he saw Ty.

Ty nodded in greeting. "You seem to be a man of many talents."

"Don't inflate his head with compliments," Sharon said to Ty. "He's hard enough to get along with." Then she turned to Dean. "The scraper is on the second shelf of the storeroom. I'll show you."

After Sharon left, Ty and Jenna looked at each other for several seconds. Jenna felt that same warm tingling she experienced every time she was alone with him. As if she were standing in a rising pool of warm water that started at her toes and slowly drifted upward until she was neck deep and on fire.

"How do you feel about today?" Ty asked.

Jenna's pulse stuttered, and she had to force herself to concentrate on the question. "Great," she answered truthfully. "Our first disaster and we got through it with some help. That's encouraging."

Ty seemed surprised. "I expected you to be upset."

"Well, sure, I know we'll miss Robert, but I figure we'll find someone else as good." She leaned closer to Ty. "Secretly I'm hoping that Dean will stay. Even though Sharon won't admit it, he did a great job, and he kept us from flying into five thousand pieces."

Ty nodded again. "I'm glad to hear it. I told you you'd be good at this."

Jenna remembered her earlier thoughts about Ty's confidence in her and smiled. As she stared into his hazel eyes, a new and more lascivious thought rose in her mind and was immediately seconded by her body. She had an afternoon she could spend with Ty—alone. She wouldn't have to worry about her son being influenced or getting too close to Ty. She could have him all to herself without any worry or guilt.

"You know, I took Jay to stay with his grandmom today," she began.

Ty simply held her gaze so she stammered on.

"I, uh, I don't have to pick him up until six or so...."

Jenna could feel heat rising up her neck, and the words seemed to stick in her throat. She didn't know how to ask for what she wanted. Ty's long-fingered hand covered one of hers. She turned her palm into his, and the friction of her skin against his made her catch her breath.

"I'll be leaving here in about forty minutes and I—" She lost the trail of the sentence as his hand tightened over hers.

"What time should I meet you there?"

All her nervousness burned away, leaving pure heat. "At four," she said.

Sharon reentered the dining room, still debating some point with Dean. The conversation faltered when she saw Ty holding Jenna's hand. Then instead of commenting, she ignored them and continued talking to her ex-husband and the Donut Wrangler's temporary new cook.

TY ARRIVED at Jenna's ten minutes early. He didn't want to seem too eager but, dammit, he was nearly crazy to be with her. There was no question in his mind what would happen when the two of them touched.

He forced himself to sit in his car for a few extra moments. He wanted to do things Jenna's way, and she'd asked him to be here at four. At five minutes till, he knocked on the door.

Jenna opened the door, and Ty's urgency to get

there faded. Now that she was standing in front of him, he just wanted to enjoy the moment. To take in every curve, every line, every emotion he could see in her blue eyes.

She'd obviously taken a shower because her tawny hair was still a little damp. He followed the line of her neck with his gaze, downward, along the low V of her fluffy terry robe. Ty thought it was the sexiest thing he'd ever seen. In a daze he managed to close the door before taking her in his arms. She murmured something into his mouth but it didn't sound like *stop,* and she was removing his hat as he walked her backward down the hall.

He already had his hands inside her robe and on her body by the time they reached the bedroom. The rest of his clothes came off in a rush, and soon they were lying together skin to skin. That's when Ty tried to slow things down. He had Jenna, naked and in a real bed. He'd been fantasizing about this for what seemed like years and he wanted to take his time. But Jenna apparently had another idea.

Every time he kissed her, she kissed him back. When he touched her, she arched to meet him and when her hands touched him as boldly as he touched her, there was no way to slow anything. They both wanted this too much.

"Ty," she said on a breathless gasp when he entered her. Her fingernails dug into his back far enough to sting, urgent enough to make him push into her harder, deeper.

Her hips rose to meet each thrust as her hands

restlessly grasped him. She moaned as the rhythm carried them both higher and Ty stopped kissing her so he could look down at her.

The sight nearly made him lose control completely. The tendons of her neck flexed with strain. Her eyes were mere sexy slits as she moved to satisfy her own need. Suddenly she stiffened beneath him, and he knew she was nearing what she'd wanted. He increased his thrusts to push her over the edge, and as she reached climax she opened her eyes.

"Oh, Ty—"

He felt his own orgasm building, the look of dazed pleasure on her face taking him past the point of no return. He closed his eyes and thrust faster until the feel of her, the smell of her, the heat inside her caused him to explode.

As they lay there together, panting and spent, Ty's mind wandered through all his past memories of lovemaking.

He'd never had better sex.

Jenna.

He wanted to make love to her for the rest of his life. Feeling vulnerable because he wasn't at all sure he'd have the opportunity, he rolled off Jenna and pulled her close to his side. He couldn't look into her eyes right then, not after what he'd just discovered.

"You are so beautiful," he said as he glanced down the length of her body.

She smiled a shy smile and ran her fingers

through his chest hair. "If you weren't such a manly man, I could say the same about you."

He hugged her closer. "Well, thank you for the compliment, but I think you're right. Best not say that to anyone else." He tried to keep talking. He needed to fight off the attack of serious feelings he was having at the moment. "Hell, I didn't mean to jump on you as soon as I walked in the door."

Jenna laughed slightly and entwined her fingers in his. "Ty Richardson, I met you at the door in a robe. If you hadn't jumped on me, you'd have hurt my feelings."

He chuckled. "I see your point. Tell you what, you meet me at the door in a robe anytime you want. I promise not to hurt your feelings."

The room grew silent except for the sound of their breathing. Ty could still hear the rush of his pulse from their earlier exertions.

"What happens between us scares me a little," Jenna said finally.

Ty turned to look at her then. "Why?"

She lowered her gaze to somewhere around his chin. "I don't know. Because I feel out of control." She ducked her head even lower. "It was never that way with Jimmy."

Ty had to swallow back the lump that was forming in his throat. It was inevitable they'd have to talk about Jimmy. Hell. He was lying in Jimmy's bed after making love to Jenna. But suddenly he didn't want to hear about anyone else who'd known

Jenna the way he'd just known her. Not even his best buddy.

"I promise not to take advantage of it, if that's what you're worried about."

She looked at him then in surprise. "I never thought you would," she said. "I'm just so used to telling you what's on my mind that it slipped out." She gazed deeply into his eyes. "I've always trusted you."

Ty didn't want to ruin the moment but he had to ask the big question. "Do you trust me with Jay? To be part of his life?"

He saw confusion in her eyes instead of an answer. He waited, giving her all the time she needed.

She blinked twice. Then said, slowly, "I have to decide what's best for him. And right now that means I want him to grow up and be proud of his father, but not want to be like him." She turned in his arms until she was looking down at him. "You're like his father in the most obvious ways. That's what scares me."

"Does it make any difference if I tell you that I love you and Jay?"

Jenna's eyes widened slightly. Suddenly Ty was afraid of what she might say. So he did the only thing a coward could do; he kissed her, deep and hard. And as he rolled her on her back so that he could love her again, he felt her body give in. He'd deal with her mind some other time.

THAT EVENING TY WALKED UP Kirby's porch steps with Buster on his heels. He'd been in a daze after leaving Jenna.

He'd wanted to stay.

But Jenna hadn't asked and he hadn't pressed. It was enough that he'd practically tackled her the second he saw her, then blurted out the *L* word. He figured he better give it a rest. He had enough guilt over lovin' Jimmy's wife; he didn't need to be pushy about it, too.

"Hey, Ty, come on in," Kirby said as he nudged open the screen door. After Ty entered, the old man looked him over closely. "You look a little peaked. Did the criminals get the better of you today?"

"No, sir. As a matter of fact the past few days have been hurry up and wait." Thinking of the missing Toolie, he added, "One of them seems to have fallen off the face of the earth. Nothin' exciting."

"Well, sit down and take a load off. I'm gonna fire up the grill and cook some burgers. You hungry?"

"Sure," Ty answered. Spending time with Kirby could serve two purposes. He'd make sure the old man didn't need anything, and he could try to keep his thoughts from Jenna and whether or not they'd ever have a future together. He followed Kirby to the kitchen, where he was handed a beer, then out back to pull up a lawn chair while Kirby lit the grill. Buster took up a position near enough to the grill to be able to claim any wayward burger that accidentally hit the dirt.

"Howz those friends of yours that opened the restaurant?" Kirby asked.

Ty wondered if the old man had a sixth sense about what was ailing him. "They're just fine. The cook quit on them, but they've got another one."

Kirby nodded and made a few neutral comments about the pitfalls of the restaurant business. Then, out of the blue, he changed the subject. "You know," he said as he placed the burgers on the hot grill. "I been thinkin' about it and I've decided that Mary Jo isn't comin' back. You should latch on to that little blonde at the restaurant."

CHAPTER SIXTEEN

A WEEK LATER Jenna had come to terms with her involvement with Ty. She still wasn't ready to make any promises, but he'd kept his word, given her some space to breathe, and he'd downplayed his job when Jay was around. In the face of his steady attention and outright affection, she found herself relaxing a bit and hoping they could make something more permanent work.

The unsettling idea of becoming a Ranger's wife still lurked in the background of her happiness. Ty hadn't asked, or even mentioned the future. But she knew deep inside that he wasn't the type of man who'd dally with her. Sooner or later he'd want the whole commitment. If, or when, he asked, it would be one of the toughest decisions of her life. Yes meant turning over her own and her son's future to a man who wore a gun for a living. No meant losing Ty for good. She hoped she wouldn't have to make that decision any time soon.

As Jenna coaxed Jay out to the car for their daily trip to the Donut Wrangler, she realized they'd only be making this trip for two more weeks. Jay would be starting the first grade.

A rush of sadness filled her. She wished Jimmy could be there, to see his son off to school. The first bus ride was a pretty important milestone in any child's life. Jay should have both his parents standing on the curb to encourage him.

Then she remembered that if she allowed it, he could have Ty. They both could have Ty for encouragement, for love, for all the things they'd lost when Jimmy had been taken away from them. She searched her mind for a clear memory of Jimmy's face. *Tell me what to do,* she pleaded silently. But no booming voice, or clear answer sprang to mind. She shrugged, not really surprised. It would be up to her.

"Come on, buddy," she said to her sleepy son. "We don't want to be late."

Without argument Jay climbed in the van. Jenna helped him fasten his seat belt, then impulsively gave him a big noisy kiss on the cheek.

"Mo-om," he huffed, and rubbed his cheek as if he'd been licked by a dog, or worse.

Jenna was unperturbed. Whether because they spent so much time together, or because he was entering a new independence stage, she knew he was growing up. Sooner than she wanted to think about, he'd be standing on his own. "You're just gonna have to put up with my kisses. I'm the mom here and I get to kiss you whenever I want." She ruffled his hair and shut the door, chuckling to herself.

"YOU'RE NOT GOING to believe this," Sharon said when Jenna and Jay walked in the door of the diner.

"What?" Jenna asked.

Sharon pulled a bent postcard out of her pocket. "We got a card from Robert."

Surprised, Jenna reached for the card. "Really?"

"Look what he sent us," Sharon said.

Jenna gazed down at the smudged postcard with no return address and realized what Sharon meant. It was a recipe. A doughnut recipe. Below it was scrawled:

Learned it at a truck stop. Best dang donuts I've had.

Sorry.

Robert.

"Well, that was nice of him," Jenna said.

Sharon took the card back from her. "Yeah, I guess it wasn't really a mistake to hire him. I wish he'd stuck around, though. Dean's going to try out the recipe." She watched Jenna for a moment. "Is everything going okay for you?"

Jenna wanted to avoid talking about Ty for as long as humanly possible. "Sure. What makes you think it isn't?"

Looking unconvinced, Sharon shook her head. "Oh, nothing. Guess I better get back to my customers."

Jenna again had the uncanny feeling that Sharon could read her thoughts like the TV guide. Soon, however, they were both too busy waiting tables to talk about personal matters.

But Sharon obviously was only put off, not defeated. Later that morning, she cornered Jenna.

''Now are you ready to tell me what's going on?'' Sharon asked as she leaned on the counter where Jenna was sorting out guest checks.

''What do you mean?'' Jenna asked absently, her mind on the checks in front of her. For once the restaurant was completely empty.

''I mean between you and Ty.''

Jolted by the mere sound of his name, Jenna put the paper in her hand down and looked at Sharon. ''Well, I—'' Remembering the presence of her son, she glanced toward the kitchen.

''Dean's got Jay back there helping him make doughnuts. But just in case.'' Sharon pulled a quarter out of her pocket and walked over to the jukebox. She punched in some numbers, and soon the dining room was filled with Mary Chapin Carpenter's voice. She returned to the counter and gestured for Jenna to sit beside her. ''Now, talk.''

Jenna couldn't keep quiet any longer. She'd violated her own rules by getting in deeper with Ty. She needed to talk to someone about it.

''Well, you know that Ty came to get me when Garland left me in the restaurant,'' she began. Sharon nodded and waited. ''That night, when we got home... I don't know exactly how it happened but we—''

''Hot damn!'' Sharon said, and smiled. ''I knew

something was different. I've been so preoccupied with Robert's disappearance and Dean—'' She glanced toward the kitchen, then squeezed Jenna's arm. ''You've finally come to your senses.'' She smiled wickedly. ''Tell me everything.''

Speechless for a moment, because there was no way she could tell Sharon about how wild and wonderful that first night had been, Jenna searched for words. ''I, uh, we, uh...'' Feeling an embarrassing wave of heat at the mere memory, she stumbled on. ''We're lovers,'' she finally said.

''I figured that out already. I want to know how you feel about it.''

Jenna looked her friend in the eye and answered honestly. ''I'm scared to death.''

''Why, honey?''

Jenna felt her eyes stinging and filling with tears. ''Because everything and nothing has changed between us. He's still my best friend and a Texas Ranger, but now he's also a man I'm having a hard time resisting.'' The tears in her eyes overflowed at that point. ''He says he loves me...and Jay.''

''But that's wonderful,'' Sharon protested before searching her expression. ''Unless you don't love him.''

Jenna pulled a napkin from the holder on the counter and swiped at the tears on her cheeks. ''I can't love him. Don't you see? He's still the man who can hurt me more than anyone. He can influence my son.''

''He could do that even if you were only friends.''

''I know.'' Jenna sniffed. ''But as a friend, I can keep him at a distance, keep Jay interested in other things.''

Sharon took both Jenna's hands and squeezed them, hard. ''Do you love him?''

''I'm not sure,'' she answered. ''But I can't sacrifice my son's future because of what I want today.''

Sharon ran a hand over her face and sighed. ''Life damned sure gets complicated, doesn't it? I wish I knew the right answer for you. All I can say is, don't give up yet. If you love him and he loves you, things will work out for the best.''

Jenna nodded but couldn't answer. She couldn't see how things would work out, but she couldn't envision her happiness without Ty, either.

The dining-room door swung open, and Dean walked toward them holding Jay's hand and carrying a plate with several doughnuts on it. When the guys reached the counter, Dean set the plate in front of Sharon and Jenna, then picked Jay up and seated him next to it so he could see. Obviously noticing Jenna had been crying, he glanced from her to his ex-wife before speaking. ''Jay and I want you to try our doughnuts,'' he said.

Jenna and Sharon each picked up a golden-brown circle dusted with powdered sugar. Sharon made a great show of examining the results of the test. ''Here goes,'' she said, and took a bite.

Jenna did the same, prepared for anything. But as she chewed, she couldn't stop a smile. She swallowed and nodded. "These are really good," she said truthfully.

"Hallelujah, we've got doughnuts!" Sharon crowed triumphantly. "You two are amazing—and thank you, Robert." She leaned over the counter and gave first Jay, then Dean a smacking kiss on the cheek, leaving powdered sugar behind. Jay giggled and Jenna pulled him from the counter into her lap.

"We did it, Mom. Mr. Dean and I made the doughnuts."

"Yes, you did," Jenna answered, hugging him.

"Can I have a doughnut store when I get big?"

Jenna blinked back the last vestiges of her tears and glanced at Sharon over her son's head. "Yes, you certainly *may.*"

TY HAD BEEN WORKING for several hours on a new county-corruption case file he'd been given when his beeper went off. He automatically looked at his watch. A little after 10:00 a.m. He dialed the number and Sheriff Temple answered the phone.

"Well, Ty. It looks like we mighta found old Toolie Mardell. 'Bout ten miles from the lake, a motorist with a flat tire stumbled across a body."

"Has he been IDed?"

"Not officially. I'm gonna ride out there now. I was wondering if you could go by and pick up Mrs. Mardell and bring her down to the county morgue."

Not knowing seemed worse than the truth, but Ty wondered how Mrs. Mardell would take the death of her husband. This was part of the job he could do without. "Sure, I'll go by."

"Thanks for the help," Sheriff Temple said. "I hate when it turns out this way. Now we have to find out how he got in that ditch."

"Yes, sir," Ty agreed. "I'll take care of Mrs. Mardell."

After he hung up, Ty looked up the number for Mrs. Mardell at work. When he called, he was told she'd called in for a day off because one of her kids had the flu and she was taking the little girl to the doctor. He found her at home.

"Mrs. Mardell?"

"Yes."

"This is Ty Richardson. I spoke to you about your husband's disappearance a while back."

"Yes, sir."

Not wanting to tell her anything over the phone, especially since they weren't absolutely sure they'd found Toolie, Ty remained cautious. He'd tell her more when he talked to her in person.

"We may have some new information about your husband. I was wondering if I could come by and take you down to the sheriff's office for one more interview?"

She didn't seem curious about why she had to be interviewed again. There were several seconds of silence before she answered. "I guess so, but I have to bring my kids. I don't have anyone to watch 'em.''

Ty didn't like the thought of Mrs. Mardell having to identify her husband's body and then driving home with her two young children in the car. Especially since one of them was supposedly sick. He'd have to arrange for a deputy to drive her. ''Do you have a friend who might be able to go with you?'' If the man in the ditch turned out to be her husband, Ty knew she'd need all the support she could get. And calling Toolie's mother would be worse than facing it alone.

Again there was a stretch of silence. ''You know what?'' she said finally. ''I just remembered that my neighbor two doors down is home in the daytime. I'll call her. Can you give me about an hour and a half before we go?''

''Sure. That's fine.'' Ty knew the body wouldn't be moved immediately anyway because of the task of gathering evidence. He'd give Mrs. Mardell all the time she needed before she was asked to identify a dead man.

''I'll see you around noon, then,'' she answered. Her voice seemed forced into a pleasant-sounding tone. Hell, Ty couldn't blame her, she'd already been interviewed five times.

''I'll be there,'' he said.

THE NEW DONUT WRANGLER doughnuts were a hit. Dean was practically strutting around the kitchen after two of the customers had ordered more.

"I told you," Sharon said, only half-serious. "His head is gonna swell so big, he'll think he's runnin' this place."

Jenna laughed. "You're just mad because he won't give you back the recipe."

"Now, that's the truth. Does he think we're gonna keep him around forever just because he can cook doughnuts?"

"That would be my vote," Jenna said, and shoved Sharon's shoulder as she walked by. "You can get used to that, can't you?"

"Harrumph," Sharon replied eloquently.

"Jenna? Sharon? You two need to get in here!" Dean called from the kitchen.

Jenna's heart seemed to rise into her throat. She had visions of her son, burned by hot grease or bleeding after touching one of the sharp knives. She burst through the swinging door with Sharon on her heels.

"What is it? What's wrong?" She looked from Dean to her son, who was glued to the picture on the television set. He turned when he heard her voice.

"Mom! Mr. Ty is on TV."

"There's some kind of high-speed chase," Dean said.

Jenna moved closer, and the hair rose on the back of her neck. A newswoman described the action.

"This is a live shot from our news helicopter. Sheriff's deputies and Texas Rangers are in pursuit of a 1989 Buick eastbound on Route 67. We've been following this story for fifteen minutes now. There seems to be a woman driving the car—''

The camera that had been shooting the chase angled farther along the road in front of the car. A roadblock had been set up with two sheriff's cruisers and several deputies.

''It looks like they've put tire-piercing strips across the highway,'' the helicopter reporter said. ''In hopes of stopping the fleeing car that has reached speeds of up to eighty miles per hour.''

Jenna had no problem recognizing Ty's car. He was immediately behind the fugitive with another deputy following close in the other lane. Praying the chase would end quickly, she watched as the fugitive's car sped toward the spikes.

Then suddenly the Buick swerved to the right, onto the shoulder of the road. Dust and rocks flew up from the tires as the driver skidded around the spikes and nearly ran the officers down. Jenna watched, horrified, as two deputies dived out of the way.

''Oh, my God,'' Sharon breathed behind her.

Jenna couldn't take her eyes off the screen.

''Is that Mr. Ty, Mom?'' Jay asked as he touched the screen and the driver's side of Ty's car.

Ty had followed the Buick through the dirt and pulled up even with the driver's window. He seemed to be waving or signaling to the fugitive. The driver's response was to push the car faster, racing ahead again, ignoring whatever signal Ty had given. In a sort of grim dance, Ty's car backed off, then angled over to the other side. A few seconds later a puff of smoke erupted from the back tire of the Buick.

The excited newscaster continued the play-by-play. "It looks like one of the Texas Rangers has just shot out the back tire on the Buick. Can't go too far without a tire."

Pieces of rubber were flying off the wheel, and sparks began to stream out behind the vehicle. The driver of the Buick tried to push on, but the car began to fishtail. Finally the driver slowed, then stopped.

Jenna, Jay, Dean and Sharon watched silently as, with guns drawn, Ty and the other officers rushed from their cars and surrounded the fugitive's vehicle. Ty lowered his gun, moved forward and opened the driver's door.

Jenna held her breath.

The driver, who looked like little more than a young girl, stepped out of the car with her hands raised. Ty indicated she should face the car and put her hands on the hood, which she did without a fight.

"Well, it appears we have an end to the exciting high-speed chase," the newscaster said. "Our news van is en route, and we'll have more details when they become available."

"Did you see that, Mom? Did you see Mr. Ty?"

Jenna reached past him and shut the TV off. Silence reigned around them. Suddenly Dean remembered some hash browns that needed turning, and Sharon decided to return to their customers.

"Yes, honey. I saw it." Jenna didn't know what else to say. Her knees felt so wobbly she had to pull out a chair and sit down.

"Wasn't that cool?" Jay persisted.

Cool. An icy hand seemed to grip Jenna's heart. She wanted to say, "No! It wasn't cool. It nearly scared the life out of me." But she couldn't infect her son with her own fears. Before she could come up with a suitable response, Jay continued.

"Can Mr. Ty teach me how to be a Texas Ranger when I get big?"

IT HAD BEEN A LONG DAY, and it was barely three o'clock. Ty pulled into the Donut Wrangler parking lot, hoping for a little pleasant, nonconfrontational conversation. He felt as if he'd been sparring with Mrs. Mardell for twelve hours. He'd arrived at her house a little early to pick her up. She'd had the children in the car and told him she needed to drop them off at the neighbor's.

Well, she'd driven right past the neighbor's and just kept on goin'. He'd chased her for almost an hour before he got to ask her why the heck she'd been runnin' in the first place. Then he'd spent two hours with her in the interrogation room listening to her confess to killing her husband.

How, on the way back from the lake, Toolie had threatened to divorce her and give "his" children to his mother to raise. It had been the breaking point for Mrs. Mardell. When Toolie had pulled over to relieve himself on the shoulder of the road, his wife had moved to the driver's side and used the car as a lethal weapon.

Toolie's mother had been right about who killed her son, and Ty hated that. He also had a gut feeling that if someone had only been more supportive of Toolie's emotionally and physically abused wife, things might not have turned out this way.

He shook his head as he walked up the steps. Now Mrs. Mardell was charged with not only the murder of her husband, which Ty considered damned close to self-defense, but also with attempted murder of the two sheriff's deputies she'd chased into a ditch with her car. Not to mention the reckless endangerment of her children, who had both been in the car with her—securely strapped into car seats.

That last part really got his dander up. It was one thing to be dumb and risk your own life, but putting two innocent children in the middle of a police chase was more than he could let go. He'd been rather hard on Mrs. Mardell for that. And now, because she'd tried to handle everything on her own, her children would go to Toolie's mother, unless Ty could find any family Mrs. Mardell had left behind in Ohio. It was a fifty-fifty chance that even if he could find someone, they would care enough to help her. He had to try, though.

Just as he was trying to clear the angry and frustrated thoughts from his head, he spotted Jenna. For a flash of a second he saw what looked like relief and joy on her face as he held her gaze and dragged his hat from his head. But right about then, Jay came flying around the counter and skidded to a stop in front of him. He had his toy gun in his hand.

"Mr. Ty! We saw you on TV. Did you shoot the bad guy?" Jay randomly aimed his own gun at the jukebox and pulled the trigger.

"You saw me?" Ty asked carefully, then glanced at Jenna once again. Her features had become unreadable. Not frowning, but the joy was long gone.

Ty squatted down to Jay's level. "No, I didn't shoot anyone but an old tire," he answered.

Dean came out of the kitchen and said, "That was somethin' when she went around the spikes."

Ty stood and lifted Jay onto a stool before he took a seat. He rubbed his forehead to ease a building headache. "Well, she said she saw the police use spikes on TV and figured she'd go around."

Dean chuckled. "What in the world was she runnin' for?"

Ty gave Jay a sideways glance. "Domestic homicide." He tried to disguise the truth from young ears. "She and her husband had a disagreement."

"Man," Dean said. "She didn't look no bigger than a sprite."

"I can tell you she looked big enough behind the wheel of that car," Ty said. He turned toward Jenna again. He was beginning to feel sick to his stomach. Why wasn't she talking?

Sharon ambled up next to Dean. "Why don't you fix Ty a plate of chicken and vegetables before you put the food away. I bet he didn't get to eat lunch."

Food was the last thing on his mind, but Ty would eat if it meant finding out why Jenna was keeping her distance. She was busy cleaning tables and too quiet for his peace of mind. He gave Sharon a tired smile. "You got that right. Some lunch sounds like a good idea."

Jenna gave the table she'd been cleaning a last swipe. When she picked up the tray full of dirty dishes and turned toward the kitchen, she realized everyone but her son was watching her. Jay had eyes only for his new hero—the Texas Ranger. It was all Jenna could do not to cry. She made an attempt at a normal smile, then pushed through the doors to the kitchen.

Knowing she couldn't hide among the dirty dishes forever, Jenna emptied the tray, placed it on the stack, then slowly made her way back to the dining room.

Dean looked up as she came through the door. "Jay, why don't you come back and help me get Ty's lunch ready?" he asked. "He hasn't had any of our new doughnuts yet."

Unaware of the tense undercurrents between his mother and his hero, Jay hopped down off the stool and headed for the kitchen.

"I think I'll help you with that," Sharon said before fleeing the dining room, too.

Suddenly Jenna was left alone with Ty. Not only

could she not think of anything to say, but her feet also seemed to be welded to the linoleum. Helplessly she watched as he stood, walked toward her and put his arms around her. He buried his face in her hair and didn't speak right away. He simply held her and she let him.

"Ty, I—" Jenna's tears soaked into his shirt. "I'm so glad you're all right."

"I'm sorry you were worried. It wasn't really that dangerous."

That dangerous. Jenna knew from past experience how men and women differed on what they considered dangerous. Jimmy had always said it was more dangerous to stop cars on the freeway or to be the first to arrive at an accident scene. He'd done his best to convince her he was more likely to be run over by an inattentive driver than to be shot.

He'd been wrong.

The warring factions inside her cranked up hostilities again, and she pushed out of Ty's embrace. She tried her best to control her tears, but she already knew what she had to do, what she had to say.

Goodbye.

And it was breaking her heart.

"Come over here and sit down," Ty said, taking her arm and guiding her to a stool. He gazed at her closely, then brought one hand up to wipe away her tears. "Please don't cry. I'm fine."

Fighting for control, Jenna reached over and

plucked a napkin from the holder and dabbed at her face. She had to calm down. She'd never be able to do what needed to be done if she dissolved into grief. There would be plenty of time for tears after today.

Making more noise than necessary, Dean and Jay paraded from the kitchen and delivered Ty's food. Jay explained that he'd helped cook the doughnuts as Ty slowly picked up his fork and began to eat.

Jenna was glad for the respite. By the time he'd finished eating, maybe she'd be in better control. She'd need all her backbone to do what had to be done. Because it was gonna hurt—not only her but Ty, and the thought of that made her resolve falter.

Her gaze shifted to her son as he chattered on about doughnuts and knew he'd never understand. Maybe the damage had already been done. She wouldn't know for sure until he'd grown up and made his choices. But right now having Ty out of their lives seemed not only safer but wiser. Why, even for a moment, had she believed she could live with another man who would leave the house in the morning and might not be home for dinner—ever again?

She couldn't lose another man she loved.

Loved.

Jenna blinked and almost started crying all over again. She did love Ty. She'd never said the words or even thought them until this moment. The possibility of losing him had shed light on her true feelings and the basis of her fear. She crushed the napkin in her fist and looked away from Ty and her son. She met Sharon's eyes through the ordering window, and Sharon just shook her head sadly.

I have to do this, she reiterated silently. She *had* to. She couldn't take chances with her future anymore.

Ty listened to Jay ramble on and answered him occasionally. Dean had gone back to finish cleaning the kitchen, and Sharon was helping him. Eating some lunch hadn't settled his stomach. He needed to talk to Jenna, to hold her and kiss away the sadness he could sense in her. But that would have to wait. He hoped to get her alone before they left, although it might be better to follow her home and talk there.

Satisfied with his decision, he took a last bite of mashed potatoes and pushed his plate away. Jenna slid off her stool and picked the plate up.

"You want some dessert?" she asked automatically.

Ty shook his head. "I intend to have one of Jay's doughnuts," he said, forcing himself to smile.

Jenna relaxed ever so slightly, and he felt a ray of hope. "Don't worry, they're better than the last one you had in here."

Twenty minutes later Jenna and Sharon shut off the lights and locked the front door of the diner.

"Can Mr. Ty come over to our house?" Jay asked.

Ty didn't say anything. He waited for Jenna's reaction.

Jenna walked over to Jay and put a hand on his shoulder. "I don't think so, honey. Not today." She looked at Sharon. "Could you stay a few minutes with Jay? Ty and I need to talk."

Unusually quiet, Sharon nodded.

Ty's heart took several wild beats in his chest. Not good. All his instincts were screaming the same warning—he was about to hear something he didn't want to know. But when Jenna indicated for him to follow her, he did. His head nodded and his feet moved while his heart ached.

Jenna led him out the back door and down the steps before turning to face him. Every line in her body seemed tense and on guard. He wished he could rub her shoulders, say something that would make her smile. But he could see she wasn't going to allow any of that until she'd said what she had to say. He only hoped—

"This isn't going to work, Ty. *We* aren't going to work. I don't know how else to say it."

His worst fears realized, he said the first thing that came to mind. "Why? We said we'd take it slow, a little at a time."

"No," Jenna said, in a final-sounding voice. "After today, after—"

He stepped toward her, but she sidled away and held up a hand to keep him at a distance.

"Today was nothin', Jenna. I was never in any real danger. You can't be afraid of everything."

"It's about Jay," she said, and crossed her arms

as if she'd suffered a chill in the eighty-five-degree heat of the afternoon.

"What about him?"

"He asked me today if you could teach him to be a Texas Ranger."

A piercing stab of pride registered with Ty. He cared more for Jay than he could admit, and the fact that Jay looked up to him made his heart expand with a new kind of joy. A fatherly kind. He'd never had that before. But then he realized what Jay's admiration meant to Jenna.

"Well, he—"

"Don't say he'll grow out of it." She looked like a woman facing a death sentence. "I can't take that chance."

"I didn't do anything to encourage him," Ty argued, although he could see she'd made up her mind.

"No. I know you didn't do anything specific. But you're like Jimmy—you want to be the hero, to save the world." Two fat tears spilled from her eyes and trailed down her cheeks. "Well, I need—Jay needs a father who thinks it's his job to be a dad. Not one who risks his life every day."

Ty's back went up at that one. "I'm not reckless, Jenna. You know that."

Jenna was shaking her head and crying. "Don't you see? You don't have to be reckless. You only have to show up for work."

Ty's mind went blank. Suddenly he found he'd bracketed Jenna's shoulders with his hands and was staring into her tear-filled blue eyes at close range. ''Please don't do this. I love you and Jay. I would never do anything to hurt you.''

Jenna's hands came up and pressed against his chest, holding him away. The pain he saw in her eyes made his throat go tight. She meant it.

''I ap-appreciate all you've done for us, and I know we'll miss you,'' she stumbled on. ''But plea-please stay away from us, Ty. I can't—I won't let this go on.''

Jenna stepped out of his grip, and Ty had to force himself to let her go. He heard the back door open and close behind him and he still stood there. The memory of Jenna's face the night Jimmy had been killed came back to haunt him. Maybe she was right. Maybe born-in-the-badge police officers didn't deserve to have a family, too. His job was his life and it had already cost him one marriage. Why should Jenna, who'd already lost a husband, take a chance on him?

Ty gazed into the afternoon sun until his eyes began to sting. He rubbed the moisture out of them and decided he needed to put on his sunglasses to keep out the glare. His sunglasses were in his car. He straightened his spine, put one foot in front of the other and walked around the building to get them.

CHAPTER SEVENTEEN

"WHEN IS MR. TY COMING BACK?" Jay asked. He was sitting on the floor of the office constructing his version of a gas station out of Lego pieces.

Jenna gazed down at him and sighed. She'd put him off and stretched the truth more times than she could count in the past week and a half. She still didn't know what to tell him. "I'm not sure, sweetie. He's doing his job."

"But he said he'd see us soon," he persisted. "And he's been gone a loooong time."

"I know he has." Jenna's heart had counted every minute of every day he'd been absent from their lives. It didn't make it any easier knowing that she'd been the one to insist on his absence. "But he'll be back," she lied. The truth was that Ty had honored her wishes—he'd stepped out of their lives. He wouldn't return unless she asked and then he might not be happy about it. How many times could she push him away and expect him to come back when she got her fear under control? Or when she wanted him more than she cared about the future? No, Jenna reiterated to herself. Ty was out of their lives for good. And the only time she could grieve the loss was late at night, alone in her bed.

Before the wave of sadness she'd been holding off managed to overtake her in broad daylight, Jenna did what all mothers do when they don't have an answer. She changed the subject. "Are you excited about going to school on Monday? You'll meet lots of new friends there."

"Uh-huh," Jay said, sounding completely *un*excited.

"Today is Friday. We'll go shopping after work tomorrow to pick up your school supplies. Then on Monday morning you get to ride the bus with Rusty." If Jay couldn't have Jimmy, or Ty, there to send him off to school along with Jenna, at least he'd have a friend to ride the bus with.

"Rusty said a kid told him the bus driver chews tobacco," Jay informed her.

Jenna fervently hoped the kid didn't know what he was talking about. "Really? That sounds like a pretty tall story to me—"

"Jenna?" Dean called through the door. "We've got two latecomers."

She looked at the clock as she pushed up from the desk. It was five minutes until closing time, but officially they were still open. Sharon had already gone home, leaving her and Dean to close up. As Jenna passed through the kitchen, she glanced at Dean. "What do we have left to serve?"

"I've got most everything, but I've already

cleaned the grill. I hope they're not hungry for a hamburger.''

The two men were standing near the front door when Jenna entered the dining room. ''Hi. You just made it before closing time,'' she said, and waved them toward a table. ''Have a seat. I'll bring you a menu.''

The men just stood there, so Jenna walked closer. ''Did you want to get something to go?'' she asked. That's when she noticed one of the men had a gun in his hand.

TY NEEDED A VACATION. As he drove down the familiar straight line of Route 82, he figured he'd take one after he confronted Jenna. He'd had enough of doing the right thing. He missed her, dammit, and he intended to tell her so. They belonged together, the three of them. Why couldn't she see that?

Ty shook his head. Maybe the police-counseling office was right. Maybe he should make an appointment to talk to them about Jimmy's death and its effect on him. Because last night he'd dreamed about his best friend, and Jimmy had looked exactly the same as he had in life. He'd even been wearing his sheriff's deputy uniform. In the dream he'd talked, and talked, and talked to Ty, but when Ty woke up he couldn't recall any of the conversation except the last few words. *Remember Jenna and Jay.*

How could I forget? Ty grumbled to himself. He

was in love with the woman. "And how do you know he calls himself Jay now?" Ty asked out loud. When no one answered, he shook his head again. *Damn. Now he's got me talking to myself.*

He was glad to see the giant doughnut looming ahead. He'd planned to catch Jenna at the end of the day and hoped the place would be empty. But as he approached the Donut Wrangler, one beat-up pickup truck remained in the lot.

"WHO ELSE IS HERE?" the man with the gun demanded.

Jenna shook herself out of the initial shock of seeing the gun. "Just me and the cook," she answered, praying that Jay would stay occupied in the office with his toys.

"Call him," the second man ordered.

All the hair on Jenna's neck rose at the demand. She wanted to scream, to run, to warn Dean, but she could only do what the man asked. She'd do anything to keep them away from her son. "Dean? Can you come here please?" she called, trying to keep her voice even.

But Dean must have heard the fear because he entered the dining room with a cautious expression on his face. When he got through the door, the man with the gun gestured to him. "Get over here, so I can keep an eye on you." Then he turned to Jenna. "Open that cash register and put the money in a sack," he ordered.

Just as Jenna pushed the total button to open the cash drawer, the other man said, "We've got a car pulling in the lot."

Jenna glanced up as the gunman turned, and her blood went cold. All the air in her lungs seemed to solidify when she recognized Ty's car. She made a sound, trying to regain her breath, and the man with the gun looked from the car to her. Before he could ask what she was certain he'd intended to ask, the second man swore.

"It's a son of a bitchin' Texas Ranger!"

The man with the gun moved quickly around the counter and took Jenna's arm. Dean stepped forward to do something, but the man aimed the gun in his direction. Dean raised his hands and spoke slowly. "Now you boys don't get nervous. We can work this out."

"You stay right where you are," the man answered. "Don't make me shoot you."

Dean nodded and stayed put.

Jenna still had the half-filled bag of cash in her hand. Terror gripped her when she realized that Ty was walking into a trap. She couldn't let these men hurt him because of her. As her panic grew, she did the only thing she could think of; she threw the bag of money toward the door.

TY, GLAD TO SEE that the last two customers were at the cash register, ready to leave, watched Jenna through the glass door. It seemed like a year since she'd told him goodbye. No matter what happened today, he felt lighter just looking at her. But then he noticed she had a strange expression on her face, and that the man next to her seemed to be standing way too close. Ty's heart began to beat hard and fast in his chest. *What the hell is goin' on?* That's when he saw something hit the door. The man standing next to Jenna pulled her in front of him and held a gun to her head.

Ty stopped in his tracks. *Back off,* his mind ordered. *Follow procedure. Don't get crazy.* But every nerve and muscle in his body wanted to shove through the door and beat the man senseless. He was scaring Jenna, and that was enough to make Ty lose all perspective on the situation. But when Jenna motioned for him to go away, he felt a searing pain in his chest. "Don't hurt her," he called loud enough to be heard. *Please God, don't hurt her.* "I'm backing off." He raised his hands, which were at the moment shaking, and walked backward until he bumped into his car. A moment later he was on the radio.

"WHAT DO WE DO NOW?" the second man said to the one holding the gun.

"I don't know," the gunman answered. He motioned to Dean. "Get the keys and lock this door," he ordered.

Jenna, relieved to see Ty unhurt, suddenly went wobbly on her feet. The man threatening her practically had to hold her upright. As Dean approached with the keys and locked the door, the man continued, "Pick up that bag and put the rest of the money in it." The gunman stepped away from the cash register, pulling Jenna along with him. Then he pushed her onto the first stool.

In less than five minutes they heard the first police siren. Within ten minutes three sheriff's office cars were blocking the parking lot and one had pulled up to the back door.

"Hell, Frank! What are we gonna do now?" The man without the gun was becoming more agitated by the moment.

"Shut up, fool! And let me think." The gunman turned to Jenna. "We could have tied up that Ranger and made a run for it. Now, because of you, one of you has to go with us. You got a car out back?"

Jenna's heart, which had been beating wildly out of fear, now seemed to stop. If he wanted her car, they'd have to walk through the kitchen to the back door. And Jay—

The man clamped a hand on her arm and twisted. "Answer me!"

"I— Yes, I have a van. But it's been having some problems—"

"That's what we'll do, then. We'll take your van, and you'll come along as insurance."

"How we gonna get by those lawmen?" the second man persisted.

Jenna shifted her gaze to Dean. Trying to convey her thoughts. She'd go with these men if they'd leave her son alone. As she stared at him, his gaze flicked to the dining-room door. Trying to move slowly and unobtrusively, she looked in the same direction. The door was opening, slowly. She couldn't see past the counter, but the only person who could possibly be coming through that door was Jay. She watched Dean's face. He slowly shook his head no, and Jenna prayed her son would understand. Without thinking of anything but distracting the men, Jenna stood up.

"Let me talk to the police," she offered. She stepped toward the front door and found herself in the gunman's grip once again.

"Where do you think you're going?"

"I know one or two of them. I'll tell them I'm willing to drive you to the interstate."

"Now, why would you want to do that?" the gunman asked, his voice heavy with suspicion. "All you've done so far is cause me trouble."

"I—I just don't want anyone to get hurt," Jenna answered truthfully.

"Sit down, lady. What you don't want is any surprises. If I get surprised, people get hurt. You got that?" He shoved Jenna back toward the stool.

TY HAD ALREADY UNBUCKLED his gun and handed it over to Sheriff Temple. When he saw one of the suspects push Jenna, he straightened.

"I don't think this is such a good idea," Sheriff Temple said. "You should at least wear a vest. Give us a half hour and I'll have the sharpshooters here."

Ty didn't trust himself to speak so he shook his head at the sheriff's suggestion. He had to go inside and get between Jenna and that gun. "I'm goin' in," he said, and started walking. He could hear the static and echo from the police radios in the cars around him, the crunch of gravel under his boots; the only other sound was the steady, determined beat of his heart.

Before he reached the bottom of the stairs, the gunman stood and put Jenna between himself and the glass door. Ty raised his hands and slowly ascended the steps. He didn't look at or acknowledge the two deputies crouched on either side of the stairs, hidden from the criminals inside. The terrified look on Jenna's face made him want to kick through the door and have ten minutes of quality time with the man who had dared to touch her.

"What do you want?" the gunman yelled through the glass.

"I want to make a deal," Ty answered.

"What kind of deal?"

"Me for the woman. Let her out of there, and it'll go better for you." Ty hoped they'd buy it because when they'd taken hostages, they'd entered the deep end of the legal pool. It would only take a couple of mistakes to cause something bad to happen. He'd negotiated before and been successful. He prided himself on telling the criminals the truth—how it really stood. In this case he'd learn to be a good liar. He'd give his word; he'd tell them *anything* to get Jenna and Jay out of danger. He held Jenna's gaze as the two men argued between themselves. He tried to send her the silent message that he loved her, that he would get her out of this no matter what it took. He saw her eyes fill with tears and knew what she had to be thinking. Then he wondered where Jay was.

A few moments later one of the men gestured, and Dean moved over to unlock the door. He stepped back with his hands raised and again moved behind the counter. The gunman indicated for Ty to step inside.

"Turn around and lock that door behind you," the man ordered. When Ty complied, turning the key but not quite locking it, the man continued, "Now face me." He seemed nervous but still a little cocky, even though Ty doubted they'd had a plan for this contingency. They didn't seem to recognize that almost everything from this point on was pretty much out of their control. Unfortunately the part that was in their control was whether or not they hurt Jenna, Dean and Jay. "Take off your boots and unbutton your shirt."

Slowly, so as not to spook them, Ty did as he was told. He set his boots near the first booth, then unbuttoned his shirt. He heard Jenna sniff once as she wiped her tears on the back of her hand. He centered all his concentration on doing whatever it took to get her out of here. He pulled his shirttail free to show them he wasn't armed or wearing a vest.

Jenna was nearing the breaking point, and watching Ty silently do what the men asked made her almost lose it. Every person she loved was in danger, not just her, but Jay and Ty. Jimmy had already been taken away from them. A few minutes before, after she'd seen the kitchen door start to open, true terror had set in. Her hands were shaking so much she had to clamp them together to keep her fear from showing. To get her tears under control, she looked away from Ty's steady gaze out into the parking lot filled with police cars and flashing lights. An ambulance had also arrived. A chill ran through her. *Please, don't let this happen....*

As she prayed, another car she recognized screeched to a halt near the sheriff's office cars. She saw Sharon jump from the driver's side and hurry toward the restaurant. A deputy stopped her. Jenna looked at Dean. Poor Sharon, the only thing worse than being held hostage would be standing outside watching helplessly as the person you loved was threatened.

"Let the woman go and I'll be your hostage," Ty said.

Jenna brought her attention back to him and took

a deep breath. She would *not* cry. She was also not about to leave without her son.

"No," she said. "I'm staying."

The gunman turned to her. "You're goin'. Get up."

With a pleading glance at Ty, Jenna stayed where she was.

"I said, get up," the man ordered again, and took a step toward her.

After that, time seemed to be suspended. Jenna was looking at the gunman when she heard a sound behind her. She turned her head to see Jay, or rather Jay's toy gun, then his hand and finally his face as he moved around the end of the counter. "Don't hurt my mommy," he threatened.

She heard a scream, her own, as the man raised his weapon. Ty shouted, "No," and lunged between the gun and her son. The gunshot, close by Jenna's ear, nearly deafened her, but all she could see was Ty falling.

Then everything shifted into fast forward. Jay ran into her arms as deputies rushed through the front door and overpowered the two criminals. Jenna didn't spare them a glance. Her son was safe, but Ty...

"Ty?" Jenna bent over him as he tried to get up. There was blood on one side of his shirt and on the skin underneath. Tears flowed down her cheeks as she gently touched his face. "How bad is it?" she asked, knowing he had more experience with gunshot wounds than she did.

The paramedics were bringing a stretcher through the door as Ty pulled back his shirt and looked down at his own wound. "It hurts like he—like heck," he answered, grimacing. "But I don't think it hit the important parts." Then his serious hazel eyes met hers, and she saw something unexpected—relief. "Are you two okay?" he asked.

Jenna hugged Jay closer. "We're fine, thanks to you," she said, sniffing back tears. Her one thought was that Ty had saved her son's life. If he hadn't stepped in front of that gun, the bullet would have hit Jay. Then her son wouldn't have seen his first day of school on Monday, let alone have the choice of what to be when he grew up. The thought brought more tears to her eyes. "You're our hero today," she added, trying to smile.

"Are you gonna die?" Jay asked, and Jenna's hand automatically reached for Ty's. His long fingers slipped around hers and he squeezed, hard.

"No, Jay, I don't believe I am," he said as he stared up at Jenna. "I can live through anything as long as you two are safe."

"Excuse me, ma'am," one of the paramedics said. "You need to move back so we can get in here."

"We'll come to the hospital." Jenna gave Ty's hand one final squeeze. Then she told the truth before she and Jay left his side. "I love you—we love you."

JENNA WALKED down the hospital corridor feeling an overwhelming sense of déjà vu. She'd done this before, over two years ago, and it had ended her old life. That couldn't happen again, not to Ty. All her refusals and fears about Ty being in her and Jay's life had crumbled into dust when she'd seen him shot. She loved him, and she didn't want to live without him. And even though he'd proved just how much like Jimmy he was, she wasn't going to push him away or let him go again. He'd saved her son's life. How much more could Ty do to prove he loved them?

The county sheriff met her at the end of the corridor and he looked so serious she almost turned around and ran. *He'll be okay,* she chanted silently. Besides, Ty wasn't hurt that badly. He'd told her so himself. She stopped and waited.

"Miz Taylor." The sheriff nodded.

Unable to be sociable at a time like this, Jenna got to the point. "How is he?"

The sheriff smiled slightly. "Old Ty's a tough one. They took him upstairs for a little surgery, but he left here talkin'. I figure that's a good sign. He asked me to wait and tell you not to worry." Then the sheriff's features hardened into a frown. "Those jay birds are lucky they were carrying a .22-caliber. A bigger gun would've done a lot more damage and we might have had to get them acquainted with our death-row facilities.''

Jenna shuddered at the mention of death in any conversation that even peripherally involved Ty. She didn't want to think about the two robbers. ''The gun looked big enough to me,'' she commented. ''When can I see Ty?''

The sheriff looked at his watch. ''They said he ought to be back down in a couple of hours.'' He extended his hand toward the hall. ''The waiting room is down this way.''

TY WAS AWAKE when Jenna came into his room. Still a little groggy from the anesthesia, he hoped he hadn't been dreaming when he'd heard Jenna say she loved him. But now, as she leaned over him, the look on her face told him this was no dream. Her blue eyes were misty with unshed tears, and the corners of her mouth trembled as she kissed his cheek lightly before resting her cool palm against his forehead.

''How are you doing?'' she asked.

''Better now that you're here.''

''Does it hurt much?''

Ty used his legs to shift slightly and felt a twinge of pain in his side. He decided not to push his luck. ''It stings a little,'' he confessed.

''The doctor said the bullet almost made it all the way through. They didn't have any trouble getting it out,'' Jenna said.

Ty nodded. He wasn't worried about the bullet. He figured the doctors knew what they were doing. He just wanted to lie still for about a week and look into Jenna's sweet face.

"It seems like a long time since I saw you," he said.

Jenna lowered her eyes briefly. "Yes, I know." She looked at him again. "And it's all my fault. I—"

"Whoa," Ty interrupted her, raising a hand. Then he reached for one of hers. "You have every right to do what you think is best when it comes to your future." As he searched for something to say to ease any guilt she might be feeling, she continued.

"I didn't do what was best," she said emphatically. "I did what scared me the least. I decided to stay the same."

"That's okay."

"No, Ty. It's not okay. Not for me, not for you and not for Jay." Tears spilled down her cheeks, but she ignored them. "I love you. I think I've loved you for a long time. And Jay—"

"Jay wants to be like me. I know how that frightens you."

"Yes, Jay loves you and wants to be like you. But don't you see? He's already like you, like Jimmy. Any one of the three of you would walk into hell to save someone else."

Ty pulled his hand from hers and used his thumb

to wipe away her tears. "I almost died when I saw him with that gun," he admitted. "I'm so sorry I gave it to him."

Jenna gave him a watery smile. "And if you hadn't, he would have come around that corner with something else in his hand. He's already who he's going to be. A man who doesn't stand by and let other people hurt the people he cares about."

Ty had no answer for that, but he knew she was probably right. "Where is he?"

He could see Jenna struggling to get her emotions under control. She picked up her purse and searched through it to find a tissue to blow her nose. "Well, Sharon nearly squeezed him in half and probably bruised my ribs after she bullied her way into the diner. But she and Dean stayed with him so I could come to the hospital. Now he's with his grandmother." Jenna rolled her eyes. "I'm sure she'll want me to sell my part of the restaurant now."

"I don't see why."

"It's a dangerous place, remember?"

Ty gave a huff of laughter and was immediately rewarded with a sizzling pain in his side. He took a deep breath. "No more dangerous than driving across town in your car."

Jenna looked pleased by his answer, but worried by his grimace. "Does it hurt to talk? Maybe I should—"

Ty reclaimed her hand. ‘‘No, you shouldn’t. You and I have some things to discuss.’’

‘‘What things?’’ Jenna asked innocently, but even in his beleaguered state he could see the mischief in her eyes.

‘‘I seem to remember you saying that you loved me,’’ he went on, determined to get to the bottom of what he hoped was true.

‘‘And I meant it,’’ Jenna said softly.

‘‘Would that be love me like a friend, or like a…?’’ He wasn’t sure what name to put on it. *Lover* wasn’t enough; *husband* seemed too much to hope for.

Jenna smiled so sweetly it made his heart feel as if it were floating in his chest. A sensation that was a hundred times better than any pain medication. He wished he could pull her into his arms. ‘‘I would say—’’ she drew the moment out wickedly ‘‘—I love you like the second thing.’’

‘‘Even if I said the second thing was…husband?’’ Ty held his breath. This had to be a dream; he couldn’t believe after weeks of miserable dashed hopes, he might actually get what he wanted. Whom he wanted.

The door to the private room swung open, and a voice called, ‘‘Excuse me, folks.’’ Two nurses came bustling into the room, and Ty nearly groaned in frustration. If he’d had his badge, he would have ordered everybody out. ‘‘It’s time for you to get some rest,’’ the blond nurse said as she slipped the blood-pressure cuff on his arm. "You've just come out of surgery." Ty could only stare at Jenna as the other nurse checked his IV and took his temperature. Before leaving, she injected something into his IV line and looked at Jenna. "He'll be asleep in a couple of minutes. You'll need to come back in a few hours."

After the nurses left the room, Jenna moved to his bedside again. Ty could already feel the pain medication making his eyelids heavy.

"Jenna?" He didn't want her to leave but he knew he was slipping into sleep.

"Get some rest. I'll be back in a little while," she said, squeezing his hand. Then she leaned over and kissed him near his ear. "And while you're dreaming, know this. I'd be proud to be a Ranger's wife if that Ranger is you."

EPILOGUE

THE SIGN ON THE FRONT DOOR of the Donut Wrangler Diner read Closed Due To Wedding. Please Stop By Another Time. The Owners. The truck driver shook his head and looked at his watch. He'd been looking forward to a homemade doughnut and coffee. Now he'd have to settle for a fast-food place on the interstate.

Across town at a little church near the North Concho River, the owners of the Donut Wrangler were sniffing back tears.

"You look gorgeous," Sharon said as she dabbed her eyes. "You're gonna make me ruin my makeup. Lord, a month ago I thought none of us would live to see this day. And now, here you are...."

Jenna gazed at herself in the mirror and, for once in her life, felt gorgeous. She wasn't wearing white—she'd chosen blue—but she still felt like a bride. Or rather, a bride-to-be. After today she wouldn't be Jenna Taylor anymore; she'd be Jenna Richardson, the wife of a Texas Ranger.

After finally making the right decision, she couldn't wait. "Is it time yet?"

Sharon checked the clock. "No. Five more minutes." She looked determined to distract Jenna any way she could. "You know? I've been thinking...."

"Uh-oh, that sounds dangerous," Jenna said.

"Well, you know the caterers are doing a great job and charging a good price. I was talking it over with Dean and thinking maybe we could do some of that."

Before Jenna could respond, there was a knock at the door. Then Barbara Taylor appeared in the doorway. A wave of relief ran through Jenna. She hadn't been sure Barbara would come because she'd been so afraid of losing Jay to another family.

"Come in," Jenna offered when Barbara hesitated.

Sharon busied herself with hanging up the clothes Jenna had worn to the church and did her best to act as if she weren't in the room.

Barbara gazed at Jenna for a long moment. Jenna could see tears glistening in the older woman's eyes and wasn't sure what she should say to ease her fears.

"You look very beautiful," Barbara said.

Surprised, but pleased, Jenna answered, "Thank you, Barbara. I'm so glad you came."

Barbara fussed with the tissue in her hand for a moment, then looked Jenna in the eye. "I wanted you to know that I'm glad you're going to marry that handsome Texas Ranger."

Jenna, taken off guard, remained silent.

Barbara rushed ahead as if she'd rehearsed the words over and over. "I know he'll be there to take care of you and James— Jay. I was wrong about losing my grandson to a stepfather. I almost lost him for real, and both you and Ty kept him safe. He's a good man. I want Jay to be part of a family again."

Unable to stop herself, Jenna hugged her. "Thank you so much for telling me that. And for being happy for Jay and me. You'll always be his grandmom."

As they stepped out of the embrace, Sharon handed them both new tissues. "We're all gonna be a mess if we don't get out there," she muttered as she blew her nose.

Jenna smiled and gazed at the other two women. "Well? What are we waiting for? I'm ready to get married."

AS THE MUSIC STARTED, Ty straightened his shoulders and glanced at Kirby, who was acting as his best man. Kirby winked, making Ty remember his first comment after learning of the wedding: "Do you suppose I can claim to be a relative and get free pecan pancakes for life?" Ty almost smiled again at the memory. Now he knew what the old man and Buster had in common—their minds were always on their bellies.

When Jenna appeared in the doorway of the

church on her father's arm with Jay walking in front of her, Ty forgot about Kirby, about the church full of lawmen and about having to wear a suit. He even forgot the almost healed wound in his side. Nothing was going to interfere with this day. He would have run through a canyon of cactus naked if Jenna were waiting for him on the other side. She looked so beautiful he couldn't take his eyes off her.

Then he thought of Jimmy.

I hope you're looking down on this with a big smile on your face, buddy. It's your fault, you know. You must have known I would love her, that I would love them both.

Ty pulled his gaze away from Jenna for a moment and looked up.

Thank you.